"But you have not told me what you expect from me when you come here, if, as you say, you will visit each night."

"I expect nothing other than your good company," he said. And that was true. In that moment, he did want only that.

A laugh escaped from her, a wonderful sound to his ears, and she gifted him with the smile he'd wanted to see. It was the first sign of joy in her face in weeks.

"And you expect me to believe that? After you have all but promised to seduce me into your bed?"

She did not appear to be opposed to it, so he would bide his time. "I would not mind that either," he admitted.

* * *

Yield to the Highlander
Harlequin® Historical #1185—May 2014

Author Note

When I wrote *Taming the Highlander* in 2005, it was a stand-alone story, and I never planned to write any other stories connected to the MacLerie Clan. I had no idea that I would become so wrapped up in their family that, in the end, I would write TEN MacLerie romances, including two about their descendants in Regency times! So it is bittersweet to come to the last story and somehow fitting that it should be about the heir of Connor MacLerie.

Aidan MacLerie has lived a charmed and privileged life and now must make decisions that will shape his future and that of his clan. Falling in love with the wrong woman is not the best choice he's made in his life, but now he faces the consequences *and* his father's ire.

I hope you have enjoyed watching these wonderful Highlanders and the women they love as much as I have enjoyed writing their stories.

Sláinte!

Terri Brisbin

—

Yield to the Highlander

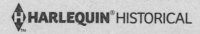

Recycling programs
for this product may
not exist in your area.

ISBN-13: 978-0-373-29785-6

YIELD TO THE HIGHLANDER

Copyright © 2014 by Theresa S. Brisbin

Printed in U.S.A.

During my writing career, I've discovered those times when the empty page mocks me and torments me, daring me to fill it with words worthy of being read. In those dark times (and in the good times, too), two particular groups of writers have proven indispensable to me during my writing years—the Hussies and the Hermits.

To the Hussies—the Harlequin Historical authors— thanks for being my safe place in the craziness of writing and publishing these last years. Whether I need answers, advice, help with titles or just camaraderie, you provide it...24/7/365.

To the Hermits—the wonderful group of writers who gather each year in Lowcountry, SC, to write on the beach—thanks for being there to help me recover, recuperate, revive and refocus!

TERRI BRISBIN

is wife to one, mother of three and dental hygienist to hundreds when not living the life of a glamorous romance author. She was born, raised and is still living in the southern New Jersey suburbs. Terri's love of history led her to write time-travel romances and historical romances set in Scotland and England.

Readers are invited to visit her website for more information at www.terribrisbin.com, or to contact her at P.O. Box 41, Berlin, NJ 08009-0041.

Chapter One

She was not the usual type of woman to catch his eye, but she had.

Aidan MacLerie decided to stop and quench his thirst at the well in the middle of the village on his way back to the keep. His men had continued on up the hill to the wives and families who awaited their return while Aidan paused. This place was one of his favourites for finding companionship of the female kind and he'd rarely been disappointed.

He dipped into the bucket and watched her approach over the rim of the cup as he drank from it. She did not walk as much as saunter, her lush hips swaying as she crossed from the path to the well. She carried a bucket in her arms, pressing against breasts he imagined were as shapely as her hips. From the kerchief she wore to cover her hair, he knew she was a married woman, or mayhap his other favourite—a widow.

Widows were fair game for his attentions. And they were experienced in lovemaking and the way of the world around them, so they held no illusions about the place any affair held in his life. She glanced up and smiled softly at him, making his body harden and ready itself for pleasure.

Oh, aye, she would be different from his usual bed-mates, but pleasure would be theirs. She would be his.

'Good day,' he said, smiling back at her and standing as she moved closer to the well. 'Here—' he reached out for the bucket '—allow me to fill that for you.'

'Thank you, my lord,' she said in a voice that sent spirals of desire through him. Feminine with earthy, lush tones that matched the rest of her. She would cry out his name in that voice soon as he filled her and as he led her to reach her own release. He distracted himself by tossing the well's bucket down and then pulling it up when it filled.

'You know who I am?' he asked. Aidan did not remember ever meeting this woman before.

'Aye, my lord,' she said, taking the now full bucket from him. 'You are the earl's eldest son.'

'Aidan,' he said. He needed to hear his name spoken by her mouth. His cock stood, his flesh tingled and his blood seethed in anticipation. 'My name is Aidan.'

'Aye, my lord,' she said. She began to back away, nodding in courtesy, but he had no intention of allowing her to escape before he discovered her identity.

'You have me at a disadvantage, mistress. You know who I am, yet I do not remember meeting you.'

'We have never met, my lord. I am Catriona Mac-Kenzie,' she answered. She met his gaze and he took note that she was older than he'd first thought, possibly older than he.

'How did a MacKenzie come to be in Lairig Dubh?' The MacKenzies had been adversaries of the MacLeries for a long time until Aidan's brother-by-marriage, Rob Matheson, had forced both clans to negotiations that eased the tensions between the two most powerful clans in the Highlands.

'I married Gowan MacLerie.' Simple and direct and it might have dashed a lesser man's hopes. But not his.

Gowan was one of Rurik's men and a good deal older than both Aidan and his wife. And he was a skillful trainer of warriors who was often away from Lairig Dubh at the earl's other holdings. He smiled then, the possibilities expanding with every moment. Not willing to let her get away yet, he stepped closer and took the bucket from her and motioned for her to lead him.

'Allow me to carry this for you,' he said.

She looked as though she would argue for her lovely mouth pursed and her deep-blue eyes flashed like ice. But after a very short hesitation, she turned and led him down one of the smaller paths that headed towards a cluster of cottages. And Aidan took advantage to study Mistress Catriona MacKenzie as she walked in front of him.

Wisps of dark brown hair escaped her kerchief and Aidan fought the urge to pull it free. He wondered if her hair would fall below that beautiful arse of hers and sway as she walked. Reaching down and using the bucket to cover his actions, he tugged his trews loose to allow for the erection that was not going to ease. At least not until he'd found a way to get Mistress MacKenzie in his bed, naked and writhing and open to his touch.

She turned down a path to their left and stopped before the last cottage. Glancing around, he listened for any sign that others were nearby. Although he did not usually seek out married women, he did not ignore them either and this was one he'd decided to pursue. He would be discreet and not embarrass her or her husband unnecessarily, but he would have her.

Soon.

She turned to face him, holding out her hands to take the bucket. Instead, he put it down and took one of her outstretched hands in his, lifting it to his mouth. A slight tug gave away her nervousness, then she acquiesced.

'My thanks for your assistance, my lord,' she said, trying to put a distance between them that his grasp made impossible.

'Until we next meet, mistress,' Aidan whispered.

He kissed the top of her hand and then turned it over and placed his mouth on her wrist. He met her gaze and slowly touched the tip of his tongue to the place where her pulse beat close beneath the skin there. Her surprised gasp echoed in the stillness around them.

Aidan released her hand, trying not to stare at her breasts as he noticed the way her nipples had tightened and were visible through the fabric of her gown. He smiled and did not hide it, as she crossed her arms over her chest and drew her shawl up on to her shoulders to cover herself.

Turning without another word to her, he strode back along the path towards the well, memorising the way as he went. Aidan could read the excitement in her body and hear it in the way her breathing became shallow and quick. His next visit would be under the cover of darkness, so he paid attention to the number of paths and cottages and other details. By the time he arrived back at the keep and reported to his father, his plans for this newest seduction were set.

Mistress Catriona MacKenzie would be warming his bed, or he would warm hers, very, very soon.

Cat stood like a statue, unable to move or to look away as the young lord strode down the path. The skin of her wrist was warm and moist from the touch of his mouth and tongue. Bold and brash, Aidan MacLerie had kissed her as though she was a young girl and as though she wanted his attentions.

Which she did not.

Still, she watched until he passed out of her view and a wicked part of her hoped he'd turn back to look at her once more. Those cat-like amber eyes of his never wavered while he studied her. She'd seen the earl one day and now she knew that his son had inherited the father's good looks and colouring, especially those eyes. She shivered now, but feared examining the reason too closely.

Cat lifted the bucket from where he'd left it and carried it inside. Tossing her shawl aside, she poured some of the water in the waiting jug on the table and the rest into the waiting cauldron in the hearth. She moved about the room, gathering together the ingredients for the stew she would make for their evening meal, trying all the time to ignore the feelings that pulsed within her. Once the meat and vegetables were in the pot, she tugged off her kerchief and laughed.

Boredom must have driven him to flirt with her at the well. Boredom plain and simple. For, truly, what other reason could explain it? She was older than he was—almost six years stood between them if she had heard correctly. She was married to one of his father's men. And, no matter if her body trembled and her skin and blood seemed on fire from his attentions, she was an honourable woman who took her promised vows seriously.

Cat laughed again and shook her head, deciding to just accept that it was the nonsensical flirtation of a young man with nothing better to do. Gowan was away and would return on the morrow, but she still had to prepare a meal for his son, Munro.

She carried out her daily chores and enjoyed a quiet meal at day's end. It wasn't until she lay on her pallet waiting for sleep to take its hold that she allowed herself to enjoy the impossible attentions of a younger man that would come to nothing more than the few minutes of excitement it had been.

Her life was not harder than most others who lived in Lairig Dubh. Gowan had offered her marriage and that had taken her from the terrible circumstances of her early years and given her an honourable place. He did not require much of her and she did not begrudge him anything he wanted from her. Being ten years older than her, he did not expect more children and he'd also long since stopped seeking her bed. With a son raised and part of the laird's warriors, Gowan was a simple man who made few demands on her.

So, the playful flirting of one young man meant nothing, but it had made her smile. And she felt a pang of bittersweet loss, too, for it reminded her of the subtle joys of courting that she'd missed in her life. As she drifted off to sleep, it was not her husband's face that filled her dreams, but that of Aidan MacLerie.

Yet those dreams were so heated and so filled with passionate bedplay that guilt filled her as she heard Gowan's voice call out as he approached their cottage the next day. How could such a small, innocent encounter affect her so much?

Gowan's return brought her normal life back and, over the next sennight, she could almost forget the way the earl's son had looked at this soldier's wife.

Almost.

Chapter Two

'What do you think of this, Aidan?'

He'd long ago given the report of the results of his latest assignment to those here, so Aidan's thoughts had drifted from whatever was the matter at hand to the lush figure of the woman he desired most. Glancing around at the clan elders and his father's other counsellors, he had no intention of revealing his thoughts, though if he stood now the matter would be quite clear to everyone there.

Aidan tried to remember what the discussion had been when he caught Rurik's eye. His father's most loyal friend and the leader of all his warriors gave him a knowing wink. Also his godfather, Rurik knew of Aidan's love of the fairer sex and Aidan had sought his advice several times when asking his father would have been too difficult or embarrassing. Rurik took it in his stride and, apparently, kept his eye on Aidan's activities. Finally remembering the last topic, he looked at his father.

'I think you should gather the newer soldiers together

in one place and let some of the experienced commanders train them,' he said, hoping his suggestion sounded like a reasonable one.

His father raised an eyebrow, but said nothing. Tempted to say something, anything, to break the silence, he knew better than that. Connor MacLerie would consider his words and weigh the merits and disadvantages of any plan, whether his first-born son's or his most trusted advisor's. Aidan watched as his father met the gazes of one after another of his counsellors and then turned back and spoke to him again.

'And who should I assign to this task?' he asked.

Aidan rose then and went to fill his cup before speaking. Several names came to mind—all experienced, capable warriors—and he offered them. 'Black Rob. Iain. Calum,' he said.

'Micheil,' Rurik offered. 'And we will need one more to work with the number of new soldiers we have, Connor.'

'Gowan.' The name escaped Aidan's mouth before he truly thought it through, but it was right for so many reasons that he repeated it. 'Gowan should be there.'

Aidan held his breath, waiting for his father's decision. This task would take several weeks, if not almost two months, and it would keep Gowan far enough away that he could not interfere with Aidan's plans for Catriona. It would give him uninterrupted weeks to follow her, weaken any resistance or hesitation she might have and seduce her and make her his. A smile threatened, one which would be hard to explain, so he took a deep swallow of his wine instead.

'Rurik, what think you of Aidan's choices?' his father asked.

Rurik crossed his arms over his chest and frowned. A good sign or bad, Rurik gave no sign of his opinion for several moments. Then, with a nod, he confirmed them.

'Give the orders and make the arrangements,' his father said, putting down his cup and nodding to several of the men there.

Aidan held his breath, not daring to believe his luck in this. Within a day, two at the most, Gowan would be gone from Lairig Dubh and he could pursue the fair and lovely Catriona without interference. He watched as the men left and his father remained with Duncan and Rurik. A discussion about several upcoming visits by various noblemen in Scotland who wanted to be in the good graces of the Earl of Douran. It was nothing new for his father or for him—people who valued them only for their name, their connections or the power and influence they wielded.

A short time passed and Aidan listened without interest to who was coming or going, caring not as long as Gowan was gone from Lairig Dubh. Then his father nodded at his closest advisors and they left.

'Send for Jocelyn, Rurik,' he called out as the men walked to the steps leading down from this tower chamber.

Aidan took a deep swallow from his cup, now puzzled over what was to come. His father alone would not be of concern, but calling his mother here meant trouble was coming his way. They passed the minute or so of time waiting for her arrival in silence with Aidan fighting the urge to ask the reason. Soon, he could hear his mother's footsteps approaching the top of the stairs and he rose to greet her.

Being forced to marry the Beast of the Highlands to save her family had brought Jocelyn MacCallum to Lairig Dubh. Capturing the heart of a man most thought did not have one had turned that marriage into a long and happy one. No matter whatever else happened, Aidan knew his father loved his mother with every bit of his heart and soul. It was there every time one glanced at the other, through good times and contentious ones.

Not that he ever expected to find such a thing as they'd found—he was more practical than that. But he did understand that his parents' marriage and relationship was not the customary one in this time or place.

'So, why did you summon Mother?' he finally asked, wanting some kind of hint about the probably discussion ahead.

His father put his cup down and stood, walking over to the door, awaiting his mother's arrival there.

'To discuss your upcoming marriage.'

Connor watched his son as he spoke of the reason they waited for Jocelyn to arrive. It could not be a surprise to him, for the boy had reached marriageable age a few years ago. Any delay in finalising arrangements had been Connor's weakness when faced with the pleas from his beloved wife to delay. So many of their kin had been married off recently, including their own daughter, that Connor gave in to Jocelyn's request. Many offers and expressions of interest had been coming in since

Aidan had reached ten years of age. A few bold noblemen had offered even sooner.

But it was time for his eldest and heir to marry and
begin to take up more responsibility within the clan and
to become an integral part of overseeing the MacLerie
estates, businesses and armies. Watching as he slept
his way through a never-ending, never-slowing stream
of women, Connor knew his son was not going to slow
down or take on more responsibility unless he married.

And mayhap not even then.

So, he could not, they could not, ignore it any longer.
His son needed to settle down and focus his attentions
on clan matters instead of those of the flesh only. Asking for Aidan's suggestions on which men were best to
send on the training mission was one way. Connor had
already made his choices, but giving his son a chance
to give his opinion had been his way of testing Aidan's
knowledge and wisdom.

Connor turned and watched as his wife reached the
top of the stairs and turned towards the chamber door,
smiling at their eldest as she caught sight of him there.
Then her gaze met his own and the warmth of her love
shot through him. As it always did.

'So, have you told him yet?' she asked as she passed
Aidan and came to stand before him. Her tone of voice
was even, but that did not fool him for a moment—she
was still not accepting that this was the time for their
son to marry.

'I awaited your arrival, love.'

Aidan glanced from him to his mother. His son
should be accustomed to the endearments that crept

in when they were alone, but from his expression, he seemed surprised by it.

'And you have what to tell me?' his son asked.

'Based on our preliminary discussions, there are three prospective marriages.'

'Our?' Aidan asked. Connor would have laughed at how his son mirrored his own posture—arms crossed over his chest, feet planted in a warrior's stance—if he had not worn his mother's stubborn expression on his face.

'The clan elders, Duncan, Rurik. Your mother,' Connor replied, nodding to Jocelyn, 'who would not be kept out of any talks that involved your future bride.'

'And? Who are the three women?' he asked.

'The first is Margaret Sinclair of Caithness,' Jocelyn explained.

'The earl's grandniece?' Aidan asked.

Rurik's father was Earl of Orkney, whose claim was through a marriage that had not resulted in a legitimate heir to inherit the title. Well, there had been a son, Rurik's half-brother, but his unlamented death some years ago ended their father's ability to keep the earldom in the family. The Sinclair family would be next in line once Erengisl Sunesson passed. And a marriage between Aidan and Margaret would link the MacLeries to one of the most powerful families of the north. 'Aye.'

'And the second?'

Connor met Jocelyn's puzzled gaze. Aidan's disinterest in his choices for a wife was stronger than either of them had expected. He nodded at her to continue as he watched their son's reactions.

'Alys MacKenzie,' Jocelyn said. With the MacLeries' recent ties to the Mathesons and their powerful Highland allies, the MacKenzies, it made sense to consider a direct link with them.

'Nay,' Aidan said, shaking his head. 'Not a MacKenzie.'

Jocelyn threw a glance in his direction, both of them surprised by his opposition at the mere mention of the lass.

''Tis early in negotiations, Aidan. Let all three names stand for now.' Connor nodded to Jocelyn to announce the third name.

'And Elizabeth Maxwell is the last.' Elizabeth was the eldest daughter of the Border lord and their family had strong ties to the Berkeley family in England. A good way to extend the MacLerie reach into the other kingdom.

Silence filled the room and Aidan's expression remained blank. Uninterested? Resigned? Which one Connor knew not. Then their son let out a long sigh and nodded.

'So how do you plan to do this? Will I have any say in the matter?' he asked them.

'Your mother has convinced me that, since all three are acceptable matches to us, you should have the final choice.' Connor walked to Jocelyn's side. 'Each of the three have been invited to visit Lairig Dubh, so that you might meet them and take measure of whether they suit you.'

'When will these visits begin?'

'I am not certain. After we attend your uncle's wedding, I think.' His uncle Athdar had claimed Rurik's daughter when she boldly hid away in his keep last winter. Handfasted when he discovered her, for honour's sake, the church wedding would solemnify the joining that was already proving fruitful.

Aidan felt the tension leave his body. He had some time yet. No matter that he knew it was his duty to marry, and marry well, for the best interests of his kith and kin, he really had not wanted to do it yet. He was enjoying his life and a wife married for alliances and treaties would make it difficult to pursue his own pleasures. And he'd become accustomed to doing what, and who, he wished.

But in this moment, Aidan gave an honest appraisal of his opposition to seeking a wife now. It was the same reason he wanted no MacKenzie on that list of brides — and her name was Catriona MacKenzie. Finding her at the well was a lucky chance, but he wanted time, and the opportunity, to discover what lay beneath that smile and behind those eyes. He wanted time, undistracted by the demands of his family, to seduce her.

'After the wedding, then,' he said, looking from his father to his mother. Aidan tried not to look too hopeful as he waited for his parents to decide.

'I will have Duncan begin approaching the families now,' his father declared, staring at him as though trying to search his thoughts. 'The roads are clear now all across the land.'

Aidan let out the breath he did not realise he'd been holding. 'If there's nothing else?'

His father nodded. Aidan walked to his mother and

kissed her cheek. As was her custom, and in disregard for his age, she ran her fingers through his hair and touched his face as she had when he was a wee bairn. 'Will you be at supper?'

'Aye, I will be there,' he said.

With nothing else to say and other tasks to see finished this day, Aidan strode from their chambers and returned to where his friends trained in the yard. His body hummed with restlessness now and he needed to work it out. Since he would not approach Catriona until her husband left, that left the other physical release of a good fight.

Aidan laughed aloud as he reached the yard and called out his challenges. With the way his blood burned for her, it would be a long afternoon in the training yard.

Chapter Three

It had been two days since Gowan departed for this new assignment and Cat's life returned to the normal one she lived when alone. Other than Munro's presence at supper several nights a week, she would be on her own to both accomplish her chores and tasks and for any plans she wished to make. She could even be lazy and remain abed when the sun rose, if she chose to.

Stretching out on her pallet, her hands extending into the chilled air of the cottage, she remembered that unless she stirred the fire in the small hearth there would be no warmth for her. Now fully awake with no hope of claiming another hour or so of sleep, she pushed back the blankets and shivered as the cool morning air of the cottage surrounded her. With some haste, she lit a fire, threw in some peat after the kindling caught and tossed her shawl over her shoulders to warm her in the meantime as she went about her tasks.

Though he'd come for supper last evening, Munro never slept here or spent any amount of time here unless his father was present. The sigh escaped her before she could stop it. Gowan's son had opposed their marriage from the day he learned of his father's plans. That it was one of convenience mattered not to the young man, for his mother's recent passing and without the presence of young bairns who needed Catriona's care convinced him it was unseemly. From Munro's occasional, intense stares, she almost wondered if there was something more there.

Shaking off her disquiet, she decided to take advantage of what looked to be a break in the unsettled weather of late winter and spend the morning clearing away brush and fallen branches from the small patch of land next to the cottage that would be her garden. When the weather finally warmed, she hoped to expand the area from what she had worked last summer to something larger. Laughing with Gowan over her pitiful crop of vegetables and herbs from last season, she'd vowed to improve this year.

Kind man that he was, Gowan suggested she speak to Lady Jocelyn, for the gardens at the keep thrived under the lady's guidance. New to Lairig Dubh and not significant enough to warrant wasting the lady's attentions, she'd declined the suggestion and, instead, took advice from some of the village women who had successful gardens.

She would prove herself a worthy wife in whatever way she could. Gowan's actions had saved her very life and she could never be able to repay him for doing so. Not that she could explain that to Munro or anyone else without revealing her shame. So, she looked for ways to make his life comfortable and ways in which she could cause him no regret for taking her as his wife. The garden would be one of those ways to make him proud.

The morning passed quickly as she pulled and tugged at weeds firmly entrenched in the hard ground. Her shoulders and back ached at the honest labour, but her spirit was lifted by the amount she'd accomplished. Cat washed up and had a plain meal of soup and bread before going to help one of the women in the village who'd just given birth. Her attempts to keep feelings of emptiness at bay faltered each time she laid eyes on her friend's newborn bairn. Even knowing it was never meant for her to be the one bearing children did not ease the tightness in her chest when she held the babe. She relied on keeping busy and filling her days to fight off the deep sadness of her barrenness.

As she was walking towards Muireall's cottage, a chill trickled down her spine as though she was being watched. Glancing along the path ahead and behind her, she saw no one paying any attention to her. Gathering the sack of mended clothing in her arms, she continued along the way. Only as she passed the last cottage on the lane and turned on to a smaller one did she see him.

Aidan MacLerie.

The earl's son stood watching her, frank desire in his gaze. He did not approach or speak to her, but he did not look away either. She nodded as she passed him, meeting his gaze for a brief moment and continuing on. The nervousness in her stomach, the tightness in her chest as she tried to breathe and the sweat that trickled down her neck and back were all signs to her that she was not unaffected by his attentions.

Cat forced one foot to glide smoothly after the other, torn between trying not to put more meaning into his presence than she should and ignoring the hope that he would speak to her. She turned to follow the smaller path—Muireall's cottage was the third one—when he spoke.

'Good day to you.'

She paused and nodded her head. 'And good day to you, my lord.' Daring a glance, Cat found him still watching her from his place. The skin on her wrist where he'd pressed his lips tingled now, reminding her of the inappropriate gesture.

'Aidan,' he said as he took one step and another towards her now. 'You must call me Aidan.'

She shook her head and dipped into a shallow curtsy. 'I could not do that, my lord. We do not know each other and you are the earl's son.'

His eyes brightened and a smile lifted the corners of his mouth then. Why did she suspect she'd just issued some sort of challenge to him—one he was pleased to rise and accept? He reached her side and she glanced about to see if any other villagers were about. Seeing none did not ease her sense of nervousness. Cat thought the earl's son might be even bolder if he knew they were unobserved.

'So,' he said as he lifted her chin to meet her gaze, 'are you saying that if we were more familiar with each other, you could use my name with ease?' Then he did not so much release her chin as he did instead caress the edge of her jaw until his fingers slid away down her neck. 'I think we should become more acquainted, then.'

His touch ignited all sorts of feelings in her, but she understood they were the wrong ones. His position as the earl's son and heir gave him much power over people like her—and she knew he had a stream of women eager to share his bed. But it could not be her. It could never be her. She would honour her word, her oath, to her husband. Her debt to Gowan cleared her mind, so she stepped back from him and shook her head.

'I think our acquaintance is what it should be, my lord. I live in your father's village and know my place. I know I cannot naysay anything you demand, but I beg you to leave me be.'

His gaze moved from her eyes down and she followed the path. During her plea, her hand had taken hold of his wrist. Shocked by the intimacy of such a thing and shocked more that she had touched him, a man other than her husband, Cat released her grip and stumbled back. Waiting those next few moments for his reprimand or retribution, she dared a look at his expression. It was not so much desire now as surprise.

'I beg your pardon, mistress,' he said, stepping off the path and clearing the way for her to walk on. 'I meant only to make your acquaintance, having not known you before. I would never demand something that you are unwilling to give.'

Had she misunderstood? Had she just accused him of something he had not done? Her experience with men was very limited and any experience with teasing as this seemed to be was worse than that.

'And I beg your pardon, my lord, if I offended you. My friend is waiting for me.' She held up her sack as proof and could not help it if it felt like protection to keep him from getting so close again. 'If I have your leave to attend her?'

'Good day, Catriona MacKenzie,' he said.

'Good day,' she replied, walking faster then. 'My lord.' That slipped out before she could stop it and it was met with his deep, masculine laughter.

What devil had made her tease him once more? Cat dared a peek once she'd reached Muireall's cottage door and found him still watching her. She knocked and entered with a call to the woman inside. Hoping that the needs within the cottage would distract her from the man outside, she walked in and greeted Muireall, who sat on a pallet feeding her newly born son.

'You look flushed, Catriona,' Muireall said. 'Are you well?'

'Oh, aye, well enough.' She put the sack of clothing on the table and began to separate the clothes according to size. When she noticed the silence, she met Muireall's amused gaze. 'Do you have any other mending to be done? Errands to run?' she asked.

'You are trying to make certain I do not take notice of the colour in your cheeks and your breathlessness.' Muireall lifted the bairn and placed him on her shoulder. Rubbing his back, she rose from the pallet and walked to Cat's side. 'Something or someone brought the colour to your cheeks.'

'Muireall, I am a married woman! I would never...'

'Enjoy a bit of fun?' Her friend laughed and reached

out to touch Cat's cheek. 'You are a good wife to Gowan, but that does not mean you should never laugh or enjoy yourself.'

'I owe him so much,' Cat began before falling silent.

'I know you believe that, but you brought joy back to Gowan's life. That would pay whatever debt you think you owe him.'

Muireall was one of very few people who knew the truth of Cat's life and how Gowan had saved it. But even she did not know all the details.

'So, who brought that blush to your cheeks?' her friend asked again.

Uncomfortable at how close to the truth Muireall was, Catriona laughed and took the bairn from his mother. Holding young Donald close and rubbing her cheek on the babe's head, she fought the longing that bairns always caused within her. But Gowan had never promised her children, only a safe place to live and someone to care of her. No matter the longings, it was still a good offer and she did not regret accepting it. Not then, not now.

'Has Hugh told you how relentless I can be when I want something?' Muireall asked her. '"Like a dog on a juicy bone", he likes to say.' Her friend laughed as she took her bairn back into her arms, cradling his head and kissing him as she did. 'So, who put that smile on your face?'

Catriona hesitated for a number of reasons. Then she whispered his name, thinking that to keep it secret was to give it power over her. 'Aidan MacLerie.'

'He is a brawny lad, is he not? He got his colouring from his father…and his size,' she said, winking as she did.

Catriona felt her mouth drop open in reaction to Muireall's candid assessment of Aidan's…size!

'I may have just had a bairn, but I'll be dead before I stop noticing a handsome young man like him,' Muireall admitted. One of the things she liked most about Muireall was her earthy, honest way of thinking and living. And she knew that Muireall loved her husband with all her heart and any noticing of brawny young men meant nothing in the face of that love. 'I would worry about you if a man like Aidan MacLerie did not make you blush.'

'Aye, Muireall, I noticed the lad,' she admitted, smiling against her will at both the admission and the memory of that brawny, young man. Cat turned back to her task of sorting the clothing, hoping all the while that the topic was done.

'Lad?' Muireall laughed. 'That lad became a man long ago!'

Cat laughed, then shrugged. ''Tis no matter to me.'

'He will lead the MacLerie clan after his father. From what my brother says, young Aidan stands well in his father's stead.' Her brother Gair served as steward to the earl and would be in a position to assess the heir's abilities, strengths and weaknesses.

Cat walked to the storage trunk next to the pallet and put the clothing away. Not having grown up here, she did not know much about the earl and his family. Not as much as Muireall did.

'How many years does he have?' she asked, curious about him now.

'He has twenty-and-two years.' So he was five years younger than she was. Munro's age.

'And not married yet?' She avoided Muireall's gaze now as she asked the question in what she hoped was a neutral tone. When her friend did not reply, it forced Cat to turn and look at her. Amusement sparkled in her eyes. Nay, more than that, merriment and troublemaking glimmered there.

'I *am* curious,' she admitted. 'Nothing more than that.'

'Ah, then you are alive! I had my doubts about you, Catriona.'

Muireall was a very special sort of woman—one who relished life and did not let a minute go by when she did not appreciate something or someone around her. Whether the sun shining after a storm, the smile of her child, the sound of her husband's voice, she savoured it all. And that drew people to her like flies to honey… including Cat herself. Muireall had everything in her life that Catriona had ever wanted for herself and everything Cat had convinced herself that she could live without.

Mayhap she had isolated herself from everyone in trying so hard to be what Gowan needed and wanted? He'd never said exactly what he'd expected of her, not when he asked her to marry him and not any other time. She did what she thought a good wife, what a second wife who had no children to care for, should do. She cleaned, she mended, she cooked, she cleaned. She was attentive to him when he was at home. Was that not what she should be doing?

'To answer your question, he should be married by now, but he has been resisting it. A young man doing what a young man does.'

'Young women?' she asked, slapping her hand over her mouth after saying something so...so bold.

From the way he flirted with her, his skills at doing what young men did were very, very good. And there were many women who would not object to sharing the bed of the earl's son. But she was not one of them.

'Aye, young women. Older women as well,' Muireall explained. 'They all seem to like him and he them. He seems to treat all of them with respect no matter how they begin or end.' Her friend looked at her then. 'Is that what you wanted to know?'

'My thanks for easing my curiosity,' she said, nodding to her friend. She had been curious. She'd heard the stories of his prowess with women and had never heard a bad word spoken about him. 'Now, what else can I help you do? If you have any errands outside, this is a perfect day for them.' Though Muireall glanced at her with a knowing eye, she retrieved a length of plaid from the pallet, clearly fighting the urge to tease Cat even more than she had.

'I need water from the well,' she said, holding wee Donald out to Cat. 'But I need to walk a bit, so I'll join ye.'

Taking him in her arms and holding him close, she watched Muireall wrap and tie the plaid to form a sling where the bairn could be carried close to her chest. Once

Donald was secured snugly in the folds of fabric, Cat gathered up the buckets near the door and tugged it open. Stepping into the sun-warmed air, she waited for her friend and then they were off down the path to the centre of the village—and the well.

They greeted people as they passed, stopping several times for Muireall to show off the wee one to all who asked. Cat could not help herself—she kept peeking ahead and behind and alongside to see if the earl's son waited there. With no sign of him, she let out a sigh of relief. She did not like questioning her response to him or suspecting she would enjoy more of his flirting attentions, so it was fine that he had gone.

The well in the centre of the village served not just the purpose of providing water, but also it was the main gathering place for any and all. News was shared. Gossip spread. Help was asked, offered or accepted by the well. On a fair and sunny day like this, a crowd gathered there.

Catriona carried the buckets and set them on the well. Muireall was welcomed by all the women, more one of them now that she'd given birth as most all of them had. The sharp sting of disappointment struck again as she watched the scene unfold. The concern about both mother and bairn, the soft caresses of his head, and shared stories and remedies for any affliction he might suffer—all just pointed out how much she was not part of this village family.

Though at first she'd welcomed Gowan's travels in his duties for the earl, now she realised that it had isolated her from a more involved place within the village and clan community. Without her husband's presence and with no other family there, she'd become even more the outsider than she was. Cat tossed the well's bucket down and turned the handle to retrieve it, trying to ignore the way this need now filled her when it had not mattered only days or weeks before.

She called out to Muireall when she had the water she needed and began to walk back to the cottage, allowing her friend to enjoy some time with the others. Just as she reached the footpath, a group of men rode through the village. Warriors like her husband, they rode as though one with their horses, calling out to those they knew as they headed towards the keep up the hill.

Cat took one last look at them as they passed and then turned back to her own path. Without really knowing why, she glanced up one more time and found the last rider staring back at her.

Aidan MacLerie.

He did nothing to acknowledge her, but his dark, scowling expression frightened her. Had she insulted him then with her words? Would she or Gowan somehow bear the brunt of his displeasure? She did not know about him to even guess, but she offered up a prayer that she had not caused problems for herself or her husband in the few, playful exchanges with the earl's son.

Time would tell.

Chapter Four

Aidan rode through the gates and past the keep, following the path to the practice yard where his friends waited for him. He'd not ridden out with the other men, but he returned with them after his encounter with Catriona. And returned unsettled by her comment. Before he could think on it and discover the reason, a friend called out to him.

'Aidan!'

He turned to seek the source of the booming voice and saw Rurik's son Dougal waving at him. Though younger by a few years, Dougal towered over Aidan and most everyone who lived in Lairig Dubh—except his father.

'We were waiting for you,' Dougal explained, waving for him to hurry his pace. 'They want to challenge us.'

Aidan glanced at the others and knew he and Dougal could and would defeat them. Other than Young Dougal Ruriksson, as he was called here, he nodded at Caelan, Munro and Dougal MacLerie along with Angus Mac-

Callum—a cousin through his mother—who all stood grinning like fools who itched for a fight. Knowing the skills and abilities of himself and Young Dougal and, even more importantly, knowing the weaknesses of the others, Aidan was convinced it was an even match, regardless of four against two.

He shrugged and nodded his acceptance and headed for the yard.

Dougal MacLerie, brother to Elizabeth and the friend closest to Aidan's own age, walked alongside him as they entered the yard and picked their weapons from among the supply there. Younger boys ran around, trying to help them all, and news of the challenge spread through all the men training there. Soon a crowd encircled the large enclosure, coin and wagers changing hands as many watching offered their opinions about the match.

'You have been spending more time in the village than is your custom, Aidan,' Dougal said, lifting a sword and swinging it to get the best grip on it.

'You know what that means,' Caelan, Duncan's son, added.

'A woman,' Angus offered. 'Another bloody woman.'

They laughed for Angus's unsuccessful attempts at seducing one of the women who worked in the keep's kitchens were known to them all.

'So who is it this time?' Munro asked. 'The widow who moved in with her brother, the smith? Surely not Old Ronald's daughter?'

They all laughed at him as they took positions on the field, expecting him to reveal his newest interest. He always did. Just as Aidan opened his mouth to speak her name, the realisation sank in—Munro was Gowan's son. Shite!

'Who says there's a woman involved at all?' he asked, raising his sword and standing back to back with Young Dougal.

'When is there not a woman?' Munro called out to him.

The others nodded in agreement with him and then all gazes were on Aidan. Better not to stir this particular cauldron right now. Instead, he stopped talking about it at all and ran at the closest one—Caelan. And then mayhem, though somewhat controlled mayhem at that, descended and they were all too busy to talk at all.

Moving in a circle, with Young Dougal at his back, they kept the others a few paces back, tiring them and then, at his word, beating them into submission. He'd fought with Young Dougal at his back, much as their fathers had fought many times, and each time they were successful. Laughing as he knocked the last one standing to the ground, he held out his hand to Young Dougal and shook it when he grasped it.

'Good fight! You will have to show me how you made that last move,' he said to his fighting partner as his friends climbed to their feet and dusted the dirt of the yard from themselves.

'Something my father showed me the other day,' Young Dougal said.

Rurik was a legendary warrior and had led the MacLerie warriors into battle for decades. That he shared his knowledge of fighting with his son, as his own father had, did not surprise Aidan.

His friends did not remain disgruntled for long after their defeat. Not insulted that others had made coins off their loss, the men accepted his offer of ale in the keep. They stopped by one of the barrels that collected rain and washed. His mother would expect no less in her keep and everyone respected the lady's wishes.

When they sat at table and had been served, done reviewing the fight and planning another test of skills, Aidan thought on Catriona's words and the fear in her gaze as she spoke to him—nay, as she pleaded with him to leave her be.

Seduction should be a pleasant process—each one taking a teasing step forward and then retreating to allow the other's invite to further the relationship. Seduction, he had always thought, should be fun and filled with even parts of laughter and breathless, hot pleasures of the flesh. Seduction might involve persuasion, but should never involve force.

Her words made him feel as though he had forced himself upon her and Aidan had never done that with any woman.

Oh, for a certain, some women he'd slept with needed more persuading and convincing than others, but each was as different as were the circumstances of his interest.

Had he misread the signs in her flirting? Had he ignored them in his desire to have her? Aidan took a couple of mouthfuls of his ale, only half-paying heed to the discussion going on around him. Thinking on their first meeting at the well, he pondered how best to approach her now. If for nothing other than his own need to know, he would speak to her, bluntly, and find out why she feared him so.

'I told you it was a woman!' Angus called from the other end of the table. Holding up his cup, he nodded at Aidan. 'To your success in another bed in Lairig Dubh! May you soon begin to share some of it with me!'

Aidan caught sight of a serving girl scurrying off towards the solar and knew word of his exploits would be shared, among the servants who worked here, his family and anyone who would listen. Everyone knew he'd stopped visiting the lovely Sima some weeks ago. That was old gossip by now and everyone who was curious, but waited for the news of his newest conquest.

He almost hoped that his parents would begin talking about their search for an appropriate wife so that attentions would be turned in that direction. And he would be free to pursue Catriona without the prying eyes and loose tongues spoiling his efforts at discretion. Mayhap he would guide the gossip down that new path himself?

'Have I told you yet that my parents seek a bride for me?' he asked no one in particular. 'They are considering potential wives at this moment.'

Silence reigned for a very long moment as that bit of news echoed through the hall. If he was correct, it would take until no later than supper this night for everyone in Lairig Dubh to learn of his impending marriage to…whomever his parents chose. That would give him the distraction he needed to find some time to speak to Catriona.

Glancing across the table as his friends mumbled

their words of congratulations for his future marriage, he realised that the perfect way to see her again sat there before him, raising a cup to his happiness.

Catriona stirred the ingredients in the cast-iron pot over the fire once more, adding a bit more water so the thick stew boiling and bubbling within it would not burn on to the metal. The aroma of the vegetables and herbs spread throughout the cottage as it cooked. The freshly baked bread lay wrapped in cloth and the crock of butter waited next to it on the table. A plain meal, but Munro said nothing more was needed for him and the friend he brought to sup with them this evening.

The recently swept floor was clean and the pallet's blankets were smoothed into place. She glanced around one more time as she heard Munro's voice and approach on the path to her, their, door. Guests of her husband and his son did not happen often and they must be made welcome or her lack of manners would reflect on her husband. So, Cat tucked the loosened strands of hair back inside the kerchief she wore, smoothed down the skirt of her gown and stood up as the door opened.

Any words of greeting she'd planned to speak to Munro's guest disappeared as she met the piercing amber gaze of Aidan MacLerie. Only when Munro frowned did she realise she must look like a gaping idiot. Dropping into a curtsy and bowing her head, she whispered a greeting as she should.

'Good evening, my lord. Welcome to Gowan and Munro's home.'

Munro nodded slightly from his place at his friend's

side, apparently pleased now with her welcome. He stepped inside and closed the door behind them. Still slowed by the shock of seeing the earl's son inside her cottage, she did not move.

'My thanks to you for your hospitality and allowing me to accompany Munro to supper,' he said, his deep voice causing the most alarming reaction—gooseflesh rose on the skin of her arms at the sound. 'And especially for being so gracious without much warning.'

Good Lord, she'd forgotten to offer him a cup! So much for hospitality and good manners, she thought as she tried to regain control over herself.

'Would you like some ale, my lord? Or water?' she asked, walking to the table and lifting a cup and waiting for his choice to fill it from one of the pitchers there.

'I brought a skin of my mother's favourite wine. I thought we could share it?' he answered smoothly, holding it out to her. The dimple in his chin became more pronounced as did the amusement in his gaze when she finally gained the courage to meet his eyes.

'That was kind of you,' she said, reaching to take it from him. His fingers grazed hers, not by accident, she suspected, as he let it go. 'And kind of Lady Jocelyn to share such a luxury with us.'

'She may not know,' he whispered to her before turning back to her stepson. 'As an apology of sorts, Munro, for beating your sorry arse into the ground today.'

Uncertain of how Gowan's son would take such a comment, she waited to see his reaction. After a short hesitation, he surprised her by laughing right in Aidan's face. And, although she usually saw his sullen, disagreeable side, his amusement seemed genuine. Cat felt some of the tension in the cottage ease. Pouring some of the deep-red wine into two cups, she handed one to their guest and then one to Munro.

'And you, Mistress MacKenzie? Where is your cup?'

Cat froze at his words. Would Munro pick up that he knew her already? Most around here were MacLeries, whether close or distant relation did not matter. Very few went by other names. Instead of waiting for Munro to point it out, she shook her head and held up the empty cup and filled it from the pitcher of ale.

'Wine is too strong a drink for me, my lord. It goes right to my head. So I will leave it to you two to enjoy and drink the ale.' At the darkening of Munro's gaze, she turned to Aidan. 'If you do not mind, my lord?' She motioned to them to sit at the table, never waiting for his reply.

'I do not mind at all, Munro,' he said to his friend and not to her. He understood that Munro would take more offence to her declining such a gift. Wine such as that was too costly for their table. 'I would not want to see your stepmother light-headed or otherwise affected this night.'

Had he actually spoken 'this night' more loudly or had she just imagined it? As though on another night such a reaction would be desired?

Shaking her head, trying to clear such thoughts, Cat took the bowls from the shelf and ladled the lamb stew into each. Though she'd planned that this would last for several more meals, she knew that these two, strong young men would empty the pot with their appetites.

Since there really was no choice in this—to offer less than everything would be an insult to the lord's son—she filled their bowls and placed them on the table.

Then with her own bowl half-filled, she sat across from the very man she'd been trying to avoid—avoid thinking about, avoid talking about and avoid talking to. If she thought this an innocent invitation from one friend to another, the merriment in his eyes as he met hers confirmed just the opposite. He'd planned this all, using Munro as the way to get here. Having no choice but to offer hospitality and company, Cat took the chunk of bread offered by Gowan's son and dipped it in her stew.

This would the longest meal of her life.

Aidan tried not to laugh—first at the surprise on her face when she saw him and then at the way she tried not to allow him to see how affected she was by him. When he'd decided that the only way to know why she feared him so was to know her more closely, Munro seemed the obvious way to do that. It was not difficult to wheedle an invitation to his father's cottage for dinner.

Now, as he and Munro talked about the day's events, upcoming duties and plans to travel to several of the other MacLerie holdings, Aidan never took his attention from her. He noticed the way the edges of her mouth curved when she smiled, the way she savoured and chewed the succulent chunks of lamb and turnips and the way she tried not to stare at him.

At first, she seemed intent on staying apart by sitting on the other side of the table from him and Munro and even staying out of any of the talk. But her nervousness seemed to ease and she offered a few softly spoken comments to the conversation. He noticed that any attempts to ask about her own life before coming to Lairig Dubh were neatly directed to another topic or turned into questions about him or Munro even.

Aidan glanced around the cottage as they ate. He noticed it was plainly furnished, but clean. Similar in size to most of the cottages on this lane, he saw nothing that seemed to say this was her home there. Two trunks sat along the back wall. Munro had told him that although she'd been married to Gowan for about eight years, they'd only moved here about two years ago. That was time enough to make this her home and yet, it was not.

As the meal continued, he watched her as much as he could. And his body reacted when he realised that she, too, stole glances of him just as much. If she was fearful or reticent, her eyes never gave it away. Though he had enjoyed the shocked expression when they'd walked in, the soft smile she gave when he offered her the loaf of bread pleased him more.

He wanted to speak to her alone, but prodding Munro into inviting him here was the first step. Put her at ease with his presence and then further their acquaintance… hopefully much, much further.

Soon, too soon for his liking, they finished eating the simple but tasty meal and he could draw out his time there no longer. They rose as he did and he shook Munro's hand, with words about their duties on the morrow. Walking to the door, he turned back and spoke to Catriona.

'My thanks again for the warm welcome in spite of the lateness of the plans, Mistress MacKenzie.'

'Any friend of Munro's will find himself welcomed in his father's home, my lord,' she said, dipping into a curtsy before him.

He reached out and took her hand, guiding her back to standing instead of the cowering position she'd taken.

'When you say "my lord", I look for my father,' he said, looking to Munro first. 'Now that we are known to each other and seeing that I am friend to Munro, you may call me by my given name. I pray you, call me only Aidan.'

She tried to free her hand from his grasp, but he held it firmly as he waited for her reaction. His body tightened, his blood heated, as he waited to finally hear the sound of his name spoken in that earthy tone of voice.

'Oh, my lord, I could not be so familiar with you. You are the earl's son, after all,' she said, laughing as she used her other hand to loosen his fingers from around hers. 'It would clearly be disrespectful to do so.' The lightness in her voice slipped when she turned to Munro, who wore a dark frown now. 'Though since it is your request that I do so…I will ask my husband for his permission when he returns.'

Aidan nearly laughed aloud at how smartly she'd slipped his noose and reminded him once again that she had a husband. With a simple phrase, she placed that husband directly between them and in his path should he be pursuing her! He could not force the issue now without making Munro suspicious, so he nodded and smiled at her.

'A wise woman who relishes the guidance of her husband,' he said, nudging Munro with his elbow. 'May we both be so blessed with wives as obedient as your father's when we marry, Munro.'

He could only describe her expression as equal amounts of anger, satisfaction and... Something else swirled in those bright blue eyes. Something he could not identify, though he hoped it was anticipation. Deciding that leaving was the best thing to do at this moment, he lifted the latch and pulled open the door.

'Good evening to you both,' he said with a nod as he stepped outside.

Aidan did not turn back to look, though he wanted to savour every moment in her company. Part of him feared the door would slam in his face, but somehow part knew that she would never dare such a thing...at least not in front of Munro.

The way his groin tightened told him he wanted to see more of the slamming-door Catriona than the one who seemed to cling to polite behaviour. Though she hid herself behind the plain garb and manners of a good-wife, Aidan suspected that there was so much more to Mistress Catriona MacKenzie.

And after this meal together and after catching enticing glimpses of the spirit of the woman that lay hidden, he knew he wanted her even more.

Chapter Five

The man was everywhere.

For someone of such a high position and with duties to see to, Cat had no idea of how Aidan MacLeric managed to be in the village so much. Or how it was always as she made her way through her days and chores and errands.

When she went to get water at the well, she spied him nearby.

When she washed clothing by the side of the stream, he sat on horseback some yards away.

When she visited the miller and the bakehouse or the butcher, he would cross her path unexpectedly.

Each encounter was brief and, if any exchange of words was possible, it was only a polite word of greeting. He always greeted any other person in the vicinity, too, so it did not look untoward to others. But the heat in his gaze was only for her and she knew it.

This morn had dawned dark and dreary with rain coming in fierce, windy waves, interspersed with only brief respites of calm. Few of the villagers braved the weather, but she'd promised to help Muireall again and she could not let something as predictable as rain stop her. As she darted along the muddied paths, holding her skirts above the worst of it and pulling her arisaid over her head to keep the torrents from soaking her too quickly, she never noticed him in front of her.

Cat hit the wall of his muscular chest and stumbled off the lane. The length of her skirts and the arisaid tripped up her feet and she careened towards a large puddle off to the side of the path. Tangled in layers of cloth, she had no chance to save herself from landing in the cold, filthy water there. She scrunched her eyes closed, pulled in a ragged breath and prepared herself for the shock of the frigid pool.

She never hit the water.

His strong arms encircled her, holding her only inches from the surface of the puddle, before pulling her up and against his body.

'Have a care, Mistress MacKenzie,' he whispered as he put her on her feet and righted her cloak, exposing her face to his. 'Running with your head so low can be dangerous.'

Cat tried to take a breath, but could not. His hands surrounded her still and she could feel the heat escaping from his body. She raised her head so she could see him from under the edge of the woollen cloak and found his gaze a penetrating one instead of the usual amused one. She tried to think of a humorous response to his admonishment so she could be on her way, but all thoughts of placating him vanished when his mouth took hers.

Hot. Hard. Wet.

Thoughts fled. Breathing stopped. The rain and everything else disappeared.

He pulled her closer then, tilted his face and possessed her mouth, sliding his tongue deep within and tasting her.

After a single, reckless moment of complete oblivion, she realised what he, what they, were doing and she pushed her way out of his embrace, wiping the back of her hand across her lips.

But that kiss could not be undone. The boldness she expected from this brash, lusty young warrior, but she should have better protected herself from this kind of embrace and kiss. This kiss spoke of entitlement and forbidden passion and dishonouring herself and her vows of faithfulness. This kiss led to more. This kiss led to....

Cat lifted her hand and delivered a stinging slap to his face. The sound of it echoed in the air around them as the shadow of her hand imprinted in red on his cheek. He blinked several times before letting his hands drop from her shoulders.

'How dare you!' she said, looking around to see if anyone witnessed this illicit gesture. 'I do not know what gave you the idea that I would violate my vows to Gowan, but I will not. I am an honourable woman and I owe....' Her eyes burned and she prayed that the rain would disguise the tears she felt pouring forth. She took a step back and lowered her voice.

'You may think that you have the right to claim whatever woman catches your eye...and you might have that right, but I beg you to look elsewhere, *my lord*,' she warned. 'I will not be a willing party to your misguided, youthful escapades.'

He'd not spoken a word. He'd not moved or in any way reacted to her slap or her words. Cat understood that there was really nothing she could do if he decided to have her, but she hoped her objections would matter before he took another step in his apparent plan to seduce her.

Suddenly aware of what she'd done, she once more lifted her skirts and ran, this time with an eye on the path ahead and without daring to look back at him. As she made her way to Muireall's, she glanced through the heavy rain to see if anyone was about and could have seen them. The paths and walkways seemed empty and she prayed no one had been about.

Arriving out of breath and soaked to the skin by her haste, she knocked on her friend's door. Cat allowed only a momentary pause before opening the door and she closed it behind her immediately, leaning against it as though it would keep him out.

As if anything would keep him from a place or a thing…or a person…he wanted. She shivered from the cold of the rain and from the heat that yet raced through her from that simple but forbidden touching of two mouths.

'Here now, Catriona,' Muireall said, taking hold of her and pulling her towards the hearth where the children huddled.

The heat of the fire there kept the dampness of the storm from spreading inside. Cat allowed Muireall to lead her there and to pull the wet woollen cloak from around her and replace it with a dry blanket. Soon, a cup of heated broth filled her hands and she tried to stop the trembling that shook her now.

'What happened?' her friend asked. Muireall's hand steadied the cup and guided it to her mouth. 'Drink more before you answer. You are still shivering.'

Cat sipped the broth and peered over the rim of it at the three little faces staring at her from their places. The eldest, a boy, was the caretaker, gently but firmly guiding his two younger sisters to a safe distance away from the fire's heat. The older girl rocked the nearby cradle while humming a tune that Cat had heard Muireall sing many times. The younger daughter leaned against her sister, her thumb being suckled noisily while she gazed at Cat.

A pang of loss struck her as she watched those bairns and tried to regain her control. She would never have children. She could never have them. No matter how much she wanted or prayed it to be so, she would not conceive and bear her husband babes of their own. At other times, she could keep the emptiness away, but the old feelings forced to the surface by the tumultuous kiss now grew stronger.

Tears threatened once more and these would be witnessed and unexplainable. So, she took a deep breath and let it out. Then she drank the rest of the broth before offering the cup back to Muireall. Hoping for the courage she needed, she smiled and nodded.

'My thanks for your gentle care.' She allowed the blanket to fall from her shoulders and straightened on the stool. 'I lost my footing and almost landed in a puddle the size of the loch. I thought my ankle twisted.' A small lie to keep her friend from getting close to the truth.

'Let me see it.' Muireall was on her knees before Cat in an instant. The bairns took it as a sign they could play and they climbed on her back, throwing their arms around her neck and pulling her over. 'Ah, my wee urchins! 'Tis not playtime now. Catriona's foot is hurt.' As Cat watched, her friend peeled the children off, one at a time, and put them back in their places with a kiss on their small faces.

With a poke and a prod, her ankle was checked with a thoroughness that any healer or physician would be proud of and declared all was well. And the time it took for Muireall to do that gave Cat the opportunity to gather her wits and calm herself. Now, the blanket was too warm, so she rose, folded it and placed it back on the trunk where it belonged. When she turned back, Muireall stood there before her.

'Are you well?' Cat could hear the sceptical tone underlying the words.

'I was out of breath from running to get out of the rain and then tripped. I *am* well *now*, though.' Cat leaned over to glance and nod at the children. 'What can I help you with today?' she asked. If she'd thought her friend would be diverted, she was wrong.

'So explain to me how a near fall into a puddle leaves you looking well kissed?'

He lost track of how long he stood there in the teeming rain. His body ached from her brief but arousing nearness and from the hot taste of her mouth. Every moment of the brief encounter refuelled his desire for her.

The way her eyes had widened as he clutched her to him, avoiding the muck and cold of the puddle. The way her mouth had dropped open as she met his gaze. The way she had tasted as his tongue explored her mouth for that brief, brief caress. His body bucked again, his cock full and aching to be within her, as he thought on the kiss.

And, though her reaction was not the one he wanted, Aidan finally saw the fire that always lay banked within her gaze. The slap had surprised them both—the flare of shock and then anger had turned her eyes to an icy blue. His cheek yet stung from the sharp reproach for his behaviour. That she had done it did not anger him.

'Twas her words that bothered him as they put his entire campaign out between them. Seduction was simply a game to play while waiting for the more serious parts of his life to commence. While waiting to take on more duties and while waiting for that much-discussed wife. It was what men, especially young men, did. But now, in the cold, steady rain that helped to cool his ardour, it seemed tawdry and small-minded.

Especially for the son of Connor MacLerie. For the man who would some day rule over the vast lands of the MacLerie clan.

No matter that he wanted her and would bed her if she came willing, this game had to end. He would no longer contrive to meet up with the lovely Catriona MacKenzie in the village, on the roads or in the keep. No matter that the kiss had fired his blood in an unfamiliar and exciting way. None of it mattered for the woman had refused him.

He wiped the rain from his face and walked back to where he'd tethered his horse. Vaulting on to its back, he gathered the reins in his hands and guided the animal through the muddied lanes and up the hill to reach the keep. With a call to the guards on duty at the gate and on the walls surrounding the yard and keep, he entered his home.

His fascination with Gowan's wife would be a thing of the past. His attempts to seduce her had gone unnoticed and would remain just some harmless fun between them.

Just some harmless fun.

His father would have tasks for him. His mother would wish to discuss his thoughts on the potential brides. As he climbed the steps to enter the great hall, leaving his mount with a boy in the yard, he realised that the one objection to any of the women named—he did not wish to consider a MacKenzie bride because he was pursuing one of her kin—was now moot.

The butcher's son was delivering supplies to the keep and was not happy about it. Young Ronald, named for his father and his father before him, had the unhappy duty of following the cart to the kitchens and unloading it. Being only ten, it was a torturous assignment for it kept him from splashing his way through every puddle in the village during a storm such as this one.

Finally finished and dismissed by his uncle, Young Ronald ran from the keep, jumping over the rivers of water that traced patterns and grooves down the hill to the village. Knowing his friends would be waiting by the end of the lane, he raced through the mud, almost losing a shoe to the sticky, gooey mud that sucked at his every step.

He spied what looked to be a deep puddle off to the side and would have raced through it, but a woman and a man stood next to it. Veering around the small house in his path, he came out the other side just in time to see the man grab the woman up and kiss her.

Shuddering and grimacing against the horror of it, he waited for them to move on so he could plunge into the puddle, which now looked deep enough to call a pool. A moment later, the woman slapped the man holding and kissing her and pushed away.

Good that, it meant they would leave sooner and he could have the puddle all to himself. Better, he knew if he told his oldest sister Meg about who was kissing whom in the shadows during the storm, she would reward him with a warm tart. Or one of her special pies. Sighing over memories of how his sister's baking tasted and smelled, he stepped closer to get a look at who these two were.

The man was the earl's son. Kissing women—Young Ronald could not help that he grimaced again—seemed to be something Aidan MacLerie enjoyed for he was always in the village visiting this one or that one. He shrugged and was ready to leave, for the young lord kissing a woman was so commonplace it would get him no reward at all, when the woman turned and he saw her face.

Old Gowan's wife.

Old Gowan was one of the earl's best soldiers. He'd even showed Ronald how to wield a sword—well, a wooden one—and shown him how to duck a blow. He knew Old Gowan and he knew Old Gowan's wife. And sure enough, that was her that Aidan MacLerie kissed.

Meg would probably give him an extra tart for this news!

The two left, each going in their own way, giving Young Ronald an open path to the puddle. As he jumped and landed in the centre with both feet, the water exploded around him and rushed in waves over the side of the big hole that formed it. Now, more empty than not, it would take time to refill.

So, he wiped his face and ran off to find his friends, the secret he carried forgotten for the time being.

Chapter Six

Once the weather broke and the storms finally ceased, the ground began to dry out. Villagers and those living in the keep all sought out the fresh air and began to emerge like ants from their nest. Though most duties could not cease simply for rain, those who could avoid going out in it had. And, as was the usual occurrence during forced time indoors, tempers flared.

His father insisted on fair challenges and fights to sort through disagreements among his warriors, so the fair weather brought forth many of those. Once the work was done for the day, those challenged and those defending gathered in the yard. Though he was neither, Aidan would not mind a chance to work out the tension in his body.

With the sun setting so early, there was not much light left. Aidan called out to Angus and Caelan when he noticed them by the fence and went to watch the first matches with them. Young Dougal, Rurik's son, stood at the ready for the next match. He probably bore no one a

grudge—the young man just loved to fight. With only
Munro missing from their group, the fight began. It took
no time at all for the crowds to gather and the betting
along the outer fringes to begin, too.

But the murmurs that passed through the crowds just
then had nothing to do with the men fighting within the
fence there. Elbows nudged and heads leaned closer to
whisper some bit of gossip about someone walking towards the keep. As he leaned away and looked to the
person causing the comments, a sick feeling hit him like
a punch in his gut, its sourness spreading into a very
bad taste of bile in his mouth.

Catriona MacKenzie walked alongside the steward's
sister, heading for the keep. He noticed that she glanced
behind her as people passed, clearly aware of the whispers and pointed staring in her direction. When those
whispers and stares began to include him, he knew for
certain that someone had witnessed that kiss.

One thing his father had taught him was that to give
scandal attention was to give it life, so he returned his
gaze to the men fighting. His attention remained elsewhere, wondering who had carried the tale. And if
everyone knew what had happened. And if everyone
thought that they had....

Bloody hell! They knew him and his ways—of course
they thought he'd taken Gowan's wife as his lover. A
twinge of guilt assailed him as he knew that he would
have if she'd said aye.

The discretion he'd planned, if that path had been
followed, was impossible now. If he tried to correct the

assumption that everyone now accepted, it would draw more attention than if he simply did not comment on it.

That plan lasted exactly four minutes—the length of time it took Munro to reach his side after entering through the gates. He hoped to explain things to his friend—after all, they'd shared a number of sexual conquests in their carousing nights and Munro would believe him.

It was the punch that connected with his jaw and landed him on his face and the taste of dirt in his mouth that convinced him otherwise.

'Munro,' he began as he pushed to his feet and wiped the back of his hand across his face. 'Come. Let us discuss this….'

He got nothing else out before the punch in the stomach knocked the air from his lungs and made speaking impossible. When Young Dougal grabbed Munro and held him, wrapping his arms around their friend and not allowing him to deliver any blows, Aidan caught his breath.

'In the hall,' he ordered. 'Gair's chamber. Now.'

Young Dougal had some sense for he dragged Munro around to the front of the keep and entered that doorway, not crossing paths with the stricken woman whose reputation was now being bandied about by one and all, embellishing the details as it passed. Aidan thought about how to proceed, how to stop this reckless talk before true harm was done, but he could come up with nothing.

Munro walked on his own as they made their way through the main floor of the keep, heading towards the chamber that Gair, the steward, made use of. It was one of few truly private places within the keep, making it a perfect place for the discussion to come. Once they were gathered inside, with the door closed and a servant outside to drive away the curious, Aidan faced Munro.

'I know not what gossip you heard, but it is not true if it involves your father's wife.' Crossing his arms over his chest, he waited for the accusations, planning to reveal nothing more than was necessary.

'So, you say you have not been following Catriona? And you did not meet with her in the village two days ago?' Munro glared at him, his posture daring Aidan to lie.

'Following her? I spend time in the village. If I saw her and greeted her, 'twas only as much as anyone else who lives there.' He evaded the question, but from the expression in Angus's eyes, he knew not well enough.

'And during the storms? 'Tis said you two were kissing in the village then. You were seen wrapped around her and her clutching you back.'

'Aye, I did see her during the worst of the storms. She was making her way to some task and nearly fell into a rut in the lane. I righted her and she went on her way and I on mine.'

Munro looked stymied then. To question him further could be considered an insult, yet it was clear to Aidan that he wanted to.

'Did you question her about these accusations? Oh, wait. No one actually accuses us. This is just gossip being spread with or without the truth mattering,' Aidan said.

'Aye, I did question her,' he spat out. 'First she re-

fused to answer me and then she denied it. Do you deny
it as well?'

'She denied it because she has been only faithful to
your father, Munro.' He lowered his voice. 'There is no
proof.'

And that was his mistake, for Munro raised his head
and met his gaze. He began to grind his jaws as he rose
to his full height.

'No proof? I think you had me invite you to supper
that night just to press your suit. Now that I think on it,
you have been in the village more than usual. And you
have not mentioned another woman's name in weeks
and weeks. That means you are pursuing a new lover for
your bed. Proof, Aidan? I have only to remember your
ways to know that there is more to this than you or she
is saying.' Munro pushed him aside and strode from the
chamber. When his friends looked to him to see if they
should stop him, he shook his head.

'Let him be.'

'Aidan?' Caelan asked the question without even saying the rest.

'She is faithful to her vows,' he repeated, telling them
exactly what they suspected—it was not for a lack of trying on his part that Catriona MacKenzie did not share
his bed.

'What about Munro?' Angus asked.

'Leave him be. This gossip will die down soon
enough. When all those who now watch us both see
nothing, it will die down.'

Now, their expressions confirmed what he already
knew—this gossip would not go away soon or well

enough. Everyone who heard it would think Catriona guilty of cuckolding Gowan. She was an outsider, from lands and a clan who were, until only recently, their enemies.

So until Gowan returned and the matter could be dealt with as it needed to be—the misbehaving wife punished and the man issued a challenge—the gossip would do what gossip did.

It would spread.

Two weeks had passed since her life irrevocably changed and there was still nothing she could do about it. In spite of knowing she'd done the right thing, everyone in the village and the keep believed she had sinned and humiliated Gowan.

Munro dogged her steps and slept at the cottage every night. He also arrived at various times during the day— unexpected and unannounced—with the hardly hidden goal of catching her in some act. It was not just his presence, it was the way he spoke to her and glared at her. So many times she wanted to strike out at him, but she held her hand and hoped that Gowan would believe her even if his son did not.

The worst part was that Munro revealed that he'd sent word to his father to return and take care of this matter of honour. Her body trembled as the thoughts of what that would entail crept back into her mind. As her husband, Gowan had the right to punish her however he chose, though to kill her would require the chieftain's permission. He could banish her or send her to a convent, but that would require money. As much as she wanted to believe Gowan would not seek such redress, Munro's taunts and threats could convince her otherwise.

Muireall stood by her when none other would, but Cat had heard the harsh, whispered words between Muireall and her husband, Hugh, and knew her friend risked much by her support. The rest of those living in the village reacted the same—treating her like a traitor and shunning her.

The butcher could not give her the meat she asked to buy and offered her only the toughest cuts instead. The baker had no space in his ovens for her bread. The women stared or walked away instead of answering her greetings. When walking through the village, she lost her footing several times when bumped or jostled from behind as people rushed past her.

The strangest thing she'd noticed was how the men of the village treated her. Before, they treated her with the respect due the wife of kin. Now, more often than not, she met lustful stares of men who saw her as a loose woman, her rumoured association with the earl's son being the only proof they needed. None ever approached her, but it did not stop them from following her with illicit desire in their eyes.

If she'd thought she was an outsider, a stranger in a place where everyone was familiar to everyone else, these last two weeks had proven how wrong she could be. Convinced that this would probably not change, no matter the course of action Gowan took with her, Catriona wondered if refusing Aidan's advances had caused more problems than accepting them would have. She brushed that sinful thought aside and tried to make it through another terrible, miserable day.

When she arrived at the well with her buckets to fill and every bit of conversation stopped in one moment, Cat knew they'd been talking about her. She nodded her greetings to anyone who would meet her gaze—only one woman did—and walked to the edge to begin filling her bucket. Somehow, one of her buckets fell off the edge and into the water below.

Fell? As she glanced around and noticed the smirks alight on most faces, she did not doubt it was done a-purpose. She had no choice but to retrieve it, so she began the task of trying to capture it with the bucket on the rope and bring it back up to her. No one, not a one, offered any assistance. The heat of their glaring stares burned her and she fought back tears as she struggled with the bucket.

Tempted to give up, leave the bucket behind and retreat to the privacy of her cottage, Muireall surprised her by arriving and helping her. Cat shook her head and tried to make her friend go away because she understood the dangers that Muireall faced being connected to her. But, true friend that she was, Muireall remained at her side, pointing and joking at the bobbing bucket until Cat's efforts met with success.

'Come to supper tonight,' Muireall said as they reached Cat's door. 'I made more than enough for one more mouth at the table and the children have missed your company.' She waited until Cat had put the buckets down before taking her hand. 'I have missed your company.'

''Tis best, I think,' Cat explained. 'I know Hugh objects…'

'Bah on his objections!' Muireall said with a laugh that was too strong and told Cat how strong the man's protestations were. 'You are my friend.'

'Muireall, I know you are my friend. Still, I will not cause you more strife with your husband or his family.' Glancing outside to see if others watched, she lowered her voice. 'Gowan is on his way home, summoned by Munro. All will be settled then.'

'Will he believe your words?' Muireall asked. She'd never once asked if they were true, she simply believed Cat. 'What do you think he will do?'

'I know not,' Cat admitted. 'He is a patient and fair man, but he can be hard, too. Now when his honour is involved…' She shrugged. 'If Munro has convinced him to return now and to these accusations, I just do not know.'

If her friend sensed or heard too much of her despair, she would never leave. So, she forced a smile and hugged Muireall.

'Go now! Who is with those bairns while you dawdle with me?' Cat walked over and grasped the edge of the door, shushing her friend out.

'You gave me no answer about supper.' Muireall stopped in the middle of the doorway and crossed her arms over her chest. 'And "no" had best not be what you say.'

'Fine. I will come,' she agreed. It would be the first enjoyable meal for her since…

'You are worrying again.' Muireall turned to leave, but glanced back again. 'Worry not over Hugh. I am not.'

It became clear to her just a short time later that Hugh was a problem. When Cat arrived at her friend's cottage, Muireall's husband stomped out with a silent stare and as the bairns watched in shocked silence. Muireall welcomed her with watery tears and a brave smile, but Cat knew this would be the last time they shared together until Gowan returned and settled this matter.

Until Gowan returned, nothing could be changed or fixed.

As she fell into a troubled sleep that night, images of Gowan's return filled her dreams. Cat prayed that the man who had saved her life once would be able to save her honour now.

But everything waited for Gowan's return to Lairig Dubh.

Chapter Seven

Aidan answered his father's summons when it came. Though he had expected to be called to answer for the rumoured actions long before this, he knew it would happen sooner rather than later. Knocking and then opening the door, he found his father, grim-faced, sitting in the chair he called his. His mother stood apart from him—not a good sign. Strife between the Beast and his mate was never good. Closing the door, he walked forward, kissing his mother and nodding and standing before his father.

The silence grew, stronger and more uncomfortable by the moment. It was a strategy, used by his father many times, and a successful one at that. He waited, as practised at this as his parents were. Oh, his sister Lilidh would crumble in tears after a few moments of her father's hard stare. And Sheena, the youngest, would have trembled by now and admitted all sorts of sins, both real and imagined or planned. But he was the eldest and could play this game.

'A married woman, Aidan,' his father finally said. Not a question as most would ask, but a statement, a judgement against him already.

'You have never taken an interest in the women I take to my bed before, Father,' he said, choosing not to answer the question even if it wasn't asked yet. At his mother's gasp, he realised his error. 'I beg your pardon, Mother.' He faced his father again. 'She said no.'

He'd never lied to his parents before. Oh, he'd told wild tales and twisted the truth when it suited his needs, but he had never lied. Would his father accept his word as truth now?

'There are problems now, Aidan. Gowan carries out his duties well. He accepted whatever tasks or assignments I set before him. If others see that their wives could become the target of your efforts to fill your empty bed with a new lover...' His mother gasped again and Aidan steeled himself for her displeasure even as his father attempted an apology of sorts.

'I told you this was not a suitable matter for you to attend, Jocelyn. I said I would handle this myself.' His father stood and approached his mother. 'Your son is a man now and makes his own decisions. And he must stand by his actions as well.'

Jocelyn MacCallum, Lady MacLerie, was not a woman to be told her place. As a matter of fact, Aidan could not remember a place or a discussion where she did not go when the need or interest rose in her. Whether matters of kith and kin or king and country, she freely offered and sometimes forced her opinions into the decisions his father considered. Telling her that it was not her place was a challenge, plain and simple, and, from the dark expression on her face, one she was not going to let pass.

'Not suitable for me, Connor? Truly, did you say that?' His mother approached, finger pointing at him. She stood only as tall as his chest and he would like to say that he did not fear her. But he did, as did his father when her eyes flashed and her finger pointed. 'He is still my son and if he has dishonoured a married woman in seeking to fill his bed, I would have my say.'

Aidan prepared for her stinging words and then he would speak privately to his father. It was the way they handled things between them. 'Before you begin, let me repeat—she said no.'

He watched as doubt and then suspicion filled her expressive eyes, the colour his sister had inherited, and then as she realised what he'd said. 'So you did not bed her?'

'Mother.' He let out a breath. He did not wish to discuss his lovers with her, but it would be easier to answer her question. 'Nay, I did not bed her.'

'But you tried? And your attempts were witnessed?' she plunged on. One glance in his father's direction told him two things—he was enjoying Aidan's discomfort and would not intervene.

'Aye. Apparently.' Short answers would be best. The next thing he knew, she would be taking him to task over…

'So now married women, older women appeal to you?' Her eyes narrowed as she asked.

The barking laugh escaped from his father's mouth. Aidan felt the edges of his own mouth twitching then.

'Not married *women*. Not older *women*. *She* appealed to me. *Catriona* appealed to me.'

There it was. This time it was a different matter altogether. He did not just want fill the empty place in his bed with another warm body, he wanted her. In a way, it was disquieting. An uncomfortable feeling tingled in his skin. It was about her and no one else.

'Connor, tell Duncan to invite the three women we spoke of here…now. Spring is too far off.'

'Here now, love…' his father had stood at some point and now walked to his mother's side '…we will travel to your brother's lands in just over a month for his wedding. On our return, the three will visit here and Aidan will make his decision. We all agreed to this plan.'

''Tis clear to me that he needs to be married sooner rather than later.'

'Which is what I have been telling you for the last year, love.' Aidan startled and glanced at his father. So his mother had been the one behind delaying his betrothal? 'We will see to it now.'

His mother seemed contented by that answer, even if he wasn't comforted by the idea at all. Especially not when he just realised that what, or rather who, he wanted was outside his reach. Games aside, seduction aside, there was something about her that was different from every other woman he'd chased…and caught before. Over these last two weeks, since the incident that somehow exposed them, he'd thought about her more than he had before.

And how he'd dragged her into this mess.

'Jocelyn, I'd like to speak to our son now,' his father said, softly. His tone disarmed whatever objections she might have raised.

'Listen to your father, Aidan,' she said, lifting on her toes to kiss his cheek. 'His counsel is wise.'

Aidan smiled as he saw his father's brow rise as his mother walked by him. They watched as she left the chamber, closing the door behind her.

'So,' his father began, filling a cup with ale from the pitcher there and holding it out to him, 'did you suggest Gowan for the assignment to get him out of your way, then? So you could pursue his wife?'

He would not lie. 'Aye.'

Aidan waited as his father drank deeply before meeting his gaze. 'And did you? Pursue her?'

'Aye.' The word came out on a whisper and echoed across the emptiness between them.

'You have not failed in that kind of pursuit before.'

Now it was his turn to raise a brow at that remark. How closely had his father watched his amorous exploits?

'As your mother will no doubt tell you, there is little or nothing that happens in my family or on my lands that I do not know about.' His father laughed then. 'And it was not so long ago that I was a young man chasing any young woman who would share a few moments of pleasure with me.'

'And marriage made you stop?'

His father's faithfulness to his mother was well known, but was considered an eccentricity among most other families. A man could have a wife and a leman if he could support both and a wealthy, powerful nobleman such as his father could afford as many as he'd want. Yet he neither sought nor kept any lovers since, according to the stories, his marriage to Jocelyn MacCallum.

Connor MacLerie's marriage stood as an example and many men in the clan followed his lead, finding happiness in the beds and hearts of only their wives. Duncan, Rurik and others remained steadfast to their vows.

'Not marriage so much as love,' his father explained. Though his father's first marriage had ended in disaster, rumours said he had loved his wife. 'That is why I want you to focus on your marriage. If you find a wife like the one I found in your mother, this restlessness will pass.' His father put his cup down and sat once more. 'So, how do you plan to proceed in this matter between you and Gowan?'

'When he returns, I expect he will punish his wife as he sees fit and he will issue a challenge to me.' That much he knew for no man would allow such an insult, whether real or perceived, to go unanswered. And Catriona would bear the brunt of Gowan's displeasure over his actions.

'And you will decline it? Handle it privately?'

Aidan shook his head and put the cup down. 'Nay. I see no way to handle this in private since word has spread. I will accept his challenge and allow him to win. His honour will be satisfied and my transgression will be looked at as a youthful escapade.' He used Catriona's words to describe it. A pang of true longing struck him then. 'Is Gowan a cruel man? A fair one?' he asked, now contemplating what actions a man could or would take against a wife who shamed him…even if she had not.

'I am glad to see you are finally seeing the results caused by your lack of control and lack of discretion,' his father said.

The heat of embarrassment crept into his face. He'd been wrong, oh, so wrong, to pursue her and had never given it much thought. Before this, he would have taken his pleasure and never thought on the conscquences. Now, an innocent woman who'd stood firm for the vows she'd taken would be chastised and, most likely, beaten for his actions.

Very much as it would happen in the future when he inherited the titles, lands and people of the Clan Mac-Lerie. His word and his actions would send men to war, deprive others of their lands, direct marriages and contracts, both binding and severing relationships—and he would bear responsibility for it all.

The image of a humbled Catriona, beaten down both by her husband's hand and the scorn of the villagers, horrified him more than he could say. To see the spirit and the passion within that woman be less than the woman he knew she could be, would be, bothered him more than he could explain.

'So? How would you take him to be?' he asked once more, glancing from under his brow to watch his father's reaction.

'I think he will do only what he deems necessary to restore his honour. I will speak with him as well.'

Aidan nodded. His father's words would carry weight with the warrior to mitigate Catriona's part in this. Feeling less burdened now, knowing that this would all be worked out, each of them playing their part in getting past the gossip he'd caused, Aidan thanked his father and turned to leave.

'Once we return from Athdar's wedding and decide on your own betrothal, I think you should take over the running of Ord Dubh. Move there. Make it to your own liking. Take your pick of the men and establish it as your holding. 'Tis time, 'tis past time, really.'

Ord Dubh, *black hammer*, was a small stone keep that sat on a round hammer-shaped hill at the southernmost spot on MacLerie lands. It was a choice parcel of land and a good place to prove himself to be his father's heir. So, while his newly betrothed wife was living here and becoming accustomed to the ways of the MacLeries, he would be preparing their home, his home, in the south.

Away from the temptation named Catriona Mac-Kenzie.

With these plans in place, all that need happen now was Gowan's arrival home to sort through things with him and see Catriona settled back into her husband's regard. No matter that he could easily see her standing on the stone balcony that Ord Dubh's keep boasted, watching his return and waiting there for him.

Not with Gowan. Not another woman waiting.

Catriona. His.

Shaking off thoughts and dreams that could not be, he held out his hand to his father.

'My thanks for your support, Father,' he said, shaking his hand.

Leaving the chamber, he made his way to the small

room he claimed as his in the other tower and went to bed. His dreams were filled with the lush images of Catriona, naked in his arms, on his bed, in his keep. Her brown hair pouring over them, shimmering in the light of candles. Her eyes so icy blue they burned as she gazed down at him, her legs tight around his hips as she rode him. Until they both cried out in pleasure.

He awakened, sweat-covered and hard, unable to find a way back to a peaceful sleep with such dreams yet tormenting him.

Hopefully, Gowan would arrive home soon and take Catriona out of his thoughts and dreams.

Catriona sat near the small window, using the sun's weak rays to light the clothing she was mending. Her back ached from the position, so she welcomed the knock at the door, knowing only it gave her the opportunity to stand and stretch out the tight muscles that complained even now. She lifted the latch, expecting Muireall to be there, on her daily errands and with wee Donald on her hip. Instead she found Lady MacLerie. Dropping into a deep curtsy and remaining there, she could not think of why the lady would be standing at her door.

'My lady,' she said, without lifting her head. 'How can I serve you?'

'May we speak inside?' the lady asked. Cat stood and moved back so the lady could enter. Though for what reason, she knew not.

'There, Peggy,' the lady said, pointing at the table.

Cat then noticed the girl standing behind the lady

and the basket she carried. With a nod to her, young Peggy hefted the basket on to the table. Still puzzled over the lady's reason for visiting her, she watched as Lady MacLerie whispered some instructions to her maid and waited for her to speak. Though a common sight in the village, visiting the sick, speaking to villagers to ask after their situations and conditions and other duties expected of her, Catriona had not met or spoken to her.

'May we sit?' the lady asked.

Cursing her own lack of manners under her breath, she pulled out the two best stools from under the table and waited for the lady to settle herself on one of them before sitting next to her. When the lady reached out and took her hand, patting it gently, alarm and fear set in. Shaking her head against the reason for this visit, Cat waited to hear the terrible words. For the other reason the lady visited here was to…

'I am so sorry to tell you that Gowan has died.'

It could not be. He was an able soldier and had been on many dangerous missions and fought in many battles for the MacLerie. His assignment this time was not one of those. This must be—

'—A mistake, my lady. Gowan was at one of your holdings, training some men. Munro said he is on his way here…to…' She stopped, noticing the way the lady's gaze slid away from hers for a moment, acknowledging the shameful incident without saying a word.

'He will arrive in a day or so,' she said, deciding she needed to look out the door to see if her husband approached even now.

But the lady's grasp on her hand tightened, not allowing her to rise. When she glanced at the face of the woman who'd tamed the Beast of the Highlands, she read the truth of it—Gowan was dead.

Gowan was dead.

'I've brought a few things you might need over the next days and will send some of the servants to help you when his body arrives. My husband said to expect that to be later this day.'

Cat could not find words to speak. Gowan dying was simply not possible. He was older than her, but as strong a man as any around. He never lingered abed and was never ill. He could not be dead. She shook her head, denying the lady's claim.

'Here now,' she said, putting her arm around Cat's shoulders. ''Tis hard to think of anything at this time. The news is such a shock to my husband as well. Gowan always served him well. But you must gather your wits and do what is expected. We must do what is expected of us at times like this.'

'Aye, my lady,' she mumbled, unsure of exactly what she should be doing now.

All she wanted to do was curl up on the floor and die with him. He'd saved her life and had asked for little or nothing in return. Now…now…all was black before her. Lady MacLerie helped her to her feet and pushed open the door.

'Some fresh air will help clear your head,' she advised. 'Do you have kin here? Or some friend I can summon?' As they stepped out of the door, Cat dragged in a breath and felt her vision clear a bit.

'Muireall,' she whispered.

'Gair's sister?'

'Aye, my lady.'

'Peggy, go and seek out Gair's sister. Bring her here,' she said to the waiting maid. 'Know you the way?'

With a nod, the girl ran off. After a few minutes in the cold air, she let go of Lady MacLerie and stood on her own. Looking around, she saw some of the villagers were noticing them now. Shivering from the shock of the news, Cat went back inside and wrapped a shawl around her shoulders.

If Gowan was dead, she should....

Glancing around the small cottage that had been her world for two years since they'd moved to Lairig Dubh, Cat realised that none of this was hers. It was Gowan's. She stood in the centre of the small world and knew nothing could be the same again. Gowan was dead.

'Cat?'

She looked up, surprised to find Muireall standing before her now. She'd not heard her friend arrive or noticed the lady's departure, but both had happened.

'Cat, we must get ready now,' her friend advised. She just could not work out what the words meant. 'Come, we need to put water on to heat.'

She must have followed her friend's directions, but she later had no memory of it. Soon, she watched the large cauldron heating over the fire. A pile of cloths sat alongside a large jar of soap. A clean shirt and a length of tartan. A large, plain burial cloth that would wrap around his body.

Gowan was dead.

The tears came then, the sorrow poured out of her.

Muireall sat with her, holding her and rocking her, and Cat held on to the only person other than Gowan to ever be her friend. Her grief stabbed deep, worse now for knowing that he thought her unfaithful in his moment of death.

By the time the commotion outside her door told her of his body's arrival and need for preparation for burial, Cat knew that she could not fail him in his death as she had in his life. She pushed all the pain and grief aside and stood to receive his body back into the cottage they'd shared here.

Her only glimpse of Munro was just then, as the men carried Gowan inside and placed him on a large, flat piece of wood. His friends stood beside and behind him, watching. And the earl was there as well, for both father and son served him.

Muireall and two servants from the keep stayed with her, but only she cleaned and washed him, preparing him for burial in the morning. The strange thing was that he looked as though he slept. No marks marred his body to tell her how he had died. No signs of recent injuries. Cat stared at his face, willing him to open his eyes and tell her this was all just a mistake.

But he did not.

As she touched the cloth to his jaw, she remembered the first time this lumbering giant of a man stood before her. The scar that ran in a jagged line down his cheek had terrified her, but not more than facing the fate her father had planned for her. She smiled now, cleaning that mark of a previous battle as she thought on how he staged another battle that day—this time for her.

Married once against her will to a brutal man who had died the way he'd lived, she ended up back in her father's control and faced whatever fate could help to fulfil her father's ambitions. Still recovering from the beatings that ended not only a pregnancy, but also her ability to bear children, her father auctioned her to the highest bidder though not for a marriage this time. This time she would simply be whored out to pay for her father's whims and wishes.

Lifting up his hand, she washed between his fingers and up his arm. His sword arm. The tears flowed freely now as she went about this intimate task.

He'd been travelling through the edges of MacKenzie lands, where the chief's power thinned and waned, and witnessed some of it, He learned more by questioning her neighbours and kin. Then he walked into the middle of the haggling, tossed a sack of coins at her father and drew his sword and dagger, daring anyone to stop him from taking her.

Cat traced the cloth down the length of his leg, washing off the dirt and then drying his skin. The other women stood silent witness to her ablutions and none tried to speak as she moved around her husband's body. They handed her a clean, hot cloth when she needed one and she continued this task. She washed his other leg and dried it.

His long strides had covered the distance between them and she half-expected her life to end when she glimpsed the fury in his gaze. He dragged and carried her out of the clearing and back to his horse. They did not stop until they'd reached the rest of his group of MacLerie warriors. There he'd offered her a meal and a choice—marriage to him or she could go wherever she wanted.

Finished with washing him, she began to dress him in the plain shirt and tartan. When he was clean and dressed, Cat took her place, sitting at his side, and the door was open for those who wished to pay a call—though with the recent accusations against her, she doubted anyone would want to enter the cottage while she was there.

The earl and lady visited first, greeting Munro, who remained outside, and then entering to speak about Gowan with her. They were brief, but their presence honoured his memory. Though she heard many people speak to Munro, only some of the men entered and said a word or two to her.

The rest of the evening passed in a blur. Muireall handed her food and drink, she thought. A few people even spoke directly to her, she thought. Nothing else sank through the wall of grief that surrounded her. Though Muireall saw her to bed before leaving, Cat could not sleep. For the first time since…since… She could not think on that now, but Munro slept elsewhere and only appeared at dawn.

Men from the earl's warriors, the keep and the village carried Gowan to the cemetery. The thick fog that morning swirled around them, their steps leaving eddies in the mist. Cat knew the priest prayed for his immortal soul, she knew the earl said some words of praise and knew that Munro tossed the first handful of dirt into the grave on his father.

But her thoughts were as opaque as the fog that morning, so she drifted along, doing what she was told to do until she found herself walking the road back into the village. She had almost reached the path leading to her door, Gowan's door, when it happened.

An older man, someone who'd fought with Gowan and drank with him, too, spat in the dirt at her feet as he passed her by. Only when another and then another repeated the insult did she realise it was aimed at her. Then the whispered words and curses followed. Loud enough for her to hear, but not so that they could be heard by others walking ahead of her.

But the stone that struck her in the back frightened her into crying out. Standing there, seeing the frank disgust in the gazes of those around her. Those who did not stare, turned away, not willing to intervene or be for her.

As she hurried back to the cottage, Cat understood that they had waited only for Gowan's burial to treat her the way they thought she deserved. Out of breath, she slammed the door behind her and leaned against it and only one thought filled her mind.

Gowan had returned to Lairig Dubh and he could not save her again.

Chapter Eight

Catriona curled her body up and pulled the blanket tighter around her shoulders. With little between her and the packed dirt floor beneath her, she shivered there, just waiting for dawn to arrive so she could rise without disturbing the others sleeping in the small cottage. As the coldness seeped deeper into her bones and in spite of it, she offered up a prayer of thanks that she, at least, was sleeping inside and not out in the relentless storms that blew through Lairig Dubh as the seasons changed here in the Highlands.

The small pallet in the corner held four small bodies, all lying askew, arms and legs in a jumbled mass, in the way of children. They slept with no regard for yesterday nor the morrows that yet waited for them. If only she had that luxury. From the sound of the echoing snores that filled the chamber, they would be asleep for a while. If only she could fall into the sleep of the innocents.

Turning once more, smoothing the blankets beneath her and tugging the one above back into place, Cat knew she actually should be able to slumber like an innocent. But everyone in the village, and most regrettably Gowan before his death, believed she served the earl's son as his leman and that woman would never be innocent again.

Munro had left the funeral and did not return to the cottage for three days. Coming back from the keep with Muireall, she'd found him and all of her meagre belongings and clothing in front of his father's house. Strewn across the path in the dirt, it was everything she called hers and he'd flung it all out of what was now his.

The worst—after tossing a few coins he had called her widow's portion at her, he'd told her not to return.

Standing mute as the meaning of his words struck her, Catriona searched her thoughts for a plan, a thing to do in reaction, and could find nothing. Munro had every right to do this and she doubted even the earl would force him to do otherwise if she appealed to him. As others began to gather, pointing and whispering at her and the humiliating debacle they witnessed, she gathered up what dignity she had left, picked up her clothing and things and walked away.

The first few minutes of complete confusion and disbelief faded as the reality of it hit her. She was an outcast, not only an outsider, now. With no home, no family, she turned around searching for a place to go. Muireall's was not a choice, not now that Munro had taken such a public stance on her. So, she hugged everything she had to her chest and dragged herself over to the only place of respite she knew—the church.

Though Father Micheil seemed more accepting and forgiving than the younger priest who'd begun his duties here, she did not expect a welcoming from either of them. Cat just wanted to sit in the quiet of the church and think on what to do. Placing her things on the narrow wooden bench in the back of the small chapel, she sat there and waited for some idea to happen.

Instead it was a some one who happened.

Though she should have known, she would not have expected Muireall to come to her aid in this now. Her husband had made his feelings known and Cat understood his reasons—he did not want his wife in the middle of such a matter as this, which could not end well.

'You must go,' she whispered to her friend. 'You cannot be involved.' And yet Muireall walked up to her, gathered Cat's belongings in her arms and nodded with her head at the doorway.

'Come now, Catriona,' she whispered back. 'Hugh's mother sits with wee Donald and she is not happy about it. Come now.'

Cat began to take back her things, shaking her head. 'You must not do this. Hugh would not allow you to… help me now.' Muireall dropped her arms to her side and glared at her then.

'Hugh was convinced to offer a bit of simple Christian charity,' her friend whispered with a glimmer inappropriate for a house of God there in her eye. 'Come. I will tell you the rest when we are home.'

So, she'd followed Muireall and that had been a fortnight ago. Since then, she'd done whatever her friend needed while fending off all sorts of disgusting proposals from various men in the village. And some honourable ones, too. Now, laying on the cold, hard floor and grappling with the facts in her life that would not change, Cat thought she might have to accept one offer or another.

Two men, widower friends of Muireall's husband and at his urging no doubt, needed wives to manage their motherless children. Another man needed help with his bedridden wife and offered her a place to live in exchange for caring for her. It seemed a fair offer, at least until the leering wink and the pinching grab of her breast as he left told her that much more was expected of her than washing and feeding a sick woman. Her stomach churned now thinking about it. She lay on her back and threw her arm across her forehead with a sigh.

This time there would be no hero to stride in and save her from the dire straits in which she found herself. Not like the last time when Gowan saved her.

This morning continued its sluggish march forward with the storms of last night moving on, leaving the ground wet and the trees dripping reminders of the heavy rains on all who walked the paths and lanes of Lairig Dubh. The wee inhabitants of the cottage woke as slowly as the day had and broke their fast in dozing silence, which suited Cat more than their usual childish enthusiasm. Hugh and Muireall came in from their chamber and sat down to eat the porridge she'd made, kissing each of the small faces as they passed them. Just as everyone settled at the table, a soft knock broke into the silence.

Hugh tugged the door open a bit and nodded to whoever stood there. A few whispered words were exchanged and then Hugh stood back and looked at her.

'Catriona. Someone to speak to you.'

Hugh would say nothing more, so she went to the door and waited as he opened it. Had Munro had a change of heart? Would he allow her back into Gowan's...his house to live? Instead, her heart beat faster as she saw Aidan MacLerie standing there. As grim-faced as Hugh when she glanced at him, the earl's son stood, arms crossed over his chest and not a hint of his purpose there. She would have just refused, but she would make no more trouble for Muireall's husband. Cat stepped outside into the foggy morning, closed the door and waited for him to speak.

'Good morrow to you,' he said, nodding at her. 'My thanks for speaking to me.'

Confused by his presence and more by his ill-at-ease manner, Cat could not imagine what this was about. Would he finally speak out and tell the truth of it? Could he convince Munro and the others that nothing existed between them?

'My lord,' she pressed. 'Why did you want to speak to me?'

He met her gaze and then looked away, as though searching for someone or something down the lane. His face had the hard angles of masculine beauty that seemed to run in his family. She'd seen the earl close by and the expression then and now in his son were the same.

Intense. Fierce, even. Handsome in a rugged way. Growing into the model his father was even now.

'I have done you wrong, Catriona. My behavior has led to your disgrace. I tried to speak to Munro,' he began.

He'd *tried*? That meant he'd failed.

'But, he would not hear me out.'

So he had tried to make things better and had stood up for her. Munro was young and had a fiery temper. That temper had led him to attack the earl's son when he first thought he'd taken Cat as his lover, dishonouring her husband.

'I cannot change what has happened, but I want to help you through this,' he said. His arms dropped to his sides and she could not take her attention from the way his hands fisted and relaxed, over and over, until she could almost feel it on her skin. 'Do you know my cousin? Ciara Robertson?'

Cat blinked several times, not following this conversation.

'What do you mean? I know who Ciara Robertson is, everyone in Lairig Dubh does.'

Ciara Robertson, stepdaughter to the MacLerie peacemaker, served as his assistant and did what no woman ever had before—carried out negotiations on behalf of the earl and conducted his business at her stepfather's side.

'She has asked that you meet her at her house at noon this day. Can you, will you, do that?'

Dozens of questions swirled in her thoughts and when she chose one to ask, he shook his head, cutting off her words.

'She will explain everything to you then. If you would prefer, ask your friend to accompany you.' His gaze softened then and he smiled, a sad one that lifted but one corner of his mouth. 'Leave your questions for now—it will all be clear to you then.'

Cat could only nod at him, agreeing to this strange request and meeting with a woman she'd only seen, but had never spoken to before. He nodded and turned to leave, taking a step towards the lane before stopping. Looking over his shoulder as though he remembered something to say, he faced her in the eerie silence of the fog.

'And I am sorry about Gowan's death. I did not…'

He paused then, and though he did not finish that thought and it seemed like he had more to say about it, he left without saying whatever it was.

Cat stood there, confused and unable to move. Within a dozen paces, he faded into the fog that surrounded the cottages and covered the village in its misty grip. She waited for some moments, standing in the silence and watching the patterns that the growing winds carved into the ghostly air. Then the sounds of children now roused for their day grew louder behind her so she opened the door and went back to the table. From the frown her friend wore on her brow, Cat knew Muireall was bursting to know what had conspired between her and the earl's son. She also knew Muireall would practise the patience of a mother until they could speak alone to find out what had happened.

Should she bring her along, as Aidan MacLerie suggested? What business did Ciara Robertson have with a person like Catriona?

Though she had expected the hours to crawl by as she considered all the possibilities in her thoughts, soon the noon hour approached and it was time to go. Mui-reall walked at her side, not chatting as was her usual custom to do, and in some way it made Cat more nervous than if she chattered away. As they approached the large house, larger than most in the village, the door opened and the young woman walked to greet them.

'Welcome,' she said. Her smile was warm and genuine. 'You must be Catriona MacKenzie?' The woman nodded at her and then glanced at Muireall.

'This is my friend, Muireall, my lady.' For how else did you address someone so much higher in position than you were? Unsure of the woman's noble blood or not, but certain of her wealth and power, she waited for her reaction.

'Not a lady,' she said on a laugh. 'You may call me Ciara if you'd like? Or Mistress MacLerie if you prefer, though with so many MacLeries about, many will answer to that! And I am acquainted with Gair's sister. Good day to you both.'

A pretty, vibrant young woman, Ciara Robertson wore her long, blonde hair in a braid, not covered the way most married women did there, but with a veil and circlet instead. Her clothing was of a quality far above a simple 'mistress', but she did not put on the attitude of those higher than Cat. Instead, she felt at ease with her immediately.

Before she could say a word or ask anything, a crunching sound on the ground behind her spoke of someone's approach. Cat prepared herself to face Aidan MacLerie and was surprised when it was, instead, Duncan MacLerie, Ciara's stepfather and the earl's peace-maker. She and Muireall sank in curtsies to him.

'Father!' she said, as she rose up on her toes and accepted a kiss on the cheek from the tall MacLerie warrior turned peacemaker. 'May I make known Catriona MacKenzie? I think that our kinswoman, Gair's sister Muireall, is known to you?'

Duncan MacLerie wore the same grim expression that seemed to be bred into men of the clan…and the same handsomeness. Still, this man had faced down the enemies of the MacLeries and brought most all of them to heel. His reputation was known and respected across the kingdom and it was rumoured that his skills had been used by even the king when needed. And now he stood before her. Why?

Cat found it difficult to breathe. Why had she been sent here? What could these two expect of her? Was she to be exiled now—thrown out of the village? That's when she felt Muireall slip her hand into hers and squeeze it, reminding and reassuring her in one slight gesture.

'You must be wondering why you are here?' the woman asked her.

Trying to gather her wits for whatever was coming her way, Cat nodded and tried to take in a breath, steeling herself for the challenge ahead. These last weeks had worn heavily on her good nature and her confidence that she could find a way of dealing with anything she faced. But now, she must.

'Aye, my la— Ciara,' she said, using the woman's given name.

'Father?'

'I am here to confirm that whatever Ciara agrees to in the…matter between you and Aidan MacLerie has the full backing and promise of the laird and she acts on behalf of both of them.' He stood behind his step-daughter with his hands on her shoulders, conferring the power of which he spoke to her.

Now she trembled in earnest, her knees threatening to buckle. The laird, the earl, had taken an interest in the gossip, too? Muireall slid her arm under Cat's to support her just then. Then, after those terribly foreboding words, the peacemaker nodded to her, patted his step-daughter on the shoulder and walked off, moving in long, lumbering strides back towards the keep.

'Come now,' Ciara said, as she slipped her arm around Cat's other one and tugged. 'Walk with me and I can ease your mind about our discussion.'

With their support on each side, Cat followed down the road, away from Ciara's large house, to a lane nearer the stream and away from the hustling noise and activity of the busy village that centred around the well. She'd not been down this way before, neither having errands that brought her here nor knowing anyone who lived in this section of cottages.

Soon, they stood in front of a cottage that was twice the size of Gowan's. A small enclosed yard sat next to it, clearly a garden, and it had two chimneys, telling her of two hearths. Although Cat wanted to remain there, Ciara released her arm, walked up the path and opened the door. 'I pray you, come inside.'

Then she realised what this was about. The laird had arranged a new place for her, mayhap to serve the lady of this house? She had no objection to honest, hard work and would prefer to keep busy at tasks and chores than sit and contemplate her recent woes. She walked ahead of Muireall, noting the well-kept look of the cottage and, once inside, the clean, comfortable furnishings, nicely arranged in what looked to be two private chambers and the one larger one that served as both kitchen and common room. No byre to hold cattle or other livestock inside—that must be out behind the house, next to the garden. This was the house of someone higher than the usual villager.

But, the one thing missing was anyone who lived here.

Ciara walked to the table and motioned for Cat and Muireall to join her there. A parchment, a small jar of ink and a quill lay in the centre there. As she sat down, Cat continued to look for any signs of an inhabitant and found none—no clothing, no personal items, nothing.

'Aidan and the laird asked my father to handle this matter, but he thought it best handled by me. "A woman's softer touch" or some such nonsense. Since he tends to be a bit more familiar with crop agreements and warriors sworn in service, I thought it would be kinder to you to do as he asked.'

'Kinder? I do not understand,' she said, glancing from Ciara's kind smile to her friend's worried one.

'Because of the results of your involvement with the laird's son, and now with your husband's death, you are left homeless and destitute. The MacLerie and Aidan wish to give you some assurances that you will be cared for.'

She wanted to argue that there was no involvement, but she could not dispute that the attention of the earl's son had dragged her good name in the dirt and caused her to become a pariah in the village.

'This house, yours now, is granted in consideration of serv—your relationship with the earl's son. A small stipend will be provided for your care and the house's upkeep. If any bairns result, they will be taken care of accordingly.'

'I cannot have bairns,' she blurted out when she should have corrected this woman's assumptions about what had or had not happened between them.

The smile on Ciara's face turned even softer then and a sadness entered her eyes. Cat saw that same reaction from any woman who'd had her own children—a mix of understanding, sympathy and utter sadness at what a lack of bairns would mean in their lives. She blinked, knowing that tears gathered and would fall, exposing her true feelings to this stranger, no matter her confidence in discussing such personal issues in the manner of a transaction.

'To protect you and to give you some assurance that this is a binding agreement, Aidan asked me to prepare this for you.' Ciara held out the parchment, which lay covered in rows and rows of words Cat could not read. 'Muireall, if you would?'

So, the earl's son either knew or suspected she could not read and had suggested Muireall's presence for just this situation. Gair's family had all benefited from his first training and now serving as steward to the Mac-

Lerie. Reading and writing had been taught to his brothers and his sister as well.

'Why not take a look around?' Ciara suggested as they sat in the still and utter silence, waiting for Muireall to read the document that would determine her future.

She smiled, nodded and rose from the chair on shaking legs. Walking to the furthest place in the cottage, she entered one of the two private chambers.

A bedroom.

A large bed, too, off the ground on a wooden frame that must be rope-strung…and comfortable.

Several trunks and a small table with two stools sat in the corners of the chamber. A good-sized hearth that promised to keep out the cold and dampness shared a wall with the other chamber next to it.

This would be warm and dry and private.

The unavoidable fact that she'd been trying not to think about came crashing down on her—this house was for Aidan MacLerie's leman. A place where they could meet and where he could spend the night in her bed. With his lover.

With Catriona.

She swallowed deeply against every sort of image and thought that brought up.

And yet, where was the righteous anger that she should feel over this? The man had sent his cousin to barter like the fishmongers she'd seen selling their wares near the river. He'd never asked her. Turning around, seeing the whole of the chamber as it was meant to be, she now understood the strange discussion with Ciara.

'Catriona?' She pivoted to find Muireall in the doorway, staring at her with a confused expression.

'Have you read it? What does it say?' she asked, crossing her arms over her chest, but unable to hide the shivers that coursed through her body at the thought of spending nights here with a man she did not know.

Muireall came close and motioned her even closer. Leaning their heads together, her friend explained everything in a whisper.

'He is publicly declaring you and claiming that you are his leman. This house…' she glanced around the chamber and then back at Cat '…this house is yours no matter what happens between you. The laird has given it to you. There is a settlement for you, he's calling it your "widow's portion", provided by the earl in gratitude for Gowan's loyal service to help you save face. And there will be money every year for your care.'

Stunned by the generosity and the nerve, Cat could not even think of questions to ask.

'And you said you did nothing with him?' Muireall asked.

'He kissed me once and I slapped him.' At the doubt in her friend's eyes, she shook her head. 'Nothing else. There is nothing else between us!'

'Catriona,' Muireall began to advise her. 'I have seen enough men to know a couple of things about them and about men like Aidan MacLerie.' She looked around to see if Ciara had moved from the table and drew Cat over to the window. 'First, this, all this…' she waved a finger at the house '…this speaks of two things to me—guilt and desire. That he feels guilty about his behaviour speaks well of him. The desire is not a surprise considering him and considering you.' Muireall's gaze fell to Cat's breasts, which she'd always thought too large. 'And he is willing to pay for his pleasure, not like most nobles.'

'Muireall!' Shaking her head, she asked, 'How many noblemen do you know?'

'I have lived here my whole life and seen my share of them, Cat. And believe me, some don't pay, they just take. At least the young lord is looking to protect you and to provide for you. Better than most women can expect to be treated, at that.'

'Are you suggesting I let him pay to bed me?' she asked.

'I believe you when you say that nothing has happened between you. But...' she glanced out to the common room and lowered her voice again '...the arrangements he's made for you, they speak of his desire for you and his hope that something will. So, make no mistake in this—he wants you and he wants you in that bed.'

'I will refuse this, him,' she said. 'I cannot whore for him.' Cat stepped back and turned to go out and refuse these shackles. And she would have, if Muireall had not grabbed her wrist to stop her. 'You think I should do this?'

'There is not a word in that document that requires you keep the arrangement between you, or requires bedplay in exchange for this house. Nothing is promised by you at all. Only him. Aidan promises in it that this is all freely given for reasons known only to him and you.'

Muireall let go of her hand and took a breath, shaking her head. 'I am no solicitor and no peacemaker as Ciara and her stepfather are, but the wording is clear and concise. This is all yours once you sign that contract.'

It made no sense. Contracts were agreements in which each party got and gave. If he was giving this, he must expect something in return? Or did he truly feel guilty over her spiral down into disgrace because of his attempts to seduce her?

'And if I refuse? If I do not sign it?'

Muireall shrugged. 'I think that is what you need to ask Ciara now and Aidan when he arrives later.'

'He is coming here?'

The smile that met her question made it clear how her friend viewed the situation and exactly what she though Aidan MacLerie expected to happen. A pointed glance across the chamber at the bed, that bed, and a tilt of her head confirmed it.

Even if everyone in the village thought she was his lover already and even though she faced a bleak future, she would not be paid to give herself to any man. She had faced death once to avoid it and she would have to find a way out this time as well.

Taking a deep breath and letting it out, Catriona understood what she had to do now. She walked back into the common room where Ciara and the damning document sat waiting for her.

'I think this is something I should talk to the earl's son about before I agree to anything,' she said.

The lift of one eyebrow was the only sign of a reaction from Ciara. If she'd thought this a matter accomplished, she gave no sign of dismay at all.

'I will await your word then, Catriona. Aidan said he would arrive here shortly so you can speak to him directly. All you have to do is sign this, or make your mark on this line, and return it to me.'

After pointing to the place to be signed, Ciara stood and nodded to both of them before walking to the door. Just before pulling the door open, Ciara turned back and smiled once more.

'I have handled many matters, both personal and legal, for my cousin Aidan. But not once has he ever done anything like this for any other woman with whom he was involved. That makes me wonder why he is doing this for you?'

She could not speak, could not think, so she just watched as the young woman left. Muireall was about to close the door when Ciara rushed back and pushed against it.

'I pray you not to be insulted, but if you wish to learn how to read and write, I would be willing to teach you. Stop by any morning if you are interested.'

Surprise seemed to follow surprise this day and that offer, an incredibly generous and kind one and not insulting at all, was the last one she could withstand. She moved across the room and sat down on one of the large, cushioned chairs there.

'I must return home, Cat,' Muireall explained. 'Are you going to wait here?' Cat nodded, not otherwise moving or speaking. So overwhelmed at this point that she could not, she could only nod when her friend kissed her cheek and took her leave.

And she waited to speak directly to the man who was at the centre of her downfall, but who might also be the one who could help her the most. Was he acting honourably as both Ciara and Muireall seemed to think? Was he making reparations for his actions? Could she trust her usually misguided sense of how men acted in something that could save or end her honour and possibly her life?

Chapter Nine

Standing before the house he'd arranged for her, Aidan felt as though he'd aged a score of years in these last weeks since first seeing Catriona at the well.

Then, bent on seduction, he had teased and followed her, expecting that she would, like all the others had, fall madly in love or lust with him and they would spend countless hours sharing pleasures of the flesh until his ardour for her cooled. And then there would be another. Even the thought of marriage had not changed his thinking on what his life would be like.

Her naked in his bed.

Then the repercussions he'd not considered had happened—she'd refused him, they'd been exposed, or his attempts had been—and she'd faced the censure of the villagers as a married woman cuckolding her very popular husband.

His harmless suggestion to send Gowan on a training assignment became a death warrant for the man. Not because of Aidan sending him off, but because the man died trying to return after hearing of the rumours. Rumours, not fact, had killed the man. Rumours that were his fault.

His father's eyes had widened when he'd explained what he wanted for her. Though he'd parted ways with women on good terms with a bauble or sack of coins to ease his way out the door, he felt he needed to do this even though she'd never shared his bed. It was the right thing to do....

Though he could not deny that he still wanted her.

Even knowing he'd caused her husband's death. Even knowing that it would seem like he was simply using her. Even though it would be better to turn the house over to her and walk away. At this moment, standing there, waiting to knock and go inside, his body readied to join with hers. His cock cared nothing for good intentions or bad ones. He knew it could be good between them and not just for him.

For he'd noticed that, as she went about her chores and errands, and other than the few times they'd exchanged words or spoke, she never smiled. Oh, a polite one here and there when greeting someone she knew, but the smile that curved those voluptuous lips of her mouth into a bow that begged to be kissed? Never one of those.

She had had a hard life, he'd discovered after seeking out more about her. Brought here about two years ago by her much older husband, she seemed to exist by serving someone else. Whether Gowan or his son or her friend Muireall, her needs never seemed to matter.

He laughed then, at himself mostly, for he stood here, in the dark, outside a house he'd given to a woman he'd never touched. He, the consummate womaniser, stood lusting over a woman who did not want him. But the worst thing? The worst thing was that he stood here with his stomach clenching and nervous sweat on his palms, waiting to knock on her door.

His feet moved without thought and, as he raised his hand to knock, Aidan realised how that would fail to do the one thing he'd hoped would happen—give her the protection that her living here in what everyone thought was his house would give her. No one would dare to treat her with disrespect. As his leman, the woman he claimed as his, none would mistreat her without worrying over the results. No other man would approach her. Now, in front of the door, he knew that a man did not knock on his own house or that of the woman he kept in his bed and under his protection.

He let his hand drop to the latch and he lifted it, easing the door open and stepping inside. In the almost pitch darkness, lit by one small lantern sitting above the hearth, he reached for the kindling and added some of the wood, chopped and piled by the stone hearth. Soon a fire began to chase away the chill of the cold room. It was only then that he spied her, sitting in a large chair in the darkened corner of this larger, open chamber.

Her head leaned back against the cushioning, tilting to the left. Her hair was loose and fell in waves, covering her shoulders and breasts. Her hands lay on the arms of the chair and she'd drawn her legs up under her. A sigh escaped her lips and she shifted—his body tightening in response to the sight of her there. Part of him wanted her to wake, but another part just wanted to savour gazing at her in such a state of repose. Aidan walked to the other chair and sat in it, trying not to disturb her.

Now he saw other things. The dark smudges that marred the skin under her eyes. The cheeks that seemed less full. The need to sleep now rather than after the evening meal. All signs of exhaustion and not eating enough. Grief and worrying did that.

And he did not like it.

He thought about carrying her in and placing her on the bed, but he feared waking her. So, he waited. The heat began to spread and warm the room. Watching her sleep, he wondered what her reaction would be? His cousin said she had refused to sign the paper that would give her clear ownership of the house and the settlement. Did she not want it or did she not want it from him?

A piece of wood in the hearth popped, sending sparks into the draught of air travelling up through the chimney while the sound echoed loudly enough that Catriona stirred. First her eyes fluttered open and then she pushed herself up to sit. He could tell the exact moment when she noticed him there. After a moment of confusion, her gaze cleared and she rose, curtsying before him.

'My lord,' she said, in a voice husky from sleep. 'I did not mean to fall asleep.'

Would she be compliant and polite now, weighed down by scandal and grief for her husband? The man Aidan had, for all other intents and purposes, sent to his death?

'Catriona. You do not need to stand before me like a servant,' he said. 'I pray you to sit again.'

He thought she might refuse when she paused for a

few, very long seconds. Then she sat once more, her back rigid, the mahogany tresses of hair flowing around her with every breath she took.

'I would have been here sooner to speak to you, but duties kept me away.' Now he stood and walked to the hearth. 'You must have questions?'

'What is this about, my lord?' she asked softly, her gaze not meeting his. 'Why this? Why me?'

'Catriona.' He waited for her to look at him. When she did not, he spoke her name again, louder. 'Catriona.' Those deep-blue eyes filled with sorrow now met his and he ached to destroy every bit of sadness there. 'I caused much of the pain you are suffering. I wanted you and wanted no one and nothing to stand in the way of that.'

'So Muireall was right, then? This is about guilt and desire? Mostly guilt from the sound of it.'

He smiled. Muireall, like many MacLerie women, was intelligent and outspoken and, most times, correct in her assessment. 'She is partly right. Guilt? Aye, guilt drove me to arrange with my father for this house and a settlement for you.' He stepped closer to her, crouching down so that their faces were at the same level. 'But never doubt that desire played a bigger part.'

A lovely blush crept up from her neck to her chin and then into her cheeks, brightening her paleness.

'I have never been alone with a man not my father or my husband or other kin,' she whispered. 'Or spoken of such matters before.'

'And I have never explained my desires to anyone before,' he admitted with a grin. 'Actually, I have never had to talk about them with the woman I want—we usually went straight to bedplay and discussed very little at all.'

Another admission, but a true one. As her blush deepened, he realised that with most of the women he'd wanted or slept with, a wink or a kiss told her she was wanted and they ended up entwined in passion. He'd never wanted or had to discuss personal matters with a woman.

He wanted her. He got her. He had her.

'And now?' she asked, her voice trembling.

'Now, you own this house. 'Tis yours along with the settlement from my father.'

'And the contract that your cousin presented to me? What does that mean? I ken you feel guilty about the rumours that spread. I ken that you overstepped, but 'tis not like you killed Gowan and owe me a widow's portion.'

Could she see the truth of it in his eyes? He looked away and took a breath. If she knew the truth, there was no chance of anything between them. If she knew he had been the one to send Gowan away, she would hate him for ever.

'My father believed it the right thing to do since Gowan has served him for nigh on a score-and-ten years,' he said.

His father's shocked expression as Aidan had taken responsibility for something he'd caused flashed in his thoughts. Though feared and ruthless, his father also lived by a clear rule of right and wrong. This was the right thing to do for many reasons, some Aidan would not share now or ever with her.

Ciara's reaction was more comical. She had perfected

Duncan's glacial expression while still young and that led to her being able to observe treaty and alliance discussions. She learned not to react, not to give away her feelings or opinions on any matter, large or small. Her experience deserted her a sennight ago when she was brought in and asked to handle this personal matter. Though it pleased him to know he could act as a man should act, it saddened him somehow to realise that no one expected him to do that.

'And the other reason?' she asked, breaking into his reverie. 'Has that faded away?' Neither from her words nor her tone could he tell if she would be pleased or not by the answer he gave.

'I still want you, Catriona. God forgive me, I want you as I have not wanted a woman before.' It was the truth.

She trembled, then, at his words. Could she tell he would have stripped off her clothing and carried her to the bed if she but gave the word? The length of his shirt and plaid covered the strength of his erection from her sight, but he felt it and knew his words were true. He'd lived in a state of constant arousal since his first sight of her at the well.

There was, though he was loathe to admit it, something more and very different about her and his need and desire for her. He'd never wanted to forgo his pleasure in the past, yet he would wait if she said he needed to. He'd never wanted to explain his actions or take responsibility for them, yet she made him want to take the right path. Now, more than before, he would do what he needed to do to see things right by her.

'But I will wait until you give the word. I know

you mourn and you are ashamed. I know this is unexpected....'

'It is too big,' she said, pushing up to stand. He moved
back to give her room.

'So only the size of it matters, then?' Another time,
another woman would have heard the innuendo in his
words, but not now and not Cat. 'No matter. It is yours
to do whatever you wish to with. Sell it. Give it. Live
in it. The choice is yours. Sign it or not—just live here
and make it your own.' He turned to face her as she
paced along the hearth. 'I just wanted to make things
better for you.'

'And for you, my lord? Is this not about having a
house where you can visit your leman?' She glared at
him now. 'Tell me true, I beg you.'

He did not tell her. With just three long strides, he
crossed the room and took her by her shoulders, drawing her to him. If she'd been afraid, he would never have
done such, but there was no fear in her gaze. Staring at
her mouth, he wondered if she would slap him this time.

He slid his arms around her and possessed her mouth
with his. She tasted sweet, her mouth hot as she opened
for him, hot as he plunged his tongue deep inside her.
Aidan slipped his hands up to her head, tangling them
in her hair and holding her mouth to his. Over and over,
he kissed her, needing and wanting to be deeper inside
her and letting his tongue do what his cock wanted to do.

She gasped for breath against his mouth when he
lifted it from her and they shared the same air, their panting breaths echoing in the silence of the room. When he
regained control, control that was stretched to nearly its

breaking point by this artless kiss, he stepped back. No slap this time, but when Catriona lifted her hand and touched her lips, it threatened to rip any control away.

Before he could fail in his attempt to put this in her control, Aidan walked to the door and lifted the latch, letting the cold air pass over his heated body.

'I want you, Catriona. As my leman, as my lover—what you call it matters not to me. I want to peel through the layers you have built up to reveal the woman beneath. I want to strip you naked and have my way with you. I want you to have your way with me,' he said, passion tightening his gut, his throat and his ballocks. 'But it is your decision and it does not change that you own this house and receive that settlement.'

Her body shivered at his words. Good, for it told him that she was as affected as he was by the restrained passion between them. 'That is the last time I will kiss you until you ask it of me.' Opening the door wider, he smiled at her.

'On the morrow, buy what you need to make this house your own. Food, linens, clothing. Whatever you need.'

'They will not accept my coin,' she whispered, the words of her shame slashing deep into his heart.

'There is a sack of coins for your use in the small trunk there,' he said, pointing to the bedroom. 'They will not dare to refuse *my* coin. And they will not dare to insult you while you live under my protection. Even if you cannot accept me, at least accept that which my name gives you.'

From the shaking nod, he could not tell if she would

follow his instructions. He would be able to tell more when he visited the next night.

'I will come tomorrow night.'

'For what purpose?'

'No matter what is truly between us, we must look as though this is what everyone believes it to be. When my duties permit it, I will visit and spend the night,' he explained, nodding his head at the smaller of the two rooms.

'Everyone in Lairig Dubh will think I am your leman,' she said.

'Just so.'

'And will I be?'

'Cat, I will try my damnedest to make that happen.'

He turned then, walking out before he changed his mind and pushed the matter. There would be time now, days, but mostly nights, when he could ply his wiles and seek her surrender.

Just so.

The door latch dropped and so did she, falling, or melting rather, to her knees. Sweat gathered on her neck and trickled down her back and down the crevice between her breasts. She ached in places she'd never paid attention to before from his kiss. His hands touched her as no other man ever had, with wanting and desire in every caress.

Was she the whore her father named her those years ago? To react so to the touch of a man she was not married to? To, worse, crave it more? If she was to be well and surely damned to hell for these sins of lust, why did she want more—more of him, more of that kiss, just more…?

She wiped her hand across her heated forehead, pushing her hair out of her face and lifting the weight of it off her neck so she could cool there.

What should she do? What could she do? Her body told her one thing and her heart said another. Or her honour said another. For even if no one but she knew she had not lost her honour to him before Gowan died, how would she face herself if she gave it to him now?

The fire popped again, drawing her attention. How long had he been there while she slept on in the chair? He'd built a fire in the hearth with wood already cut into pieces, she noticed, not peat. The basic foodstuffs filled the jars and tins on the shelf in the cooking area. The large bed waited, covered in clean sheets and warm blankets.

Looking around now, she noticed that full night had fallen, so it was too late to return to Muireall's home. Climbing to her feet, she walked aimlessly around the large room, trying to decide what to do. Exhausted from nights of too little sleep and days of too much work and shame, Cat made the only decision she decided to make this night—she banked the fire and walked into the bedchamber.

The bed was too inviting to ignore, she discovered, so she washed with water from the jug someone had filled and placed there on the table. The tips of her breasts tingled as she drew the tunic over her head. The slide of the fabric over them reminded her of his arousing words… his promises, really…about stripping her naked and having his way with her. Moisture pooled between her legs as she reacted to only the memories of his words.

Her eyelids drooped in spite of her arousal as she washed quickly in the chilled chamber, and when she slid under the bedcovers and the clean sheets she was falling asleep as she rested her head on one of the pillows there.

The rest would have to be faced in the morning.

Chapter Ten

'Good day to you.'

Who would think that just four words, spoken with a pleasant tone, could demonstrate the power of the earl's heir in influencing how she was treated by the merchants and villagers? But, when it was uttered by every person she passed and called out by those who saw her walking along the paths of Lairig Dubh the next day, it was hard to miss or to misunderstand.

The butcher sold her his best piece of beef. The miller promised the finest milled flour would be sent to her house on the morrow. The weaver offered her some lengths of fine cloth for new gowns. The alewife spoke of a brew that Aidan favoured and assured her some would be sent to the house when it was ready. The village women smiled and nodded, greeting her and asking how she fared.

How could their treatment of her change so much from just one day to the next?

Aidan MacLerie.

He'd changed her from cuckolding wife to the heir's favoured leman with one signature on one deed. All attempts to hide his efforts and intentions regarding her before Gowan's death brought gossip and disdain. His purchase of a house for her—and all that supposedly meant—now that she was a widow brought acceptance.

As he'd said, no one would dare to insult her while she was under his protection. The news of that protection raced through the village even as she stood in that house and tried to decide her answer and her fate. The MacLerie kith and kin took the choice out of her hands and made it a thing already done.

If he was true to his words, nothing of what they believed mattered to what, if anything, happened between them. The power to say aye or nay remained with her. Muireall's words of advice, spoken early this morn when Cat returned to her cottage, echoed in her thoughts all day as she made her way back to the house.

In spite of sharing the beds of many women since gaining manhood, he has never made these kind of arrangements with any woman. No matter how this began, you are a widow now with no family. More importantly, for the first time in your life, this is your choice. Accept the house, accept him in your bed, or do not. It is up to you.

So, if Cat could believe it, this was not something he did often. He was offering her not just protection, but property of her own. He offered her a future better than she ever expected, which was more honourable than she had expected.

Muireall was a practical woman and she understood

the MacLeries better than Cat ever could. And though married twice, Cat had never felt part of either clan or place. If everyone believed she was Aidan's mistress, she would have a chance to meet more people and gain friends. Then when it was over, for it would have to end, she would have a house and have more friends.

Most of all—do what you wish to do. You deserve some happiness and if you will get it from being with him, then be with him. No one can plan what will happen on the morrow, so seize what happiness you can now.

That had been her advice all along. Muireall knew Cat's deepest sorrow—to never bear children—and urged her to seek whatever would give her the happiness she needed instead.

So, the only decision she made that day was to take each day as it came. If Aidan wanted her, if he pursued her as he'd promised to do, she would do only what felt right to her. Accepting the house did not, so she would accept only the hospitality of it for now. Living there, living on her own, finding her own place among the people here, would give her a chance to set down some roots here.

Walking through the shady path that led to her…the house, Cat could not figure out why she was the target of his efforts. Her experiences in the marriage bed had been unappealing at best and painful and unwanted at worst. Though Gowan always had a care for her during those early, infrequent times in their marriage when he'd shared her bed, her first husband had not.

She shuddered then, forcing away the memories and images she swore would remain in the past.

Men certainly seemed to gain pleasure from joinings of the flesh, but she'd never experienced what so many women whispered about at the well or while gathered together to share chores. And she knew many happily married couples whose morning glances spoke of such pleasure. Cat wondered if the damage caused by losing her bairn prevented her from feeling such things?

Lifting the latch, she carried her purchases into the house. Across the room, she saw the spot where she'd stood during *that* kiss. Heat coursed through her now, telling her that pleasure might not be an impossible thing between Aidan MacLerie and the woman he wanted in his bed.

But could she allow it? Could she be happy as a wealthy man's leman?

This time, it was different.

Aidan walked up the path and noticed light from within. Smoke escaped up the main chimney as did the smell of something wonderful. His stomach growled in anticipation, even though he'd shared the evening meal with his family and even though he did not expect Catriona to cook for him.

She was not his servant. Nor would she become one.

Opening the door, he found her in the same chair where she'd sat last night. He nodded and closed the door behind him.

'Good evening, Catriona,' he said, hanging the skin of wine on a hook near the cooking area.

'And to you, my l-l-l—' she began and then stuttered.

'Will you now call me Aidan?' He laughed. 'If nothing else, no one will hear it but me.'

'Good evening, Aidan,' she said softly. It was only one of the ways he wanted to hear his name coming from that mouth, but he would take it…for now. 'Have you eaten yet?'

'I have,' he said, noticing the table set with two bowls and spoons. 'But the smell of it is making me hungry again.' He approached the table. 'You did not wait your meal on my arrival, did you?'

She did not answer, she only put down the clothing she was mending and rose, going over to put some of the aromatic stew into the bowls. As he sat in one of the chairs, he noticed that her portion was smaller than his and his was not the same amount that he'd eaten the first time she cooked for him.

'Are you not hungry? Especially since you waited?' he asked. Realising he'd brought the wine for her, he retrieved it and poured it into their cups.

'My l—' she began to say and he frowned at her. 'Aidan, I am not accustomed to such rich wines.'

'Become accustomed,' he growled. He wanted her to savour the finer things he could give her now. He softened his tone. 'Surely you would not refuse a taste to honour the first meal in your new house?' Instead of arguing, she lifted her cup up and nodded. 'To many happy hours in your new house,' he said, touching his cup to hers.

'To your new house.'

He laughed when she changed the words, but his laughter died as he watched her lift the cup to her mouth and drink from it. Her chin lifted, exposing her graceful throat to him. When the wine rushed too quickly past her lips and threatened to spill, she licked them quickly with the tip of her tongue.

Aidan stood and was leaning halfway across the table, wanting to taste the wine on her lips, when he remembered his vow to her. With a grunt, he sat back down and drank deeply from his own cup, hoping the strong wine could ease the powerful desire that coursed through his veins now. And he cursed his foolishness at giving such a vow when all he wanted to do was kiss her!

The meal passed and they spoke of Ord Dubh and his father's wish that he move there soon. He did not want to mention betrothals or wives to her. As she asked questions about the southern holding, he wondered if she would move into his keep and be with him there? As he finished the savoury stew, he knew there would be time for all of that.

'So, have you decided to keep it?' he asked, as she cleaned the table, washed the bowls and put things away.

He was more familiar with the large keep, a large family and servants to do what she was doing, but watching her fascinated him. This is how it would be to live with her. Not that the son of Connor MacLerie would ever be allowed such a wife or such a life, but it appealed to him in some way he could not explain.

'I have only decided to live here for now. Muireall's cottage is too small to add me to it. She even asked if I would give this house to her and Hugh and live in hers instead.' A smile brightened her face and made her eyes sparkle. 'I think she was serious.'

'It is yours, though I wish you would keep it for yourself. Mayhap take in your friend's family as boarders?'

Catriona looked around the room and then at him, her unease clear in the way a frown marred her brow. She took a step towards the chair and then back. Another in the direction of the door and then back.

'What is wrong?' he asked, approaching her and fighting the urge to take her in his arms. Would resisting that urge ever get easier for him? Or would he reach the point when he gave in to it?

'I ken not what you expect of me now. What should I be doing?'

'Have you never had a time of leisure to yourself, Cat?'

She shook her head. A forlorn expression darkened her eyes now as she shrugged. 'I am not accustomed to being lazy or free from chores or errands to be done. I would rather work hard.'

'Ciara said she invited you to visit with her. That will be hard work.'

He'd learned his letters and numbers as he'd learned how to wield the sword. For him, it took little practice to read or write, but he watched as others struggled with each. Aidan did not underestimate just how much effort would be needed to master such tasks. And, in working with Ciara, he knew that his cousin would include other topics and introduce Cat to others who were influential in the clan.

'I would not want to embarrass you if I failed. Not if her offer to me was truly in regard for you,' she said.

'Again, you miss my point, Cat,' he said. 'Just as this

is your house, spending time with my cousin, learning to read or write, is for you. Those skills could help you when…' he paused just before uttering the words he'd first thought of—*I marry* '…when you might need them.'

She thought on his words and nodded. He'd seen signs of her bright mind and had no doubt that she would succeed at whatever task she set herself to.

'But you have not told me what you expect from me when you come here if, as you say, you will visit each night.'

'I expect nothing other than your good company,' he said. And that was true. In that moment, he did want only that.

A laugh escaped from her, a wonderful sound to his ears, and she gifted him with the smile he'd wanted to see. It was the first sign of joy in her face in weeks.

'And you expect me to believe that? After you have all but promised to seduce me into your bed?'

She did not appear to be opposed to it, so he would bide his time. 'I would not mind that either,' he admitted.

Sometimes, in battle, a warrior must sacrifice in order to win the war. Aidan could tell this was one of those moments when a retreat might be the strongest move he could make.

'I will take my leave of you,' he said, stepping back. 'If you ask what I expect of you, I would say I want you to make this house your own.' He nodded and turned to the door, but her words stopped him before he could take a step.

'Aidan,' she said in nothing more than a whisper. 'Kiss me.'

He shook his head, standing his ground when his body urged him otherwise. He tried to speak, but words dissolved before he could say them. He only knew that if he kissed her, he would have her. As long as he stayed where he was, she was safe.

Did she know the danger that she faced right now? Clearly not, for she began to take one step and then another towards him, all the while his breaths becoming laboured as though he was going into battle. Then she was in front of him, gazing at him with desire and curiosity, and only a few scant inches separated them.

'Do not do this, Cat. If I begin, it will not end with a kiss. I will not be satisfied,' he said. Knowing his proven abilities to give pleasure to the women who'd shared his bed, he assured her, 'You will not be satisfied.'

'Kiss me. I pray you, kiss me now.'

He'd warned her. He'd given her notice that he would not stop at just a kiss. It was in her hands now. Then she said the words that threw his world off-kilter.

'I trust you, Aidan,' she whispered.

Aidan shrugged. 'More fool you,' he said as he fell towards what he knew would be his damnation.

Chapter Eleven

In that moment, when he'd turned and begun to leave, Cat knew she must stop him. Whether curiosity or some need to have something she'd never had before, she only knew that she would regret it for every day in her life if she did not. Was this just sinful desire for him? She knew not, she just felt.

And for only the second time that she could remember in her pitiful life, she wanted to reach for something. She wanted to fight for what she wanted.

Her body became a thing unknown to her as soon as he arrived. Her lips burned. Her body ached and grew moist with his every glance. Every word spoken in that deep voice he had caused the growing heat to spill into her veins. Even her breasts swelled and her nipples tightened with each passing moment of trying to resist his call.

She wanted him.

The thought shocked her, but it was the truth.

The feeling of it shocked her.

Cat tried to ignore the ever-present desire she read in his eyes all through their supper and tried to vanquish its effect on her with more of his fine, rich wine, but every second with him stoked a response deep within her.

She wanted him, God and Gowan forgive her.

She'd been honest when she offered her trust. Oh, she had no doubt about how this night would end, but he'd shown her more consideration and more honour than any man had, for he'd not done what he wanted when he wanted whether she said aye or nay. And now that she'd said the words, she waited and watched as he delayed what she now accepted was inevitable, for he had seduced her and she had fallen.

After a scant few breathless moments, he reached for her and dragged her up to him. His mouth was hot against her. This was no mere kiss—he meant to possess her, to bend her to his desires and to take her completely. This kiss foretold it all.

Cat let go and fell into him. She felt his arms wrap around her, holding her up, holding her to him.

He moved around her like a storm then, his mouth on hers, tasting her, his hips grinding against her so she could feel him. Parts of her long dead came alive then, every place on her skin tingling as she let him lead the way to damnation.

He lifted his mouth and traced a path of kisses and touches of his hot tongue along her chin and down on to her neck. Her head fell back, allowing him closer, and he took it with a masculine chuckle that she heard and felt. Cat closed her eyes and waited for the next touch, the next caress, the next.

Then he was gone. But not really, as he moved around behind her. His hands covered her breasts, holding her up against his hard body. She let her head rest back on his chest and he nudged it to one side and found her neck, suckling on it and kissing it as she could only gasp and surrender to his every touch.

When would he join with her? When would he enter her body? Would it hurt as it always did? This pleasure coursing through her, something unknown before, seemed a fair exchange for the pain she knew would come when he took her.

She arched against him then, as his hands slipped inside her gown and shift to her skin and she felt his strong fingers and hands cupping her flesh. When he began to rub the sensitive tips and the underside of her breasts, she might have moaned. When he laughed, she knew she had.

'Ah, Cat,' he whispered in her ear. 'I so like to hear you being pleasured.' He licked and then bit the edge of her ear, causing her body to arch again. 'Let me hear your pleasure,' he urged.

He moved again, one arm across her breast, holding the other, teasing it, rolling the tip between his fingers, making her wetter with each touch. She felt his other hand sliding over her stomach, over her hip, getting closer to the place between her legs. She wanted to open to him, let him touch there, make him touch there. She lost her breath as he rubbed her through her clothing, panting and waiting, always waiting.

He gathered up the length of her gown and shift and took hold of her leg in his hand. The shock of such a caress forced another gasp, but now, the cool air of the room against her naked skin did not make her cold. His hand caressed up and up, sliding between her thighs until he reached the curls there.

Her legs fell open then and, if he'd not still held her up with his arm around her and his hand there, she would have crumpled to the floor. She reached up and grabbed at his shoulders, trying to keep from falling.

'I have you now, Cat,' he whispered again in a heated breath against the skin of her neck. 'Let me have my way as I've dreamt of doing. Let me pleasure you, lass.'

Catriona could not have said any word at that point, let alone nay. She craved the next movement of his hands, she wanted them…there. She wanted to feel him there.

When his fingers slipped into the moisture beneath the curls, she screamed. It was too much. Too much. But each touch, each caress, made her want more. By the time he stroked her deep and slid his finger forward, she wanted him to go back. The flesh there swelled as he urged her towards something with hushed, heated words.

He never took his hand from between her thighs, but he moved and she found herself on the floor with him at her side. The candles made the room too bright for such a thing as this for he could now see her, see her flesh exposed, see her breasts and now her legs and that place. So she closed her eyes, afraid of his appraisal after having had so many women before her in this very position.

'Open your eyes, Cat. Look at me.' His voice, always so deep and appealing, now grew deeper and huskier as he ordered her. When she did not, he took her mouth again, plundering it with his tongue until she lost her breath and her mind. 'Look at me while I show you what pleasure can be between us.'

Could she watch this? Could she look upon him as he touched her so intimately? Opening her eyes, she met his gaze. Intense, heated, his amber eyes seemed to glow with arousal as he moved down to kneel between her legs. If she'd forgotten that his fingers remained between the aching folds of flesh there, his caress reminded her. Now, when her body arched, they could both see it. Embarrassed only until she watched how his eyes darkened and his nostrils flared in arousal, she let her legs fall open to him and waited.

His black hair reflected the glow of the candles in the room as he leaned down closer and closer to her legs. What was he doing? As his mouth kissed the skin of her thighs, his gaze never wavered from hers. He would not. He could not. He…

Did.

Her vision dimmed as his mouth claimed the place where his fingers had caressed. Strong and hard, he slipped his tongue along the flesh there until she could not see or breathe or think. Her fingers scratched along the wooden planks of the floor, seeking some hold that would keep her from screaming out.

As her blood raced through her pounding heart, her body arched and arched, forcing her hips from the floor and pressing them against him, begging for more, for deeper, for more. He never slowed or quickened his pace, his tongue teasing and exciting and tormenting her flesh in even, long strokes until she screamed. But it was not enough. Something waited ahead of her, of them. Her muscles tightened, waiting, just waiting.

When he found some spot there and latched on to it with his lips and even his teeth, she lost everything that she was and shattered beneath his touch. Pinpricks of light flashed through her eyes, her body undid itself, pouring out some release. Aidan's voice pierced the silence, urging her on in a fierce whisper she could not resist. The vibration of his voice against that sensitive, swollen flesh gave her more pleasure as she did as he ordered and screamed out her pleasure to him.

Barely able to open her eyes, she lifted her head and looked at him. The smile on his wicked mouth spoke of his absolutely male satisfaction at proving a point, but when it turned into something else, something more intense, she shuddered against the promise. He turned the promise into something real when he leaned forward and kissed her again. Open-mouthed, she kissed him back then, mimicking his tongue's actions with her own, sliding hers deep in his mouth, tasting all that he was.

Cat reached up and wrapped her arms around him, sliding her fingers through his hair and allowing herself to touch him as she'd wanted to for too long. Aidan pulled back for a moment and unbuckled his belt and untied the laces on his trews. He lifted his manhood out and skimmed his hand over the engorged flesh.

He would join with her now. He would take his pleasure now after giving her so much. Cat laid back down, took a deep breath and waited for the inevitable pain that would follow now.

'Are you well?' he asked her. She'd gone from alive

with passion and in the throes of her release, one he gave her, to…to…this almost dead thing that laid beneath him unmoving, hardly breathing. The lovely flush of arousal was being replaced with a gaunt shade of what passed for fear. 'What is wrong?'

Though his cock would argue, he would not simply take his pleasure on her without regard for that fear. She'd closed her eyes tightly and would not look at him. Aidan reached out and caressed her cheek with the back of his hand. 'Catriona, I pray you, tell me what is wrong?'

Cat opened her eyes then and shrugged. 'I am just readying myself,' she whispered in a tone that was so wrong, as though she expected the worst from what they would do now.

Rage filled him and he wanted to find and tear apart whichever man had caused her to act like this. She mistook what his expression must look like and began to shake her head.

'Take your pleasure. I am ready,' she pleaded, grabbing for him as he moved off her and tied his laces. Her eyes appeared huge in her ashen face and he could see the tears gathering.

Aidan MacLerie had never once forced himself on a woman not willing and this would not be the first time. Whether she spoke the words or not, Cat did not consent to this joining. He leaned back on his heels, took her hands and helped her to stand.

'Do you not want to…?' she asked, in a quivering voice.

'Aye, I do.' He showed her the proof of his raging

desire by taking one of her hands and placing it over clothed but still erect flesh. She gasped, but did not pull her hands away from him. 'But that can wait until you are ready.'

Or until I can make you ready, he thought.

And he would. Aidan wanted the woman writhing in an explosion of passion, not barely able to suffer his touch as she was now, shaking and filled with fear or some strong hesitation that spoke of past mistreatment.

He helped her retie her laces, closing her shift and gown and shielding the voluptuous breasts he'd discovered hiding there. His cock throbbed again, reminding him of their thwarted satisfaction. With the musky smell of her own arousal and release still on his fingers, he helped her to one of the chairs and sought the cup and wineskin.

'Here,' he said, placing the cup in her trembling hands. 'Drink this down.' He'd not noticed any whisky among her cooking supplies. He would bring some or send some to her on the morrow. Sometimes wine was not a strong enough spirit. Sometimes only the brewed and aged *uisge-beatha* would handle life's woes.

She sipped from the cup until he gently guided it up so that she drank it faster. Then, he went into the bedchamber and brought a blanket out and wrapped her in it. After stoking the fire in the hearth, he sat and watched her, waiting for the shaking to stop. Once he realised it was taking too long for her to calm down, he lifted her in his arms and carried her into the bedchamber.

Aidan half-expected her to struggle, but she only watched in silence as he stood her on her feet, tugged down the bedcovers and lifted her into the centre of the large bed. The look of acceptance baffled him until he comprehended that she thought he just wanted to tup in the bed and not on the floor. He had been the fool—he'd paid for a bed large and comfortable enough to suit him and instead, he'd almost taken her on the floor in the other chamber.

Shaking his head at his own stupidity, he tucked her into the bed…alone. Her hand on his stopped him from leaving.

'Aidan,' she said. 'I would ask…'

This was, he decided on hearing it, one way he didn't wish to hear his name said. He pressed his finger to her mouth, stopping her from any kind of pleading.

'Sleep now. We can talk on the morrow.'

'But you…' She tried to explain something, but he did not like the way it sounded either.

'Take your rest. We will sort this out between us,' he promised.

And they would. He'd felt too much passion within her to not want it all. He knew there could be even more. And he wanted to be the man, mayhap the first man, to taste it all. She laid back against the pillows then, her pale complexion nearly the same shade as the linens that covered the bed.

'I will bank the fire and put out the candles, worry not,' he said, leaning over to kiss her.

He wanted to taste her mouth, but settled for a soft touch of his lips to her forehead. He blew out the candle on the table by the bed and took some time to light a fire in this hearth, though with the thick layer of blankets on top of her, he doubted she would take a chill. Aidan knew her gaze followed him as he worked on the fire and then left, pulling the door closed a bit.

Trying to do the gallant thing and leave her be was the most difficult thing he'd done in a very long time, but it felt right. He laughed to himself then—he'd done more 'right' things since meeting Catriona MacKenzie than he had before. She could be very good for him.

She would be very good for him.

They would be good together.

He walked around the common room and put out the candles, banking the fire and preparing to leave. Instead, he sat in the chair she seemed to favour and waited for her to fall asleep. In the silent darkness, her breathing echoed to him. Some time passed and he thought on her reaction to him.

What could have been done to her that she reacted so? Lying like a dead thing, eyes scrunched closed tightly, her body lifeless beneath him? He suspected he knew the truth of it, but it turned his stomach to think of a woman, any woman, being misused like that.

Oh, he could not deny it happened, and happened regularly, for the Church and the law proclaimed a woman was the property of her father and then her husband to do with as he wished. It was the way of things among men and women and the world.

His father took a harsh view, though, of his kith and kin if they mistreated their women. So, either men did not or they kept it hidden from the earl's gaze and that of his wife and those who served him.

Would Gowan have done such a thing to her? He let

out a breath. The man travelled on the earl's business and spent much time away from her. She never seemed in fear of him, even when Aidan was pursuing her. Nay, from what he'd discovered about Gowan, he seemed to genuinely care for Catriona. Both his mother and father spoke highly of the man and a few casual words shared when they did not know he listened about the couple's arrival in Lairig Dubh reaffirmed that.

Unless he asked her about it, there was no one else to ask. In spite of Munro having known her for nigh to eight years, Aidan would not bring up his stepmother or her history to him.

That left Catriona and, though he wanted to ask her, her reaction left him convinced she would not speak of such matters with him. Deciding that she must be sleeping, he rose and took careful steps across the floor, trying not to wake her. His hand was on the door latch when he heard it.

Crying. And crying while trying not to be heard. Muffled by the pillow more likely than not. It drew Aidan to her, the desire to ease her pain and her fears stronger than he would have expected towards a woman he wanted for nothing more than bedplay.

Or did he want only that?

He pushed away any ideas of the sort and walked back into the bedchamber. The crying stopped as soon as he entered as though waiting for him to leave once more.

'Cat?' he whispered softly enough that he would not wake her if she did indeed sleep.

The fire's glow cast shadows across the chamber and across the bed, distorting everything around him and making it impossible for him to see her. She turned to face him and the tears streaming down her cheeks let him know he was right—she was crying.

He did not think about what he should do then. Aidan sat down on the bedside, the ropes creaking beneath his weight, and he removed his boots. Then he leaned back against the headboard and pulled her up into his arms, holding her head under his chin and brushing her hair from her tearstained face.

'Hush now,' he soothed.

His actions and words had the opposite effect of what he was trying to do, for instead of easing her misery, she cried even harder. So he waited, much as he used to for his sister when she came to him with her heartaches or other feminine disasters that befell younger sisters.

Aidan wondered if she'd not grieved for Gowan's loss yet. The days and weeks since his death had not been easy for her and she may not not have let her weakness show, even with her friend Muireall. He'd only watched her from afar during the funeral and saw only the stony, shocked façade worn by those who have suffered a great loss.

His conscience bothered him once more. If he had not seen her and decided to pursue her, he would not have sent Gowan away. If Gowan had remained, Aidan would have lost interest at some point and moved on to easier quarries. Even with all of that being true, he still wanted her in a way that was new to him.

She began to quiet in his embrace and, as she relaxed against his chest, he wondered where this would all lead. Somehow, he knew that it would be very easy to get deeply involved with her and that it would not end just as easily. And once more, that thought did not frighten him off as it should.

'I think you may have got the worst part of this arrangement between us, my lo— Aidan MacLerie,' she whispered in between sniffling. 'I have never been good at anything in my life and now I cannot even be a good whore to you.'

'You are not a whore, Catriona.' He smoothed her hair again. 'You could never be any man's whore.' She pushed back to look at him then and he released her from his embrace. 'And what else have you failed at in your life?'

'But that is what you wanted me to be, is it not? What else do you call a woman who gives herself to a man not her husband, to a man who could never be that?' She ignored the other question completely, not willing to share her past with him yet. Or ever?

Words flew through his thoughts—words to ease her pain and confusion—but he could not say any of them. No matter how she felt, he would never have thought her his whore.

'Just so,' she said with a sad shake of her head before he could explain. 'I have been thinking about how to end this.'

He sat up then as she sat back on her heels in a shift too thin to hide any of her body from his sight—even if the fire did not light the bedchamber the way he'd like it to be lit. 'End this? Have we even begun it yet?' he asked her.

'No matter,' she said, brushing off his words. 'If you

would but lend me a small sum of money, I can leave and make my way—'

'To where, Cat? Where would you go?' He wanted to know because, at this moment, the thought of her leaving him did not sit well with him.

He wanted her. Damn it to hell, he wanted her!

His question stopped her then. She had not thought it out, that much was clear. She shrugged then and tossed her hair over her shoulder. Her full breasts strained against the thin fabric, visible there to him. His erection sprang to life on only a threadbare hope such as that.

'I will accept Hugh's cousin's offer of marriage, I think,' she said without a hint of awareness of the danger rising in him about her leaving with another man. 'He lives in the north and has need of a wife. Well, his five motherless bairns have need of a new mother.'

'Need of a wife?' he growled out the words as he grabbed for her. 'You will not be his wife.'

Aidan's fingers slid along the shift, grazing those breasts and finally sliding in under her arms. Holding on to her waist, he lifted her and dragged her up to sit on his lap. With her legs spread on either side of him, the wee beastie between his legs surged between them. She gasped and slid back just enough so that she did not sit on top of it.

'Again?' she asked.

'Still.'

'Oh.'

Her mouth formed the sound, but it was the wonderment in her gaze, reflected by the fire's light, that undid him and his efforts not to try to tup her this night. That and the way her gaze followed her hands down his body to where he really wanted them to be. Now he, Aidan MacLerie, heir to the earl and the consummate lover and seducer of women, found that it was his turn to beg.

Chapter Twelve

She was truly a failure in life.

She had killed her mother in childbirth.

She had failed to be a boy who could have helped her father more than a worthless girl.

When she was grown and could have helped his aims by accepting the marriage he'd arranged, with a pretty purse of coins going in his pocket, she had refused. He had beaten and starved her until she gave in, barely able to see or speak at her wedding due to the bruises on her face and body.

That had mattered little and had not stopped Torcaill, a vicious, dangerous man, from claiming his marital rights on her whenever and wherever he wanted. And he'd wanted. Insatiable in all things, his desires for fleshly pleasure were known throughout their village. Whether wife or whore or unfortunate in his path, he swived his way through life, as though it mattered more than breathing or eating did. Refusal on her part was not an option. He demonstrated that well and frequently, shaming her before her kith and kin and even strangers passing through the village.

Fighting back aroused him even more, making him more and more vicious, so she learned to lie still and let him do what he would do to her. When he realised what she was doing, it infuriated him. Then he would slap her and pinch her until he got a reaction, leaving marks and bruises all over her. Once he caned her so badly she could not sit for days.

Even when the healer had told him she was carrying and that treating her harshly could end both the pregnancy and her life, Torcaill shrugged and took what he wanted anyway—as he always did. She tried to say no and tried to explain that she was beginning to bleed. Incensed by her attempt to refuse him, he finished tupping her and then beat her until she lost the babe inside. And, as the healer told her when she came to after the bleeding and the fever that racked her for four days, she had also lost the ability to bear other children.

She prayed as she faded in and out of consciousness that day—prayed for her own death and his. And when the Almighty answered part of her plea and ended Torcaill's life, she smiled for the first time in months. Catriona had outlasted him and would survive.

Her father showed no remorse at all for her treatment at Torcaill's hands. He belittled her for not taking rightful care of her lawful husband and set out to find her another one. He needed coin and decided that whoring her out would make more of it faster than trying to find another husband for the barren, worthless woman she was.

Barely out of her sickbed, he dragged her to the village centre and began offering her to any man who would meet his price. And, for the first time in her life, with nothing left to lose, she fought back. Her loud struggles were what had drawn Gowan's attention and his intervention.

She'd cost him a huge sum, all his coins, not something a simple warrior could earn back quickly in service to his chieftain, and she could give him nothing in return. Even those few, early attempts to please him in bed turned into horrifying and embarrassing encounters. So she turned her efforts to being whatever kind of wife he needed.

Yet not a day passed that she did not feel that she had failed Gowan. He said he needed and wanted no more children, but a few words spoken in passing made her believe he did.

He stopped sharing her bed years ago, never returning after those few attempts proved so much a failure. It was not for a lack of need on his part, for she knew he paid coin to lie with one of the village whores from time to time.

And she could not even be a good mother to his son, for Munro had rejected her place in their household from almost the first day she returned with Gowan.

Then, not knowing how to deal with the flirting of this handsome, young, bold man, she'd dragged Gowan's good name into the dirt along with hers. It all proved she was the worthless slut her father had called her all those years ago.

Laughter bubbled up inside her, threatening to escape, while tears began to burn her throat and eyes. Worse

than either of those, she wanted to touch this man who'd
bought her way out of poverty on just the promise of attempted seduction as his collateral.

In the dark of night when emotions and guilt attacked
her, she was tempted to get up and walk away. To walk
until she could walk no more. And then to lie down and
let go of life. The temptation to do that this night tor-
mented her and Catriona might have done that except
for Aidan's words.

'Touch me. I beg you. Put your hands on me now.'

Startled at the vehemence of his words, she felt the
tension increase in his hard thighs beneath her. His
breathing grew shallow and fast and heat poured off
his skin. His body readied itself for pleasure and she
watched as his flesh pressed against the lacings of his
trews. She'd seen it earlier, naked and bold in his hand,
and now hers itched to release it and hold it.

She shivered then and it shook her whole body. But
it was not in fear or because the air chilled her—it was
plain and simple desire that coursed through her. When
once and always in the past, the thought of pleasing a
man turned her stomach, now she wanted to touch him,
to taste his skin, to caress the hard, rising flesh to its
full size. What had once been a weapon of terrible pain
and fear now intrigued her.

So, could she? Was she ready to invite her seduction to reach its conclusion? Or should she walk away
before this fire of passion that threatened to ignite between them did, burning them both in ways she could
not even contemplate?

'Cat. Pleasure me.'

Those words, usually a demand followed by forced measures, should have stopped her, but they did not. They were not an order this time, but a plea and spoken by a man who could have forced her the same way others had. The flesh between her legs began to ache with the same need he'd caused in her earlier—one that he could incite and then soothe with his touch. Now he asked her to take control of his body. To touch him.

To please him.

She remembered watching him fight once, in the yard, surrounded by his friends and the men who would one day serve him. His tall, muscular body had glistened in the sun as he and Rurik's son took down all the others. Now she wanted to caress his skin to see how it felt under her hands.

Reaching for the ties on his long shirt, she tugged them loose and leaned up to pull it over his head. Cat gasped as her breasts slid along his skin as she pushed it up his arms and off. Though he did not resist, he did not help much either, forcing her to move closer to him to do it. Tossing the shirt aside, she sat back and tried to decide where to touch first.

The dark curls on his chest that trailed in a narrowing path from his neck down to his manhood beckoned her hand, so she began there. She ran the back of her hand across his chest, swirling in the curls, and discovered that touching his nipples drew out a gasp from him. Empowered by such a reaction, she grazed her fingers over them, watching as his eyes darkened and his mouth opened. He'd put his mouth on hers and caused a fiery heat to burn throughout her body—could she cause the same to him?

Leaning forward, she kissed the side of his neck and then she kissed one of his nipples. He shuddered under her. Doing it again brought another shudder. When she tried to suckle on it as he had hers, his body bucked beneath her. Cat liked the way it felt, to be the one causing him to respond with her touch.

She caressed his chest, running her fingers over the curls and tracing them down, down, down until she reached his belt. Without looking at him, she unbuckled it and then tugged on the laces of his trews.

He stopped breathing then. Aidan closed his eyes and leaned his head against the board behind him, giving her leave to do as she willed to him. So, she loosened the leather laces and spread the fabric apart to take him in her hand.

Smooth, like a rich fabric she'd felt once, and hard, his flesh rose against her palm, the skin drawing back to expose the tip of it. A bead of moisture appeared at the tip and she rubbed her thumb across, causing the flesh to surge against her hand. Aidan's breathing stopped and his body tensed under her. Cat slid one hand down the length of his manhood and touched the rest of him there.

'Cat,' he growled through tightly clenched jaws. 'You are killing me!' The guttural tone caused vibrations to echo into her, deep inside of her, and her body began to tighten at the sound of it. When she glanced up, her hands still encircling him most intimately, the desire glowed in his eyes.

'Should I cease?' she asked, not knowing if this was pleasure or pain for him.

'Nay,' he shouted aloud. Then he smiled at her. 'Nay.' A bit softer then, but still thick with his need.

She was teasing a caged animal and she knew it. His control would break and it would be her doing. That should have terrified her and yet it did not. Somehow she knew she was safe in his arms. At least her body was. A man like this could be dangerous to a woman's heart.

He raised his hands and covered hers then, guiding her into a pattern of caressing the length and then around the width of his flesh. His breathing grew louder and raw, his jaw still clenched and his body tensed beneath her. In her grasp, he hardened and she knew his release was nigh.

'Cease,' he whispered, lifting his and her hands off his flesh then. Leaning back on her heels, she knew he wanted to finish within her body.

But could she?

'You have that look in your eyes again, Cat.' He shifted and lifted her off his legs then. Sliding from the bed, he stood and pushed his trews down and off. 'I do not want that look to be between us.'

He stood before her then, bathed in the fire's light, exposing himself to her and letting her just gaze on him. Unashamed. Unabashedly male. Hard everywhere, strong muscles that tensed as he moved towards the bed. His manhood rose from the curls at its base, inviting her touch once more.

'That is the look I wish to see in your eyes,' he said. 'What do you see?'

'You look hungry and curious at the same time,' he said on a laugh. 'Your tongue keeps peeking out of the corner of your mouth as though you would...' His words became strangled then, as she did what he was describing.

'Taste it?' she finished.

His flesh pulsed then, his body tensed and hers answered with the same. She reached out, but he stopped her questing hands.

'Not this time.' He shook his head and reached for her now.

Pulling her on to her knees, he grabbed hold of her shift and pulled it over her head. Tossing it aside, he climbed back on the bed and knelt before her. After only a moment's delay, he tugged her towards him and embraced her. The heat of his skin shocked her as their bodies touched.

'Do not think, Cat. Just feel what I do to you,' he whispered as he tilted his head and touched his mouth to hers. Her body understood and reacted to his promise now.

She let go and let him do as he would then, her body a thing unknown to her as it blossomed under his touch. Whether hands or mouth and skin, it mattered not for he used every part of him to bring the need within her to life, to stoke it like the fire and to promise to vanquish it before she burned up from it.

As the first moments of release began, he moved between her legs and drew them up around his hips. Instead of fear, she felt need. The need for him to fill her emptiness, to take her over the edge to mindless pleasure.

And he did.

His flesh slid into her, the moisture of her body easing its path. He lay over her, his face intense from his own building arousal, as he moved deeper and deeper within her flesh. Ever did he watch her, waiting for some sign he needed to stop, she supposed. Then all thoughts evaporated as he took her to the edge of release over and over before letting them, nay, pushing them to, both crash over it.

He toppled on her and then rolled them both to their sides, never letting her go. They lay in the silence, not speaking, as she listened to the pace of their breathing. A while passed as their bodies calmed and his flesh withdrew from her. But she would never lose the sense of awe or forget what he'd wrought within her during this joining.

No pain. Oh, as she shifted against him, she knew her body had been entered and filled, but the place there felt empty now. No pain.

He reached down and tugged loose the bedcovers beneath them. Pulling them up, he covered them and then rested his chin on her head and encircled her with his arms.

Sleep captured her then and she sank into a rest unlike any before. She was replete. She was emptied.

She was safe.

In the morning she could not remember how many times they'd joined. A touch of a hand. A kiss. Shifting bodies. Any small caress seemed to ignite the heat between them.

Cat remembered the second time, for Aidan drew it out in anguishing, slow strokes that made her cry out in need. Even when he entered her, he made her feel each moment of his flesh in hers.

The next time he took her, he stoked her arousal fast and hard until she screamed out her release.

Then....

She did not remember the rest for they faded into a sensual fog of excitement and release, torment and easing, touching and taking and possessing. He'd taunted her, teased her, caressed her, tasted her through the whole of the night. Even now, her body wanted to respond to even the memories of it all, but exhaustion prevented it.

So, how did one greet a man in the light of morning after a night of such abandonment and pleasure? When sleep finally gave up on her, Cat knew she must face the dawn and find out.

Opening her eyes, she found herself alone in the bed. Sitting up, she stretched, trying to ease some of the overused muscles and realising that Aidan's youth and strength would wear out her older body very quickly. Laughing, she reached for her shift and found a clean gown to wear.

When she opened the door of the bedchamber, she found an empty room. Aidan was not there.

The silence surrounding her told her he was gone. Gone without a word to her. But a fire burned in the hearth, so he had at least thought of that.

She poured some water into a pot and put it on to heat. Her one luxury, the one thing she spent her pennies on that was not a necessity, was a special tea from the healer. The healer's herb garden was the best in Lairig Dubh and she provided Cat with betony leaves that steeped into a wonderful concoction.

Taking out a leaf and crushing it into a battered metal mug, she poured the steaming water over it and set it aside to brew. With a drop of honey to sweeten the taste, she went looking for something to eat and found the oatcakes left from the day before wrapped in cloth. A simple way to break her fast, but she wanted nothing more this morn. Making her way not to the table but to the cushioned chair, she sat down and sipped the tea.

Her body, though not well rested, felt alive for the first time. There was not a place on her he had not touched last night. He'd pleasured her so many times and so much that she lost herself in it. She should be tired. She should be exhausted, but she was not. Truth be told, she wanted to run laughing along the lanes and share the joy she'd had with anyone who would listen. She wanted to tell Muireall that she understood now what she'd meant.

But she would do none of those things for to do so would make them all question whether or not this affair had begun before Gowan's death. They would look askance once more, in spite of Aidan's protection, and she could not bear that.

And now? Now what would she do?

Even the betony tea did not soothe the slight of his wordless leaving. Looking around the empty house, the truth struck her—this is how a man treated his leman.

No explanations, no excuses, no leavetaking. None of that was necessary when a man paid a woman for her time. He did not answer to her, but she did to him.

That stung even more.

Oh, Cat had accepted that he was not hers and would never be, but the truth of her circumstances was harder to ignore in the cold light of day. A night of passion spent did not grant anything more than that. Many questions turned over and over in her thoughts and the betony tea provided no clarity. She allowed herself only until she finished, before deciding that she would seek out Muireall and offer her help this day.

The sharp rapping on the door surprised her, for no one had come to call on her since she'd moved in just days ago. Walking to open it, she found a wee lad who stood there, holding out a flower torn from some bed.

'The laird's son bid me bring this to you and say...' He paused, shuffling his feet in the dirt there and shaking his head as he whispered to himself.

'What is your name?' she asked, crouching down so she could look him in the face. His mop of red hair stood on end and a thick sprinkling of freckles on his face reminded her of the miller's oldest.

'Alasdair,' he said, before returning to his whispered words.

'Aidan MacLerie sent you here?' Her heart lightened in that moment. Mayhap it was better than she thought? 'He sent this flower?' She brought the blossom, one that grew along the paths in the forest, to her nose to smell its scent. Aidan must have passed them on his way out this morn.

'Aye, he did. And he said…' His face filled with misery then and tears threatened to spill. 'I have forgotten the rest, mistress.'

Catriona reached out and lifted his chin so he would look at her and not the ground. 'You do remember the words, Alasdair. If you take a deep breath and let it out, the words will come back to you now.'

'Do ye think so?' His bright green eyes showed his doubt, but he shrugged and nodded. 'I could try.'

Cat smiled and urged him to, knowing it was really just a way for him to calm down and then he might remember whatever message Aidan had sent to her. 'Go on with you now. Try.'

With all the seriousness of a warrior going into battle, he sucked in a breath that filled his wee chest almost to bursting and then pushed it out with great force. So great a force that she nearly coughed in response. But she waited as the smile grew wider across his face and he nodded.

'He said to bid ye to visit his cousin this morn. And he will speak to ye further on in the day.'

He let out a shout and jumped up and down, clearly thrilled with himself for carrying out his duty. She stood then and smiled at the boy.

'I will tell Aidan that you carried out your task well, Alasdair,' she promised.

She bade him to wait a moment and went into the house and found the last oatcake. Boys his age were hungry every moment of every day and he snatched it out of her hand with a quick word of thanks. He reached the end of the walk where it joined the lane and turned back to her.

'Just call me if ye need a message sent back to the laird's son, mistress. I am good at carrying them and will find him for ye.'

Wee Alasdair did not wait for an answer, for he stuffed the last bit of oatcake into his mouth and ran off, holding a penny in his fingers which Aidan must have paid him for his services.

The day grew brighter then, no matter the clouds that rolled overhead and threatened that the springs rains would fall. A smile blossomed on her face as she looked at the single flower in her hand.

He had left, but he had thought of her.

And he placed a task before her—a reminder, a request more, that she visit Ciara and learn to read and write. Aidan said it would be hard work to learn her letters and numbers and she did not doubt that.

Now, though, with the possibility of a future ahead of her, she realised that knowledge and a skill like that could give her opportunities once Aidan married. So learning with Ciara could help her to be on her own. Right now, this morn, that felt right to her.

She finished dressing and went to begin a new part of her life then—one in which she could make decisions for herself. One that included some joy.

And one in which there would be a large measure of passion.

Chapter Thirteen

Aidan walked towards the keep, regretting with every step that he'd left without seeing her smile this morn. And though he had taken her without ceasing all through the night, his body ached for her even now.

Catriona was everything he'd hoped for in a lover even if her innocence in bedplay was clear. She opened to him and he brought her to release and to pleasure for what must be the first time in her life. Her body answered his every touch and he had so much more to show her. How it should be between a man and woman. How pleasure should be shared and should be for both of them. His blood surged and his cock rose in spite of how many times they'd joined all through the night.

Duty, his father, summoned him to his side this morn. When his parents left for his uncle's wedding, Aidan would stand in his father's place. And make judgements in his stead. Today, he would hear disputes and resolve them, just as he would once he took over control of Ord Dubh.

He passed through the gates and waved to the guards. When his friends saw him and followed, he wanted to sing out Catriona's praises to them, but he held the words. Though ever eager to share stories of their prowess with each other, somehow, exposing her to them felt…wrong.

So, as they recognised the signs he could not seem to hide on the morning after a good bout of sex and asked for the details, he brushed them aside.

'Just tell us her name?' Angus said.

'You are daft!' Caelan said, smacking Angus on the side of his head. 'Everyone knows who she is. He's been after her for weeks.'

'I was not sure which of the rumours spoke true of it, but I can tell from your stride that you have been well f—' Angus stopped and changed the word when Aidan glared at him. 'Well tupped.'

Aidan stopped then and looked at them. 'Speak of this, of her, to no one lest Munro hears of it. And I will not have it said she dishonoured her vows before Gowan's death.'

He needed them to know that truth. Something within him would not allow her to be shamed by his actions.

'Munro kens of the house you gave her,' Dougal said. 'Everyone kens.'

Aye, everyone would know every move he made, that was the way of things. And what they did not, his father would anyway.

He'd counted on everyone knowing, to ease her way and to keep her safe from harassment. But he did not wish to speak of her openly with his friends. Not in the way they usually shared details of their conquests and their bedding of this woman or that one.

'My father waits on me,' he said, walking towards the keep then. 'Do you wish to watch?'

Though the others strode off, not interested in anything but fighting and swiving or talking about doing those things, Young Dougal walked silently at his side into the keep. Dougal, unlike Angus, knew when to keep his mouth shut and Aidan liked that about him. Entering the great hall, Aidan found both of their fathers at the high table, though Rurik sat at one end while his father sat in the centre with his mother next to him. With a nod of his head, his father directed him to the other side.

The disputes heard this morn were not serious in nature, but they needed the chieftain's wisdom and his support of whoever won the argument. One farmer claimed another had stolen livestock. A man asked approval for a marriage between his son and a woman from outside the clan. About ten matters in all needed to be heard.

He bowed to his mother as he walked up the steps and then took the seat next to his father. When he looked at Rurik at the other end of the table, the man's gaze narrowed and then he nodded. A flurry of exchanged glances between his parents and Rurik ended with them all looking at him with some awareness in their eyes.

Did he wear the fact that he'd finally shared Catriona's bed like a garment? The good thing was he saw no censure in their glances, but he suspected they would have words with him about it soon.

* * *

The morning passed slowly as villagers and men sworn in service and merchants came before the earl to settle their disputes. Though not with each, his father had asked for his counsel as much as he did his mother, so Aidan thought he must be meeting his father's expectations. When the session was done, it was time for the noon meal.

As the servants prepared the table and then brought forth platters of cheese and roasted quail and other meats, his father called him to speak with him and Rurik. His mother was too busy directing the servants to notice.

'So, 'tis a thing done then?' his father asked him.

He did not pretend not to understand the question.

'Aye.' He crossed his arms over his chest, mimicking the taller, stronger, older Rurik's stance.

'No matter that she has taken you to her bed, arrangements are moving forward for finding you a suitable wife. Think not to delay it because you've found a pleasing place between her legs.'

Anger filled him then, but he held it in check. So, his father thought this was no different than all the other women before her? He could not blame him or anyone else who thought this was the same as his past behaviour. But it wasn't. He didn't know how this differed, but it did.

'I know my duty and she knows her place, Father.'

'It is easy enough to forget once the chase is done and the quarry is in your grasp. Success in capturing what, or whom, you wanted and pursued at such a cost as she did can lead to a loss of control over your feelings, Aidan. Do not let yours run loose and unbridled.'

'As I said, I know my duties and she her place.'

His father's only reply was a curt nod, while Rurik grunted. Aidan knew not if it was in approval or something else.

His mother called them to table and Dougal joined his father there. They ate then, speaking mostly about their journey, who would accompany them and what tasks would be most important during their absence. All they waited on was for the warmer air to allow the snow in the higher passes to melt and they would be on their way.

All through the meal, his thoughts wandered to that house on the far side of the village. How had she looked when she awakened? Had her paleness been replaced by the rosy blush she wore as he pleasured her? Would she sink back into the demure, unassuming demeanour or would she remain the woman who boldly took her pleasure and screamed out her delight throughout the night?

Did his message arrive? The boy was so excited by the offered penny that Aidan wondered if he'd even heard the words he wanted said to Catriona.

Did she seek out Ciara for lessons this morn? Was this day like any other to her or had last night's intimacies changed her?

'Aidan?'

His mother's voice broke into his thoughts. The silence around him let him know everyone noticed his distraction.

'Aye, Mother. What did you say?' A few deep chuckles down the table confirmed they'd all noticed.

'Join me in my solar before you leave the keep, if you will?'

She rose then, as did everyone at the table, when the lady left. Others walked away then for all had duties to be seen to. With a word to Dougal that he would seek him out later, he followed his mother across the hall to the chamber she called hers. They entered and he waited until a servant poured wine into cups and served them before speaking.

'How can I serve you, Mother?' he asked, taking a sip of the wine and taking note of the shelf of books there.

'Tell me about this woman you have set up in the village,' she said. 'I met her once under the worst circumstances.'

'Why do you question this? I have had women in the past and you never raised a concern,' he said. Drinking some of the wine, he turned to face her.

'You have never arranged a house for any of them. That speaks of an ongoing arrangement between the two of you,' she explained. 'I am concerned because of the upcoming negotiations on your behalf.' The same issue his father had raised. When he began to say that, she held her hand up and waved him off.

'More than that, it makes me ill to think you are preying on an unfortunate with no choice in the matter. Taking advantage of her misfortune after her husband's death to get her into your bed.'

'What have I ever done that you would think me so cruel as that?' he asked. 'What has Father said of the matter?' Anger at being characterised as someone low enough to do what she accused him of made his voice rise.

'Your father said you are old enough to see to your own matters now.' His mother walked to the table and put the cup down.

So, his father had warned her off, yet she still meddled. That was a weakness of hers and one she would never change.

'And yet you trust me not to see to them?' He placed his cup next to hers. 'Be advised that the house I arranged is hers regardless of what happens between us. A settlement on behalf of her husband's service to Father will make certain she is never in poverty again. Does that satisfy your concerns, Mother?'

'Sometimes we defend the actions we take because we know they were for the wrong reasons. Or we sense our own mistakes, but are not ready to acknowledge them,' she said quietly.

She approached him then, placing her hand on his arm.

'Just have a care in this. You have a few choices to make in the coming months and I would not see her harmed because you mistook your father's assistance as permission.'

'Twas natural, he supposed, for his mother to worry over the women who lived in the keep or the village. As lady and countess, they were under her control and supervision. Well, usually 'twas only the women of the keep, but the Beast's mate had extended her control and he'd allowed it. Nothing about the MacLeries was done according to the usual custom of things.

He nodded. As he turned to leave, he caught sight of a book on her shelf there. An old one that he thought he remembered from his childhood. Filled with letters and stories and prayers, it had beautiful colours and images throughout its vellum pages.

'May I borrow this?' he said, lifting the book from its place.

'This is not what I would have expected you to borrow. Mayhap the book of battle strategies? Something about Carthage?'

''Tis not for me,' he said. 'Catriona is learning her letters and numbers and I would share it with her.'

'Take it then,' she said. He glanced again at his mother's face, for her voice had shaken then. 'She can borrow another one if she would like.'

Aidan found a piece of oilcloth and wrapped the precious book in it to keep it safe. He had no doubt that Cat would enjoy seeing it. He kissed his mother's cheek as he left, deciding to see if Cat had gone to his cousin's after all.

If he realised that he'd almost never visited any of his previous bedmates during the day, he did not remember. And he did not see the shocked expression on his mother's face as he pulled the door closed.

Aidan arrived at Cat's house and tethered his horse outside her door. He heard no one moving about inside, so he went in and found it empty. She must be still at Ciara's or, more likely, at Muireall's, so he gently placed the book on the table and turned to leave. He smiled when he noticed the flower he'd pulled from beside the road now sitting in a cup of water there on the shelf above the hearth.

The softest snore echoed through the air, catching him unaware. Walking softly to the doorway, he found her curled up on the bed, sleeping. On her side, with one hand tucked under her face, she looked relaxed, though dark circles smudged the skin beneath her eyes. Had she slept the morning through then and not gone to Ciara's?

Nay, the gown she wore spoke of her dressing. The worn and dusty leather shoes by the bed told him she'd left the house. Some aromatic brew sat steeping near the fire, so he knew she'd had something to drink this morn. Walking to the pot and lifting the lid, he inhaled and recognised the smell of betony—his mother's favourite tea when she was aching or overwrought. He dropped the lid harder than he'd planned and he heard her stir behind him on the bed.

'Aidan?' she said, her voice still thick with sleep. She pushed up on her elbow and ran her hand through her hair, dragging it out of her face.

And he wanted her. Now. Again and again.

In the dark of night. In the light of day. It mattered not.

He wanted her.

'I did not mean to disturb your rest, Cat,' he said softly, trying to make himself believe the words as he uttered them. 'Are you well?'

It had been cruel of him to keep her up through the night with little sleep, but, try as he might, he could not feel guilty about it. Part of him, the randy lad below his belt, urged him to take her now. He resisted, knowing she needed to rest if she was still abed. If not grief, then becoming accustomed to this new place, would keep her from resting well for some days.

The first step he took proved difficult, his cock hard and aching. Why could he not control this overpowering need for her? He'd lusted after many women, but this was something too strong, too different.

She pushed up to sit and let her legs slide over the edge of the bed. He swallowed hard as the skirt of her gown caught beneath her and exposed her shapely legs to him.

'I pray you, pardon my laziness,' she said, standing next to the bed and pulling her shoes on. 'I would have been ready to greet you, but I did not expect you until later.'

His pride swelled as she blushed then. She thought he'd arrive at night to bed her.

'I doubt you have had a lazy day in your whole life,' he said, with a laugh. The dark, enigmatic expression that filled her gaze for only a moment surprised him. 'I meant no insult by it, Cat. You answer to only yourself now, so if you are tired and sleep, so be it.'

'I do not know how to be on my own, Aidan. I have always answered to someone else's demands on my time.'

'Then you need to set things to be done on your own time. Your errands and chores are yours to command.' She studied him silently and he could have believed she agreed with him, save for her doubting expression. 'If you would like, you can hire someone to help you. There is coin enough for that.'

'I have nothing to fill my days now and you would have me pay someone to work for me?' she scoffed.

They were so different from one another. Their lives were so different. He'd grown up with servants and teachers and soldiers who lived to serve him and to fulfill his every need. She'd worked from dawn to dusk, serving her family and then her husband. It would take more than a few days for her to accustom herself to having her own house and money to support herself, if she could at all. He'd seen those who rose from poverty and adversity to new wealth and somehow their thrifty ways followed them through life.

"Did you go to my cousin's?" he asked. 'Surely that will fill some of your days?'

'I did. I tried not to embarrass you with my efforts,' she said. She leaned over and smoothed the bedcovers, tempting him in so many ways that he forgot to breathe.

'What did Ciara say? About your efforts?' he said against the rush of heated blood through his veins. Aidan moved away from her and the bed as the chamber grew hotter each moment.

'If you promise not to laugh, I will show you.'

She went into the other room and he followed, waiting to see what she thought would make him laugh. Her hips swayed enticingly and her hair swung around her like a curtain moving in the breeze. Would it always be this way between them? He was completely lost in every move she made, every word she spoke, every expression that shone from her eyes?

Cat opened the drawer in the cabinet in the cooking area and lifted something out. Turning, she held it out before him. He must not laugh, no matter what it was. A small piece of flat slate with something scrawled on it with chalk. Aidan reached out and turned the slate so he could read it and saw clusters of numbers written on its surface.

Her first attempts to learn and write. His heart swelled with pride as he said the numbers and she pointed to them.

'One. Two. Three. Four. Five. Six. Seven…' He paused and turned the slate a bit. The next one did not look like any number. But it mattered not for she had tried…for him. 'Eight. Nine. Ten.'

'Two small circles should not be difficult to draw, but I struggled with them,' she admitted. 'Ciara gave me this…' she held out a small piece of parchment '…as a guide so I can practise.'

'I brought you something that could help you as well,' he said. Her gaze moved to the table and the book that lay there. 'From my mother's books.'

'I could never,' she protested. 'Even if my skills improve, 'tis too costly for me to touch.'

'We can read it together. I will begin it and, as you learn, you can say the words. Or the numbers, for it contains both.'

She looked on him with an expression of such adoration then that Aidan knew he must get out or he would touch her. She would be safest from his lust if they were outside, where people would see them and he could not throw her on the table, toss up her skirts and have her… many times…to slake his hunger for her. The randy lad approved of that second plan.

'Have you eaten?' he asked, taking her elbow and guiding her towards the door. ''Tis a beautiful day and we should not waste it.' He knew he was speaking nonsense. Her questioning gaze confirmed it. 'I sat with my father to hear disputes this morn. You sat with Ciara, hard at work on those. Come, let us walk a bit.'

Chapter Fourteen

Cat kept glancing at Aidan as he took her by the hand and led her outside. He guided her along the path that led to the centre of the village.

When she'd returned from Ciara's and from hours of intense concentration, determined to learn her numbers, her head had ached. Her body reminded her of their more exquisite exertions of the night and her exhaustion pushed her to a short rest on the wonderful bed he'd bought. She never thought she would awaken to find him there, staring at her.

Unsure of his intentions, she'd dawdled there in the bedchamber, expecting—from the fierce desire that he ever wore in his eyes—to be tossed on the bed and tupped. Though she should have been too exhausted by his efforts of last night, all night, her body already warmed to the thought of joining with his.

When he did not, she decided to show him what she'd learned so far and he gifted her with the warmest smile over the curling, tilting, scrawled numbers there on the slate. She would practise for hours to see that expression again.

Now, they walked together, her hand in his, and, for the first time since becoming his leman in fact, they would be seen so. And she could not do it. As they approached others, she tugged her hand from his and walked a step behind him instead of by his side. He paused as though he thought she would speak to the two women and waited for her.

She let them pass with just a nod and waited for him to walk again. He did not.

'Catriona? Is aught the matter?' he said, holding out his hand to her once more.

'I...cannot,' she said, shaking her head at the proffered hand. He startled at first and then dropped his hand to his side.

'Ah.'

Was he angry? Did he understand she could simply not proclaim their relationship to one and all, not now, not in the village where everyone saw and judged her?

'Come, then,' he said. 'Walk with me.'

This time he walked without touching her, pacing his longer strides to hers so that she was near him. When people passed, they bowed or nodded to him and greeted her as well. The same men who had leered at her just days before now only gave her respectable words or glances. Several men asked Aidan's views on various matters affecting the village or the fields. It would be time to plant very soon and his opinion about when that would happen and which crops would do best this season seemed to matter.

He was his father's son, after all, and would own and control all of this some day.

The one person she did not see and had not seen in days was Gowan's son Munro. It was as if he did not live in Lairig Dubh any longer. No one mentioned him to her, not even Muireall, so she had no idea of his whereabouts or his circumstances. She just feared seeing him here while Aidan escorted her, his leman, for all to see.

When one discussion went on for several minutes, she considered how inappropriate she was for him. He was wealthy, learned, heir to a huge estate and titles that would take him even to the king's court and possibly beyond that. She was the impoverished daughter of a whoremonger who'd barely survived with her life and could offer him nothing of worth. Not even a fertile womb. She'd been lost in her thoughts when his hand took hers.

'Catriona?' he said.

To pull away now would be an insult to him in front of these people, so she left hers in his larger one and walked with him along the path. He took it another step when he moved her hand on to his arm and placed his hand on top to keep it there.

They continued as such as though it a natural thing. Once, nay, twice, his hand slipped and touched the side of her breast. She thought it an accidental slip until she met his gaze and realised he did it a-purpose. Then, even as in the darkest part of last night, her body answered the slightest hint from him.

'Again?' she asked, the words escaping before she

could stop them. He turned and pulled her close, now those aching breasts leaned fully on his arm.

'Still.' One word, said on an exhale and she was ready to lose herself in the passion he promised.

'Now?' How long would it take them to return to the house? she wondered. Not as long to get there as it had to reach this point, if they spoke to no one and rushed their pace a bit.

'Now.'

One word and she was his. He began to turn back towards the house when a young boy called out to him.

'My lord! The laird calls you to the hall. There are guests, he said.'

The momentary insanity that gripped them dissolved as duty called him to the keep. She knew he must heed his father's summons and do it with some haste. Her body ached for his to ignore it and come with her. He nodded to the boy and faced her.

'Later.'

Her body trembled, hearing all the promise in that one word it wanted to hear. Another night spent being pleasured by his skilled and questing hands and mouth and… She shivered again at the memories that flooded her now.

'Your horse,' she forced out. At first he frowned and then he laughed for clearly he was not thinking of his horse either.

'I will leave it. I'll send a boy to tend to it.'

He released her and she nearly melted there at his feet. Her body was not her own any longer. She was not her own. In only one night, she had lost herself to him and his, their, desires. She belonged to him and it had taken hardly any time at all for her to fall from grace completely and utterly. Far less time or effort than she thought it would have taken.

As he walked away, she understood one thing—this would not end well at all, for she was already half in love with a man she could never call her own.

She dared not seek her bed. Or should she?

Would he wake her with a word? A caress? A kiss?

Cat paced around the room that had once seemed so large to her and now could not contain her restlessness. The wrapped book on the table caught her gaze, but she'd decided to wait for his return before opening it.

Was this to be her life now? Waiting on him? She shook her head in denial, yet here she stood, not knowing if he would return or when. Duty came first so it was possible she would spend this night alone. She would spend many nights alone.

Cat promised herself in that moment that she would move past this infatuation, enjoy it for all the pleasure and joy it brought, and then find a balance and a pacing to her life.

Once she had learned to read and write, she had a skill she could barter with—for the cost of a monk or brother to teach those skills was far more than anyone here earned in a year. But she could trade that for the goods and supplies she needed.

Once he left her behind to carry on with his life.

And, oh, aye, he would do that sooner rather than later. Word of three possible brides and all sorts of guesses spread through the village the same evening as the announcement was made. His younger sister had been married twice to join clans. His cousins and other kin the same. As the heir, his marriage would be grander than anyone else's.

Shaking off these thoughts of weddings and of a time too far in the days to come to worry, she filled the pot with water and pulled it over the heat to boil. Surely a cup of her tea would calm her nerves while she waited.

The slate still lay on the table, so she gathered the chalk and a damp cloth to clean the surface and practised her numbers. She knew how to use the numbers to add up purchases and to tally her coins. Writing them was another thing. She'd promised to take the lessons seriously, so she leaned down and concentrated on getting them right.

When the cleaning cloth dried out too much to work, she stood to rinse it in the bucket and saw him there. When he'd entered, she knew not. He stood, leaning against the door, his arms crossed over his chest, just watching her.

'I did not hear you,' she said. 'Why did you not say something?'

'You were bent to your task and I did not want to interrupt you. My cousin would be pleased,' he said, walking towards her. He inhaled as he bent down to review her work. 'That is betony that you use in your tea?'

'Aye,' she said. 'Would you like some?'

At his nod, she fetched a cup, poured the tea in and added a dollop of honey, making it the way she liked it before asking him. He took a drink of it and laughed.

'This tastes just how my mother makes hers,' he said.

'Does she grow betony in the keep's garden for it?' she asked. Cat sat down on the bench at the table and sipped her cup. The tea had soothed her, but her body and the rest of her reacted to his presence, his nearness.

'Aye, along with so many other herbs. You should visit her and let her show you.'

'I hope to plant it here,' she said. 'My garden at home is quite pitiful.' She realised her error as soon as the words were out. 'At Gowan's,' she corrected. 'Was.'

'What else did you grow in your garden there?' he asked.

She spent a few minutes while he finished his tea telling of her successes—few—her errors—many—and her hopes for this new garden. Once his cup sat empty, her mouth went dry.

'You did not open the book.' He nudged it towards her.

'I waited for you,' she said. 'It is your mother's?'

She peeled open the oilcloth and moved it aside to place the book flat on the table. Careful not to move the candles too close, she marvelled over the elaborately decorated, thick leather cover. The colours sparkled in the flickering light.

'Aye,' he said, with a frown. 'But I do not think that is the book I thought it to be.'

'Should you return it now?' she asked, picking up the wrapping to prepare it.

He opened it and let the pages separate. She saw numbers, large ones, painted in bright colours and gold and silver on their edges.

'Will you read it? Some of it? Even if you must return it?' she asked, leaning her chin on her uplifted hands. His voice always thrilled her, so she could not wait to hear him read passages from it. 'Is it in Latin? Greek?' Since she could read neither those nor any other, it mattered not. Only that he could mattered.

'Neither. French, the language of the royal court,' he said. 'Choose a number you have practised and I will read that page.'

Aidan walked around the table and sat next to her. The bench was not so long that she could get very far from him. And that was a good thing, for he wanted her close, under his hand, able to be kissed when he wanted to.

'As you can see,' Cat said, pointing at the slate, 'I struggle with even the simplest number. So, page one.'

Aidan carefully lifted the pages until he found the one embellished with the number she chose. Opening it and spreading it out before them, he noticed the illustrations were of a garden, filled with many flowers and plants and trees. A voluptuous woman, with the same colouring as Cat, stood in the middle with her arms open in welcome.

'My beloved is mine, and I am his. He feedeth me among the lilies.'

The images might have been tame enough, but these words were words of love and desire, expressed by a king. This book was not the storybook he thought he'd taken from the shelf, but another kind of book completely.

'Let me try another,' he said, turning to Catriona. 'Choose another page.'

'Four,' she whispered.

Aidan turned back to that page and read the verse at the top to her. This one was covered in vines and grapes. Barrels of wine sat in the centre of it.

'Let him kiss me with the kisses of his mouth: for his love is better than wine.'

These verses were the infamous Songs of Solomon, words of love and passion and desire. Words usually kept hidden from those not educated to read in Latin. But these words were in French, the language of the English court. And he doubted that this book had been created by the holy monks.

He was about to close the book when Cat tugged on his arm.

'Page six, I pray you,' she said on a sigh. She did not lean away this time after making her request and he could feel the weight of her breasts against his arm and her thigh against his. So could the randy lad.

'A bundle of myrrh is my well-beloved unto me. He shall lie all night betwixt my breasts.'

'Oh, my.' Her voice was breathless and her own breasts strained against her gown. She leaned over to look at the images on this page and she gasped.

No flowers. No vines. No plants, except for the small pouch of leaves resting between the breasts of the same voluptuous woman from page eight, now naked and lying with a naked man.

'Page eight,' she said, her hand on his thigh now, urging him on. Aidan turned to it, not daring to glance at the illustrations first.

'Awake, O north wind; and come thou south. Blow

upon my garden that the spices thereof may flow out. Let my beloved come into his garden, and eat his pleasant fruits.'

Catriona was panting now, pressing against him and stroking his thigh. Did she even realise she did these things? Or was the spell of the words and images so strong that her body reacted without thought? His gaze took in her open mouth and her breasts against his arm, threatening to spill out of her gown, and he dared a look at the images that she saw there.

The naked woman reclined on a bench while wisps of wind blew above her. Her legs lay spread open and her lover… He closed the book, nearly catching her nose as she leaned in to look more closely at the forbidden images there.

'What kind of book is this, Aidan?' she asked.

'A forbidden one,' he said, his own body ready to experience the delights described within it. 'One meant to entice and arouse.'

'Are you enticed, Aidan?'

He swallowed and swallowed against the desire pouring through him. He would have thought her innocent and unaware had her hand not slipped at just that moment and touched the very proof of how aroused he was. 'Aye, Catriona, I am that.'

Pleased by her growing boldness, he slid his hand up under her gown and shift and sought proof of her body's reaction. The folds of flesh between her legs were moist and she arched against his hand, pushing his fingers in deeper.

'As am I.' She sighed.

Boldness to meet hers, he pushed the book aside and lifted her on to the table. It took no time at all to throw her skirts out of his way, loosen his trews and fill her. She grabbed on to his arms, her head tossing side to side as her flesh tightened around him, urging him on to the oblivion of release. Faster than he could have imagined, his erection tightened within her, pouring his seed deep in her womb. Her own release, coming in waves of spasms he felt surrounding his flesh, milked him dry.

Their breathing echoed through the chamber and it took some minutes for them to gather their wits. How did she drive him so mindless with desire? 'Twas not as though he was some untried youth, never having tupped a woman before. He was practised and experienced, yet he acted in an artless, hungry manner whenever he could have her. He could blame it on the long interval between taking a woman to bed, but he'd had longer. He could blame it on the length of time it had taken to have her, but he'd pursued other women for longer.

So, it came back to her. Catriona MacKenzie caused this reaction, this constant need for her, this growing desire to be with her, to be in her.

He stepped back and tied his laces and then held out his hand to her.

'You must object, Cat, and not let me treat you so,' he warned. 'If you do not require better behaviour from me, you are likely to find yourself—'

'Tupped on a table?' she asked. Pushing her skirts down and sliding from the table, she looked back at it. ''Twas more pleasant than I expected it would be.'

'Catriona!' he pleaded. 'You must set bounds, for I

have none when it comes to seeking pleasure with you.'
'Struth, he would have her in any manner at any time and in any place, if it were up to him.

'Are there bad places to…tup?' she asked, gathering her tangled hair and shaking it loose over her shoulders. Those breasts pressing against her gown… All this talk of tupping right after they'd tupped was not good. It would lead to more. Still, she *had* asked.

'I have not found any yet, though I do seek comfortable places. A bed is my favourite place.'

'Let me wrap the book so you can take it back,' she said, reaching for the cloth and the book.

'Ah, but there are so many numbers you have not learned yet. Let us keep it for a while longer.'

The flash in her eyes told him she wanted to find out what other pleasures were suggested in the ornate book. For now, he needed no other inspiration but her. Aidan brought her closer, wrapped the length of her hair around his fist and drew her mouth to his, tasting the sweetness he knew he would find.

The night passed quickly and he left her sleeping the next morning with a whispered word and soft kiss on the mouth that showed she'd been well loved during that night. And over the next days and nights, Aidan showed her that there was nothing and nowhere forbidden between two lovers who sought pleasure together.

Though she balked at displays of affections when others could see them, she never refused him anything when in private. His favourite had been finding her on her knees in the garden, digging out weeds. He'd crept up from behind her, wrapped his arms around her to hold her up and taken her that way—fast, deep thrusts with her not moving except to push back against him until they finished. Then, he discovered that cleaning off the mud had brought as much pleasure as getting dirty had been.

As the time came for his parents to leave for MacCallum lands, Aidan knew that this time of having who and what he wanted was coming to an end. He just worried over Catriona's reaction when he asked her to remain with him after his required marriage.

For he had discovered that getting who he wanted this time made him want her even more. And he did not wish to part from the woman who gave him all that she was, asking nothing in return.

Chapter Fifteen

The snows had melted from the high mountain passes and, in two days, she and Connor and the others would journey to the lands of her family for her brother's wedding to Rurik's daughter. She still marvelled that Athdar had survived Isobel's pursuit of him when her father had been opposed to the match. But, Athdar saving the man's life could have been the turning point in taking him seriously.

As Jocelyn walked through the village, visiting the sick and checking with the merchants and the healer about supplies, she looked for any sign of Catriona MacKenzie there. Connor had done as she'd asked and sent Aidan off on a task that would keep him from the village this day for she wished to have words with the woman who'd clearly captured her son's heart…whether he knew it or not.

The signs were there for all to see—he spoke of her often, whether at table or while carrying out his duties. He praised her abilities and her attempts to learn to read and write. He spoke of her garden. He spoke of her quiet sense of humour. That he spoke of her at all—a woman he'd pursued, set up as his leman and now spent every possible moment with—told Jocelyn how serious this was.

He was a healthy young man and, like any of that age, had a string of women in his bed and he in theirs. 'Twould always be so when their blood ran hot and they had only to beckon with a soft gesture or word. But Aidan had never once spoken the names of any of the ones before Catriona to his parents. Never once paid his own coins to buy her a house. And he'd never cared whether his exploits spread through the village or keep.

But he did now. Other than him speaking so highly of this woman, no stories passed through kith and kin about them. He did not boast to his friends, he did not include his friends in drunken reveries that resembled orgies of olden days and he allowed only Rurik's son Dougal to visit the house he'd bought her with him.

Jocelyn headed towards the cottage of Gair's sister now. Ciara was busy with her father at the keep, so Catriona could not be there this morn. From what Peggy had learned, the woman kept to herself most of the time, spending time with Ciara when she was available and helping her friend Muireall with her chores. Now reaching the path to Muireall's cottage, she let Peggy knock on the door.

'Good day, my lady,' Muireall called out as she came outside, a wee babe on her hip. Jocelyn recognised the family resemblance between this woman and her brother, their steward.

'Good day, Muireall,' she said. 'How does the wee one fare?' The babe gifted her with a gummy smile and drool spilt down the boy's chin. His mother wiped it without pause.

'Teething early, my lady. The youngest of mine so far.'

'Is Catriona MacKenzie about?' Jocelyn asked.

'Oh, nay, not now. She stopped by earlier, but has been gone for an hour or more.' Muireall's frown declared her friend worried. 'Lady, she is a kind and gentle woman,' she began to explain. 'She—'

'Muireall, have no worries over my enquiry.' Jocelyn was struck by two things—Catriona's friend's loyalty and her fear. 'Aidan spoke of her garden and I bring her some cuttings from mine.'

Muireall's face lightened, but concern still filled her gaze. 'Do you know where…?' She shook her head. 'I am certain you do, my lady.'

'Aye, I know the house. Good day to you,' Jocelyn said, walking on towards the edge of the village.

There was no doubt in her mind that everyone who saw her this day knew her path and knew whom she sought. News travelled quickly and Jocelyn also knew that her son would hear of her visit when he returned. But, it was time to assess for herself how far this relationship had gone and how dangerous it was.

She knew the house and its location for she'd visited it when some kin stayed there some years ago. Connor kept it empty for use when guests came to call and when discretion was necessary, for its location and position close to the forest gave it a measure of privacy that many village houses, cottages and crofts did not have.

Perfect for a man and his leman.

Peggy walked to the door and would have knocked if a loud and very bold epithet had not echoed from the walled yard next to the house. Guessing from the feminine tone that Catriona worked there, Jocelyn approached the wall and followed it around until she reached the gate which, convenient for privacy, was positioned facing the forest and not the lane. She found Catriona sitting in the middle of the garden in the dirt.

'Good day, Mistress MacKenzie,' she called out in greeting.

'My lady.' Catriona pushed to her feet, shaking the dirt from her gown as she quickly came to the gate. 'Good day to you,' she said, curtsying before her. 'How may I serve you, my lady?' she asked, as she rose and pushed open the gate.

'Aidan spoke of your garden and your love of betony, so I brought you some cuttings from the garden at the keep.' She held out her hand to Peggy and the girl handed her the basket she'd brought. 'There are also some herbs and a few for flowers,' she added. 'Every garden needs some colour, I think.'

'Your generosity is appreciated, Lady MacLerie.' Catriona motioned to the door. 'May I offer you some cool water inside? I fear I have little else other than some ale. Oh, or some whisky that Aid— Your son brought here for his use.'

Jocelyn followed the woman inside, sending Peggy

back to the keep. She wanted a private discussion with Catriona and wanted no other ears nearby.

She did not know what she thought she would find inside, but the house was clean and neat with few decorations or personal belongings. A few cushioned chairs sat near the hearth, with some plaid blankets tossed over the backs, making an inviting scene. The cooking area was clean and the table clear. On a shelf near the cooking area sat a certain book, wrapped in oilcloth, most likely to keep it protected and to keep it covered.

'I was surprised when he took this book for you.'

Jocelyn laughed then as she remembered not knowing how to ask her son if he realised the book he'd chosen was not a storybook. But how did a woman explain to her son, grown or not, that his father had brought it back to his mother as a special gift for the two of them to share? And shared it they had, many, many times. 'I notice it has not been returned to me yet,' she said.

From Catriona's blush, it was clear her son and his leman had shared it as well.

'How are your lessons coming?' Jocelyn asked. As the woman's blush deepened and she stammered, Jocelyn knew her words had been taken wrongly. 'Your reading and writing lessons? From Ciara?' she clarified.

'Forgive me, my lady,' she said. 'I thought you meant… But then you could not have meant… Forgive me,' she said. Catriona offered a seat in one of the chairs and then went to the pantry, still mumbling under her breath.

'A cup of water, if you please, Catriona,' she called out.

Soon they sat together in the silence.

'The last time we spoke, it was a difficult time for you. How do you fare now?' she asked.

'I thank you for your help when Gowan died, my lady. He was a good man and he sav…' Catriona paused then for a moment. 'He was a good man.'

Had she started saying that Gowan had saved her? Jocelyn wondered about that, but let it go for now.

'My son said you refused him while Gowan yet lived?'

'Aye, my lady, I did. I held true to the vows I spoke with Gowan. No matter what the rumours,' she said. Catriona shifted in her chair and drank from the cup.

'Were you forced to this? Did he, did Aidan, pressure you to this?' Jocelyn motioned her hand to the house. 'I pray you, tell me true and do not try to protect him. I know my son and he can be…persuasive when it comes to women and filling his bed.'

If she was shocked by Jocelyn's candour, the woman did not show it. Instead, she answered the personal and prying, her son would call them, questions in a calm, thoughtful manner, keeping her dignity as she was questioned about things a mother rarely spoke of to her son's woman.

'His guilt caused him to arrange this house. I ken he thinks that his pursuit of me robbed me of house and home, but I think that would have happened on Gowan's death, no matter.'

Catriona had no idea of the true part in her husband's death that Aidan had played. If she did…

'But I gain so much from this arrangement, my lady.

A house for my use as long as I need it. An education in letters and numbers that someone like me would never have had. And a short respite from grief and pain.'

'A short respite? Is he leaving you?' He had tired of women quickly, moving from one to another in a ceaseless process over these last several years. But surely not already?

Catriona stood then and walked to the open door. Staring out it, she shook her head and then met Jocelyn's gaze.

'Oh, nay, not yet,' she said softly. Taking a breath and letting it out, she turned and faced her. 'But I know you seek a wife for him and I know he must marry soon. And, lady, I know my place and it will not be at his side.'

Jocelyn stood and walked to her side now. Her heart hurt somehow at this woman's sense of how things would work. There was no regret or shame in her voice, no disrespect in her tone. But there was also no hope, only a clear understanding of Aidan's future and her own separate one.

'Worry not, if that is what brought your visit here,' Catriona said. 'I will make no demands on him. There can be no bairns and I will not keep him from what he must do.' She smiled then, a watery one, and she shrugged. 'You see, I am taking advantage of all he offers me even while you think he takes too much from me. I will leave here with a skill and some coin to ease my way wherever I go.'

'Does he know this? Does he know you will not stay?' Jocelyn asked.

'I have told him so, but you know men, my lady. He hears only what he chooses. But we women know how it must be,' she finished.

What struck Jocelyn in that moment was that in different circumstances a woman like Catriona would have been the perfect wife for her son. And the sadness of that revelation brought tears to her own eyes. Blinking them away, she walked to the door. She took Catriona's hand in hers.

'If you have need of anything, you have but to call on me and I will do whatever I can to help you. Do you understand?'

'I thank you for your generosity, my lady. But I will not have need to call on you. I know what I'm doing.'

Jocelyn looked into the face of the woman her son loved and who loved her son and nodded, knowing she would not argue the point. The offer had been made and Jocelyn would honour it.

'Good day, Catriona. My thanks for your hospitality.'

She walked away quickly, the tears that had threatened pouring down her face now. Jocelyn waited until she turned the corner and Catriona would not see her before tugging a linen square from her sleeve and mopping her eyes and face. By the time she entered the gates, she had herself under control. She spied her husband standing in the place high on the walls of the keep in the spot he liked because he could see all the comings and goings.

Jocelyn must speak to him now. He must know what they were up against.

* * *

Connor watched as she walked with purpose towards the stairway that would bring her to him. This was a place where they could speak without being heard. This was a place where they could do other things without being seen as well.

The original castle builder had created this gap for his assignations with the lord's wife at the time. That did not end well for either of them, but the sad story of their ending did not stop him from enjoying this place with his wife whenever he could coax her here. No matter that all knew what happened here when the guards were directed elsewhere. It was the Beast's lair where no one would trespass.

Now, she reached the top of the stairs and motioned the guards away. He could not see her face yet, but her manner did not bode well for his hoped-for seduction this day.

'Connor,' she said.

'Jocelyn,' he replied. When the expected kiss did not happen, he took her by the shoulders and pulled her to him. 'Wife,' he growled, possessing her mouth until she melted against him.

And still he did not cease tasting her, dipping deep and fast and hard into her mouth with his tongue, hoping to spur her on to take of him. Several minutes of very pleasing kissing happened before he gave up his efforts. Placing her back on her feet, he held on to her until she steadied. At least he knew she was affected by him.

'Husband,' she said, putting her hands on her hips in a stance he knew well. 'We must discuss Aidan.'

'You went to speak to his leman.'

He did not ask, for he knew she had. His mate did not leave his presence without him knowing where she was. He would never cease protecting her whether she knew it or not. Connor owed her his very soul and so she would always be under his protection and observation.

'Certainly I did,' she snapped back at him. 'We have a problem.'

Though love had come to him in the most unexpected way—in a marriage brought about by threats and blackmail—it did not mean he could not see it. Aidan was maturing from a callous, randy young man into a young man worthy to be his heir. And much of it had been brought about by his attraction to Catriona MacKenzie. His actions had caused harm and he'd done the right thing in trying to sort through the consequences of it.

And he'd fallen in love in the process.

Even Connor could see it.

'What problem is that, Jocelyn?' he asked the woman who held his heart in hers.

Their love had developed after their marriage—in spite of it, he sometimes thought—and had grown deeper as they faced the adversities and challenges of life. He did not doubt that his son could do the same thing, once he married the right woman.

'What do you know about this woman? Surely your spies have reported to you about her marriage with Gowan? And before that? I know you are careful about your son.'

'Spies, Jocelyn?'

He preferred to call them by other names, but as long

as they provided him with what he needed, he cared not the name. And provide they did. Whether important information or small bits he tucked away for future need, his sources kept him well informed about everything and everyone who lived under his control—and those who might affect him or his interests.

So far, they'd said nothing alarming about the woman his son had chosen as his leman…and more.

'She said something about Gowan saving her. I was curious and thought you would know by now. And, aye, spies, Husband. You have your creatures everywhere.'

'And the matter you think is a problem?' he prodded her. He tucked away that bit about Gowan and would have someone look into it further, for it might prove valuable.

'They are in love.'

He let out a frustrated breath. 'I know. It has no significance to our plans. You know that. He will marry an appropriate bride and they will find happiness. Hopefully, as we did.'

'Connor! How can you say that?'

'You spoke to Catriona. How did you find her to be?' he asked, knowing the answer already, for he'd observed the woman his son had taken under his protection.

'She is circumspect and loyal and does not overstep like that last one,' she said, shivering at the memories of the histrionics of Aidan's last lover, one he'd kept, thankfully, for a very brief time.

'Then she understands that she cannot stand in the way of our plans for his marriage?'

'Aye, she understands, but—' she began to argue.

'She understands, Jocelyn. Let it go.'

The fire in her eyes that he wanted to see was, instead, replaced by anger that said he was not going to get the chance to seduce his wife after all. She screamed out her anger then, stamped her foot and walked away from him, cursing and muttering under her breath as she went down the stairs and through the yard to the keep.

Those who witnessed the exchange turned back to their tasks when the door slammed behind her. She was soft-hearted and, no matter how much she claimed to understand the necessities of life as it involved her son, Jocelyn would never give up hope now.

Connor walked back along the battlements, watching as his men trained below.

He would do what was necessary to see his son, his heir, settled with the right bride, one who brought an equal measure of wealth or power or lands to the marriage. It was Connor's duty and would be Aidan's when he had a son.

If Catriona wanted to remain as his leman, so be it. Most men of his position married as required and kept a leman for love as well. Connor would not demand that Aidan give her up, just keep her in the right place in his marriage.

One day, Jocelyn would see the wisdom in his plans and understand that it had to be this way.

And Aidan?

Well, he was as stubborn as his mother at times, but as a man he would understand the necessity of it. As his son, Aidan understood the absolute necessity of doing his duty.

Connor entered the keep and went about his tasks. Their journey would take several weeks and Aidan would stand in his stead while they were away.

Once they returned, the potential brides would arrive and Aidan would be too busy to worry over Catriona.

It was just the way of things.

Chapter Sixteen

The first week of his parents' absence had passed and Lairig Dubh still stood as it had for ten generations. Its people lived on and everything had been uneventful. Aidan's only disappointment was he'd been too busy to spend time with Cat. She visited the keep once, with Muireall, but she would not remain with him.

She'd finally accepted his invitation to come and eat supper with him this evening here. It was a near thing, for she said it was not her place. He thought that only using the boy she seemed to favour, wee Alasdair, to send the messages convinced her to join him. She did not, he suspected, want to give the boy the task of sending her refusal to Aidan. He cared not the method, he was only happy she accepted.

And yet, he wanted it to be her place.

He wanted her at ease in his home, with his family and his friends.

He wanted her with him, day and night.

But each day and week his parents were away meant

he was one step closer to losing her. For each day they were away, it meant that the women, one of whom he would marry, were that much closer to arriving here.

Now supper neared and Aidan grew nervous. Would she come? When he approached the high table and the servants prepared to serve, he despaired that she would not. Then he saw her near the back of the hall with Muireall, ever at her side, and seated with some others from the village who'd had business in the keep this day. He began to stand, to call her forward when the hall grew silent in response to his action.

Catriona dipped her head then, the only one there not looking at him, and he realised she was embarrassed. Not wanting to make her more uncomfortable, he took his seat and nodded at the servants to begin. Gair sat at his side, discussing several issues, but he noted that her embarrassment faded as he watched her partake in the simple meal offered.

When she smiled, he did. When she laughed, he drank in the sound of it, wondering about the cause of it. When she took a few sidelong glances in his direction, he saw them and nodded to her.

'Aidan?'

He sighed. He lost his ability to think when she was there and when she was not. He must learn to push her from his thoughts and concentrate on his duties. Turning to Gair, he waited for the man's words.

'I received word from your parents. The wedding is scheduled for three days hence and they will return a sennight after that. There is a message for you in your chambers, though I do not think it anything of a pressing nature.'

His uncle. His sister. His cousin Tavis. They had all recently married and their marriages had joined clans or made alliances stronger. It was the way of it.

It would be the way of his life and marriage.

He pushed aside what must be and thought instead of what was—Catriona was his. And he planned on keeping her, no matter what.

After waiting for a polite amount of time for everyone to finish the meal he'd barely tasted, he stood and walked to the place where he wanted to be. Everyone stood as he passed and he greeted a few of those familiar to him as he made his way down one long aisle of tables to her. She stood as well, head bowed before him, and she would have dropped further if he had not taken her hand and stopped her.

'Come,' he said. 'I would show you the rest of my home.'

'My lord,' she whispered, allowing him to lead her though he could feel the resistance in her body.

Just as they approached the doorway to the tower where his chambers were, a group of warriors entered the keep. Recognising several of them, Aidan knew who else served as part of that group, recently returned from a mission escorting an important trade partner of his father's back to the coast. When the group went off to find food and drink, one man remained in place.

Munro.

He thought he might get Catriona away before she

saw him, but she lifted her head at the wrong moment and he knew from her stumbling step she'd seen him. Hatred filled the man's eyes and he fisted his hands as he saw them leaving the hall together.

Catriona stopped then, out of surprise or some other reason, and the hall fell into silence, waiting to see how this encounter would go. Munro took a step towards them but Young Dougal and Angus intercepted him then, drawing him away with boisterous talk of food and ale and women.

He owed Dougal a debt of thanks for that. As he headed once more for the stairs, Catriona stood frozen, a desolate expression in her eyes.

'Come now, love,' he whispered, taking her arm under his. 'We can speak more about this in private.'

That seemed to move her along so he led her up the stairs and into the tower where his chamber was. Twice they climbed until they reached the floor where his room sat. Opening the door, he allowed her to enter first.

Cat circled the large, very large, chamber, taking in the comfortable luxury in which the earl's heir lived. She thought her cushioned chairs were so, but his furnishings put her modest ones to shame. She paced mostly because of seeing Munro here—or rather him seeing her on Aidan's arm.

The hatred shining in his eyes was too much to bear and thankfully one of Aidan's friends had stepped in to ease the tension of it. But now, her stomach threatened to empty and her head ached. She thought she might shatter from within. Cat stopped walking and looked for a chair on which to sit before she toppled over.

'Here, sit,' Aidan said, holding her and guiding her to one of the chairs. 'I did not know he would return this day or I would have warned you.' He left for a moment and returned with a fine glass filled halfway with an amber liquid. 'Sip this, it will clear your head.'

The powerful whisky he favoured burned a path down her throat and into her stomach, sending fire, then warmth throughout her body. He sat next to her, watching her every move.

'So you knew where he was?' she asked.

'Aye. He was assigned to guard one of my father's allies—a man from Flanders—back to the coast.'

'Did you send him?' she asked. It would make sense. Once Catriona had moved into the house Aidan set up for her, Gowan's son had disappeared from the village, easing things as he made her his leman in fact. 'Is that what you do? Send people away when they are inconvenient?' An impossible thought tickled the back of her memory, but she brushed it aside.

'He made things difficult for you, Cat. I did not wish to see you distressed by his presence and his actions. You saw what happened just now. He believes you were unfaithful to his father and nothing will convince him of the truth,' he argued.

'He made things difficult for *you*…for *us*,' she said. 'Is that what you will do when I become a difficulty for you? Send me away?'

She did not know why she asked that question, for she had already decided she would leave him when that time came. Some strange mood held her in its control and she could not banish the worrying thoughts and feelings from herself.

'I want you to stay with me, Catriona. I want you with me.'

'And your new wife? She will accept this?' Catriona knew how wives felt. She knew Gowan sought comfort in the harlots' beds and she knew how humiliating it felt to her—even when his doing so was her fault. High-born or low, no woman liked it.

'It matters not. You are the woman I love and I will not set you aside.'

The devil teased her now, prodding her to say things she should not. Or mayhap the whisky or the strange mood had loosened her tongue and the words she'd thought about during the hours he was not with her. Once he married, he would be spending those hours with his wife. The woman who would bear his name and his legitimate heirs.

'So you will keep me in the village and come to me from your wife's bed? Will you wash her scent from your skin before you do? Or will the taste of her yet be on your tongue when you come to claim me?'

The words poured out then—all of the feelings and fears she kept within, exploring them only in the dark of night and all the while knowing in the light of day how it would be.

'Catriona,' he said, walking towards her. 'This can work between us. Any wife will know of your place in my heart before we marry. She will have to accept it, for I will not let you go.'

She pushed out of his embrace and walked to the

other side of the chamber, crossing her arms over her chest and rubbing her arms.

'I knew that Gowan slept with the harlots to find the pleasure he could not find in my bed. I knew it was my fault,' she stated plainly. 'Yet that did not ease the humiliation from knowing it.' Then the deepest truth pushed its way out. 'And I did not love Gowan as I love you, Aidan. I know I have no right to say this, but it will kill me to share you, even with your lawful wife.'

She sank to her knees, unable to stop sobbing into her hands, as she admitted her greatest failing—not that she had failed Gowan as a wife but that she'd allowed herself to fall in love with a man she could never claim. She should never have come here this night.

He wrapped her in his arms and held her there, kneeling next to her, as she cried. All the feelings of hopelessness and pain and guilt and sorrow bubbled up and tears flowed. He whispered words and held her until the worst had passed. Then he lifted her in his arms and carried her to his bed. But, when she thought he would lie down, instead he held her on his lap.

'You love me?' he asked quietly.

Of everything she'd said in her emotional tirade, those words were what he'd heard?

'Aye, you daft man,' she whispered back, touching his face. 'I love you. In spite of my efforts not to.'

He kissed her then, soft and sweet. Then he kissed her cheeks and her chin and her eyes and then her mouth again.

'Say it again, I beg you,' he pleaded.

'God forgive me, I love you, Aidan MacLerie.' He shook his head.

'Just the words, Cat. Just the words.'

'I love you.'

'And I love you, Catriona.'

The world tilted then for her. Words she'd never believed she would say to a man, she'd said to him. After so many years of pain and suffering and loneliness, he'd given her pleasure and passion, a time to heal and a chance at a new life. Now, he returned his love to her.

'Do not think of what we will face, Cat,' he said, kissing her again. 'Think only of my love for you and we will find a way through it all.'

He followed his promise with a string of unending kisses that left her breathless. Then Aidan eased them back onto his bed and he held her close to him. Some time passed and she tried to empty her thoughts of all the worries she had over the end of what they had now.

'Stay with me, Cat. Stay with me this night.'

His words echoed into the silence of the chamber and into her heart. She wanted to refuse—she should refuse. Her heart decided the matter then. If she would need to give him up and walk away in just a few months, she would enjoy every moment that they did share. She would make enough memories that she could live on them for the rest of her lonely life.

Cat turned in his arms to face him, decision made.

'Love me, Aidan. Just love me.'

And he did, drawing out each touch, every movement, until she lost herself to him. Undressing her with his hands and mouth and teeth and tongue, he drove her to the edge of need and madness for him. He moved between her legs and gazed into her eyes as he entered her. Her body accepted the length of him, fitting around him until she could not remember being a separate body from his.

This time when flesh filled flesh, there was no beginning or ending to either of them. Joined in the most intimate way, she let him in and accepted that love made this time different from all that had come before. Release came slowly, their bodies melded and she felt every contraction and shudder of his through her.

The tears surprised her. She did not think they were tears of sadness for she did not feel sad then. Catriona felt....

Complete.

Healed.

Fulfilled.

Strong enough now to leave him when the time came.

It was the darkest, quietest part of the night when he finally slept next to her. Their fingers entwined, his body tucked tightly behind hers, his arm draped over her, keeping her there. Their hearts beat at the same pace; their breaths matched the other's.

And in that dark, quiet time and place, she decided to stay with him until his parents returned. Then, things would spiral out of her control or his and she would need to leave. Catriona would claim these next days as hers.

And she did.

Though she had left the keep to go and collect some clothes from the house, she remained with him. She would not sit with him at the high table, but she ate her meals in the hall from a seat much closer than the first night.

She discovered that she liked his friends, especially Dougal, Rurik's son. They mourned the loss of their companion, but seemed to accept her company now.

During the days, she tried to keep herself busy and useful in the keep. The servants accepted her help, she knew some of the women from the village, and things went smoothly. She was careful not to overstep or make decisions that were not hers. Cat did not want it reported to the laird or the lady that she had assumed a position she did not have.

And the nights…the nights were filled with love.

On the night before his parents would return home, they retired to his chamber right after supper and talked and loved, knowing it would somehow be different on the morrow.

Exhausted and ready to sleep, the loud grumblings of her stomach surprised both of them.

'Did I not feed you enough?' he asked. They had shared food earlier, but little of it was eaten. Most of it had been smeared in places and removed in a delightful way she'd never thought of before.

'We rushed through supper, Aidan. Worry not, for it will pass,' she said, rubbing her hand over it.

Her appetite had grown steadily over these last weeks. So had her exertions, especially spending nights in bed with this younger man. He tired her out so much that she found herself creeping into his chambers in the middle of the day to rest. She would never tell him for fear he would not keep her awake all night long.

When it rumbled again, he got out of bed and searched in one of his trunks. Handing her a robe and pulling a shirt on, he held out his hand.

'Come. I know where the cook leaves some food for those who arrive back later than supper.'

'Aidan,' she said, holding up the robe. 'I cannot walk through the hall wearing only this.'

'You need only walk down the steps,' he said, pulling her hand until she slid off the bed and on to her feet. Holding out the robe for her, he waited as she wrapped it around her and tied the belt. It was too large and too long for it was made to his height and not hers. 'I will carry you along the back corridor to the kitchens. Fear not, no one will see you.'

Once he'd made his mind up, there was no refusing him. She'd tried and lost that battle more times than she could count, so she let him take her hand and lead her down the steps of the tower to the main floor of the keep. He did scoop her up into his arms and carry her as he'd promised and they arrived in the kitchens without anyone seeing them.

He placed her on her feet and began collecting food from different bins in the larder and pantry. It was simple fare—some cheese, bread, dried figs and ale. They used a small table there, one she'd seen the cook use, and he found two stools for their use. Her stomach quieted as she ate. They continued in companionable silence. Aidan would offer her more from the various plates and she ate more than she expected.

When it was time to return to his chambers, he took her up in his arms again and she wrapped hers around his neck. If anyone who slept in the hall saw them or heard them, no one acknowledged their passage along the corridor back to the stairs. He began to put her on her feet when the doors opened and people poured into the keep.

Gair came running down the stairs now, dressed and heading for the door. As he passed, he handed a length of plaid to Aidan, who looked down at his shirt and shrugged. Wrapping it around his waist without a belt, he at least was covered. Cat tried to get around him to go up to his chambers for her garments when the laird's loud voice rang out.

'Aidan, come and meet Lord and Lady Sinclair and their daughter Margaret,' he said.

She wanted to sink into the shadows then. Caught unclothed with the earl's son by noble guests and a potential bride, Catriona thought that this had to be the most humiliating moment of her life. Worse even than when the villagers spit on her after Gowan's burial. With nowhere to go and no way to avoid being seen when Aidan moved forward at his father's summons, she closed her eyes and waited to be shamed once more.

'Catriona, love,' he whispered.

She opened her eyes and found him in front of her, shielding her from the people streaming into the hall.

'Go upstairs and dress. I will send someone to see you back to the village.' She nodded and began to turn away, when he touched her cheek. 'Remember that I love you.'

His father called him again, but Aidan remained there, like a wall, waiting until she was out of sight up the stairs. She ran the rest of the way, knowing that servants would be roused from their sleep to welcome the laird and lady back and to help in getting the guests settled into their chambers.

She dressed and straightened the bedcovers and the rest of the chamber while she waited. When the knock on the door came, she was surprised to find Dougal Ruriksson there. He said little, but saw her back to the house.

The night crawled now as the reality of her situation crashed down around her. On the morrow, she would ask Ciara for her advice. Where could a widow seeking a new life settle?

Chapter Seventeen

When the lesson was done and Ciara pleased with her progress, Cat cleaned the table and put her slate and parchment in her sack. She'd been distracted all morning by the true task she'd set for herself three days ago and had not yet had the courage to complete. Ciara had excused herself to give instructions to the woman who cooked for her and left the chamber. Ciara's children were napping, looked after by their nurse, so the house was quiet now.

The perfect time to discuss her quandary with someone who was so worldly and yet so much like any other woman.

Cat laughed then, for Ciara Robertson was unlike any other woman she'd ever met or heard of. Brought to Lairig Dubh and raised by Duncan MacLerie when her mother married him, Ciara had an education like no other and could read, write and speak in several languages. Trained by Duncan, she travelled for the laird on his business and, as she'd found, could handle delicate situations easily.

Her husband, Tavis, was Rurik's second-in-command and high in the laird's esteem and trust. Their marriage had happened when Ciara was abandoned at the altar by her betrothed. From what Muireall told her about that, it seemed to end well for everyone involved for Ciara and Tavis had been in love with each other for years.

So, with her education, experience, travels within and out of Scotland, surely she would have some ideas for Catriona. Where to live, what to do, how to spend her money wisely…

'You look deep in thought,' Ciara said as she walked back in, carrying two steaming mugs.

'I would speak to you on a personal matter, if you have a few minutes more, Ciara.' There. She said the words that would now force her to carry through with it.

Holding up the mugs, Ciara smiled. 'You had that look about you all morning, and yesterday morning, and the day before, and…' Laughing, she took a sip of her drink. 'What do you wish to talk about?'

Catriona sat at the table once more and pulled the cup nearer. Instead of the usual smell she expected, this was something else. Something pungent. Something… bad. Trying not to offend, she slid the cup away without taking a taste.

'I need to leave Lairig Dubh and I would be grateful for any advice you can give me.'

'Where will you go?' Ciara asked, drinking more of the now noxious-smelling liquid.

'That is what I wanted to ask you. You have travelled

widely on the earl's business and I thought you might have knowledge of a small village or town where I could live and seek employment.'

It made her dizzy. She could not identify the ingredient that bothered her, but the smell turned her stomach and she gagged. Pushing up from the chair, she ran out the door and into the fresh air. Her stomach lurched and she wanted to vomit. Standing there, trying to breathe while her stomach rebelled, she was surprised when Ciara stood beside her, holding a cold cloth on her neck.

'Have you been ill?' Ciara asked.

'Nay, not ill exactly,' she explained. 'I just have not been feeling well.'

'All this upset, no doubt,' Ciara said, though her tone echoed disbelief. 'Come, sit here and talk.'

They settled on a bench there by the door and soon the coolness of the cloth made her feel better.

'So when do you plan to leave?'

'As soon as I can make arrangements to go,' she admitted. 'Soon, it will be difficult to stay.'

'And the house? Will you sell it?'

'Ciara, I have not signed the papers. It does not belong to me,' she explained. 'I told Aidan I would use it while I needed it and not accept it from him.'

'I thought I was clear—that contract was for your peace of mind. The house is yours. The laird, not Aidan, put the deed in your name.'

She blinked. She owned the house after all. She would have to sell it or rent it if she left.

'Would you consider staying and working for me?'

'For you?' The offer was quite unexpected.

'Aye, for me. Not that you will have to, but I need someone to oversee my household. The children adore you, you know both the cook and the nurse and we work well together.' Ciara shrugged. 'I am guessing that you want to leave because Aidan will marry?'

'I...I cannot stay. I cannot be his leman once he marries, Ciara. I have seen it and I cannot.'

'Can you stay and make your own life here? You do not have to see him. He will be moving to Ord Dubh as soon as he marries.'

Cat knew that much, but there were so many memories here that would always remind her of him, of them. And then one day, he would return as laird and earl in his own right.

'I am guessing not. Well, at least now you have the means to go or come as it pleases you.'

'Thanks to him, I do.' Catriona felt the sadness descending on her. 'So, have you any ideas? Muireall's husband has friends in one of the northern villages and I thought that might be a good place.'

'Will you tell him of the bairn before you leave?'

She frowned at the younger woman. Was Ciara carrying again?

'What bairn? What do you mean?' she asked.

Her stomach began churning again and this time she could not dispel it. She fell to her knees and vomited right there in the grass. It went on and on, until her belly emptied itself completely. Sitting back on her heels, she tried to take a breath in. Ciara was back with a cold cloth and a cup of water for her to rinse her mouth.

'That bairn,' she said with too much joviality for the

situation. 'The one you are carrying. The one, if my counting is correct, will be born in about a seven month.'

'I am barren,' she said aloud, needing to remind herself. Catriona's hand drifted to her belly. 'The healer said when I lost the babe that I would never conceive or carry again.'

'Ah, so you did lose a bairn, then? I wondered.'

'So you are mistaken, Ciara.' Ciara stood and tugged Cat to her feet and away from the distressing sign of her illness.

'That is what my cousin Lilidh said when I recognised her symptoms as well,' Ciara said, a wise smile perched on her mouth. 'Their son Tavish is nigh to two years now.'

Whether Ciara had guessed Lilidh's condition correctly or not, it was not possible that she was pregnant.

'No matter,' Ciara said. 'Time will show if I am correct or not.'

She sat down hard on the bench, unable to think it a thing that could happen. If she was, it changed everything. Aidan deserved to at least know that she was carrying a child of his. Born out of wedlock or not, if the child was a boy, he was his father's responsibility. Bastards were accepted more easily into their families here than in the Lowlands or, God forbid, England.

Catriona glanced at Ciara then. If this was true, she did not want Aidan to hear about it before she told him.

'I beg you to keep your suspicions quiet for now, Ciara. I pray you not to share them with anyone until I know for certain.' She searched the woman's face for some sign of acknowledgement but it was blank. 'I may just be ill.'

Standing, she left, not realising she'd not spoken a farewell to Ciara. She must think her a madwoman, wandering off in the middle of a conversation, but Cat needed to be alone then. She did not go back to the house, to her house. Instead she spent hours simply walking along the paths of the village, thinking about this new impossible possibility that would change everything.

Her *easy* way out of this situation—leaving Lairig Dubh and him behind—had just turned incredibly difficult.

Four long, frustrating, infuriating, boring days.

He'd had no sight nor word of Catriona since that night when his parents arrived unannounced and early with the Sinclairs. It had taken hours to get them, their retainers and guards settled in for what looked to be an extended visit. Lord Sinclair explained that they had been travelling and the roads had been better than expected. So they passed through MacCallum lands a day or two earlier than planned and travelled the rest of the way back with his parents.

Margaret Sinclair appeared just as thrilled as he was at the prospect of marriage, at least when she was not under her parents' glaring sight. In view of her parents and his, she was beautiful, polite, knowledgeable and well educated. His father pointed out privately to him that she was also wealthy, endowed with much lands and those lands had access to the North Sea. Her family was in line to inherit control of the earldom of Orkney and had direct ties to the king of the Norse.

In other words, a woman worthy of the heir of the MacLerie clan and all that he would bring to the marriage.

She left him as cold as a frigid night's air.

So, he found himself escorting her and her mother and her maid across their lands, spending a few days at their southern holding, the one that he would control shortly. She rode well and nodded and smiled and laughed at just the right times in conversation. But he recognised the same uninterest in her gaze that he was trying to hide in his.

As they entered the village, he could not help but to look for Catriona. Glancing down the road that led to the edge of the village where she lived, he saw no one.

'My lord,' Margaret said, riding up next to him. Following his gaze down the path, she asked, 'Is this where you keep your whore? Or do you have her with you in the keep?'

He pulled on the reins so heavy and hard that his horse danced up on his hind legs. Aidan brought him down and under control, but he could not say the same for his temper.

'You dare much, lady,' he warned in a low voice so only she would hear. No matter his attempt at discretion, everyone in their travelling group halted as they had.

'Mother, go on ahead. Lord Aidan will see me safely to the keep,' she called out.

Her mother glanced from her to him and back again before agreeing. His father would be insulted by any suggestion that his guests were not safe on his lands. He waited until they were alone before speaking.

'Have a care before speaking on matters not of your concern, Lady Margaret,' he warned.

His horse reacted to the tension in his body, moving skittishly beneath him. Deciding it was safer to speak to her from the ground, he jumped off and pulled the reins down, trying to calm the horse. She sat silently on hers, watching him. He glanced around to make certain no one could hear their words before speaking.

'Do not call her whore, for she is not one,' he warned. 'Now, what is it you truly wish to know?'

For he sensed she had something to say on the matter and now was the perfect time to determine if she would abide by his intentions to keep Catriona. He knew he could convince her to stay, he just needed time.

'You misunderstand me, Lord Aidan,' she said, dismounting easily with no help. Her skills were admirable. Walking to his side, she placed her hand on his arm. His skin crawled beneath it.

'I do not mind at all if you keep your wh— Woman after we marry.'

'If we marry,' he corrected.

'I am not inclined to share in the…pleasures…of the marriage bed, so I would prefer you slake your lust for such things on her,' she said directly. 'I prefer a quiet life of contemplation and prayer.'

'What of an heir?' he asked.

'I will do my duty as is expected of me, my lord,' she ground out in the only fit of temper he'd seen her display, 'but I will not like it. So, you can do what you must until I conceive,' she said, shuddering in distaste or disgust, 'then I pray you will find your way to her bed and stay out of mine.'

He almost laughed. Aloud. He had hoped to find a bride who would understand, but this was even better. A woman who did not want to explore the joys of the marriage bed. But, why not?

'Do you come to this untouched, lady?' he asked.

Her eyes narrowed and she threw her frozen gaze at him. The fury there at his question nearly singed his skin. 'I would never dishonour myself and do otherwise.'

'Then how do you know that you will be content in an empty marriage bed?'

'My priest has counselled me that it is the way God would like marriages to be, filled with prayer and not lust. I would seek that in my marriage.'

Aidan kept his tongue behind his teeth now and kept all the comments he wanted to make silent. He nodded at her and offered her his foot to regain her seat.

'I appreciate your candour, Lady Margaret,' he said.

'As I would appreciate your accommodation if our families agree to this marriage,' she replied.

They rode back to the keep in silence and Aidan could not believe his luck in this matter of marriage. Should he tell his parents that he and Lady Margaret would suit and end the speculation over the other two women?

Could he marry such a woman as this? Cold-hearted, cold-natured, a woman who would place her devotion to the Almighty between them? What kind of sons would she bear him? His stomach soured at the thought of taking her to his bed. Considering his history of bedding any woman willing, it made him cringe at the irony of it.

After meeting the first woman, he was more certain that taking another woman as wife would just not be possible for him. He understood his duty, especially as first-born son of the chieftain and the earl, but he was growing to dislike it.

As he guided the lady to the keep, he realised that the one thing Cat feared the most—being thought of as a whore—would then be true, for she would be sharing the bed of a married man.

Fear struck him then, for he was being the veriest of fools. He loved Catriona and did not want to soil that love by sharing a bed with another, even if the other was his wedded wife. No matter if the other woman gave her permission or not. He wanted only Catriona and must find a way out of this madness before he lost her completely. But then, this was for naught if he could not convince Catriona to stay.

As the visit continued for several more days, Aidan only knew he needed to see Catriona. His father had forbidden him to do so while the Sinclairs were staying with them. So, he bided his time, strained his control and good nature to be a good and polite host and prayed they would tire of Lairig Dubh and leave.

After a fortnight, Lord Sinclair announced they would be leaving in another day to travel to visit other kin before returning home. Aidan could feel the end of this torture approaching.

Now the truly challenging work would begin—to

find a way to keep Catriona at his side. He could not figure out whether the more difficult person to convince would be her or the Beast of the Highlands. For very few crossed his father and lived to tell of it.

Chapter Eighteen

Munro watched as Lord and Lady Sinclair and their daughter rode through the gates. Their visit had extended for just over a fortnight and he'd observed as Aidan did what he did best—charmed and cajoled and convinced. To anyone watching the scene that had played out over the last weeks, they would think Aidan infatuated with the woman who was but one possible bride for him.

But he could see through the falseness of the mask his former friend wore to the cold-hearted, conniving bastard beneath. No matter his protestations that he had not dishonoured his father's wife, the way he took her to bed as soon as he could get her proved Munro's suspicions.

He slammed his fist into the stone wall at his back.

He'd always known she would be trouble.

When his father returned with her, he'd been ten-and-four years and he yet mourned his mother's death a six-month before. How his father could bring another woman into their house befuddled him…until his own growing body and young man's urges made it all clear to him.

Catriona MacKenzie had the body of the Greek goddess he'd seen when Aidan showed him a book from the laird's collection. When he spied Catriona wet from the water splashing while she washed clothes, with the fabric of her gown plastered over her curves, his body reacted for the first time as a man's would and he understood why his father brought her home.

Over that first year, she had gained some weight and her figure filled out, creating soft, lush breasts, hips and legs that would welcome a man between them. And, to his disgrace, he had wanted to be that man.

And so, with every timid smile or soft word to him, he hardened in lust for his father's wife. As the years passed, his desire for her grew until he could barely be in her presence without reacting. Whether his father recognised it or not, Munro knew not, but he found himself assigned away more and more. When he fell in with the laird's son and his small group of friends, Munro travelled more and more.

But even the women drawn to Aidan MacLerie and those he took did not lessen the desire he had for Catriona.

Then Aidan began sniffing around her as he did so many others. Munro knew she would be weak and end up in his bed, just like the rest had. When the son of the powerful, wealthy, titled Earl of Douran wanted you in his bed, there was no way to refuse.

And worse, it would be his father who would wear the horns of a cuckold this time.

When his father had gone off on an assignment that would keep him away for some time, Munro kept a close watch on them both and his suspicions were confirmed by the rumours—Aidan had succeeded in his quest and taken Catriona.

Even now, his anger seared his blood and he wanted revenge on the man he once called friend.

For it was that friend who had caused Gowan's death.

If Aidan had acted with honour, if he'd been a true friend, he would have walked away from her. But when he chased and then caught Catriona, Aidan had forced his hand and Munro had to summon his father home to deal with it. And that resulted in Gowan's death.

He could forgive his former friend many things, but not that.

He moved along the battlement, watching below, and took a new position near the corner of the wall. Standing there, letting his anger brew, Munro could hear a couple of the other guards talking about Aidan.

'He's a lucky lad,' one said.

'A hot piece in his bed and a rich one in marriage. 'Tis not so bad a life,' the second one said. A husky, lust-laden laugh followed. 'I wouldna mind that one he has sharing my bed.'

'Nor I,' the first one agreed. The red haze of fury filled Munro's vision.

'But I hear it was not luck at all that got her there,' the second one lowered his voice. 'I heard he was the one who sent her husband away so he could have at her as he wanted.'

'Shite!'

'Oh, aye. And have at her he did, swiving her even while old Gowan lay dying in the woods.'

'I would not mind swiving her,' the first one admitted, his voice lowered now, too. 'Not that he'll give her up.'

'Not that she'd have either of us after having him. 'Tis the way of things among their kind, lad,' the second one advised. 'He'll need heirs and she canna give them to him. His father wants more than a whore as his son's wife and he'll make certain to get it.'

Munro was about to turn and crush them both against the walls when the commander called out to all of them.

He completed his duties that night in stunned silence—going through all the motions of guarding the walls even as his mind turned over and over the one thing the guards had said.

Aidan had been the one to send his father away.

All this time, Munro believed Aidan had simply taken advantage of his father's absence to pursue Catriona. Now he knew the truth—Aidan was responsible for it all.

He'd sent Gowan away, pursued and seduced Catriona and then been there to take her in when his father died. Munro had reacted in anger, throwing her out of his house, just to give her a taste of how it would be without a man to protect her. And he'd always planned to be the one to do that—planning to offer her shelter once his anger cooled.

And that would put her in his control and then…

Well, then, he could have her for himself.

Instead, Aidan had been ready, probably expecting Munro's reaction, and had given her a house and coin and made her his leman in fact before the whole village and clan.

He slept little that night, mulling over his choices in his mind. Munro only knew that it would not be right for Catriona not to know of Aidan's machinations to rid her of a husband to get her in his bed. Especially since she'd fallen into his plan. And especially since she'd now be placed in the one situation she claimed she was not—any man's whore.

But the sun's weak light at dawn found him still awake and no closer to a solution than last night.

As he reported for duty this morning, he planned to simply confront Aidan and then he would make certain Cat knew the truth—Aidan was responsible for her downfall and her husband's death.

Aidan joined his parents for the noon meal, as ordered by his father, and knew that there were more orders and directions coming his way. His father had spent last night's supper extolling the virtues of Lady Margaret Sinclair to him. Tempted as he was to inform his father of the one virtue he liked about her—that she would let him keep Catriona without argument—he kept his tongue and words behind his teeth and let it all pass over him.

He looked for signs on his father's face that would hint at the purpose of this call, but his father had perfected the blank stare decades before Aidan's own birth. If his father wished to give nothing away, to friend or foe, he did not. So, the meal went on and his patience wore thin.

Aidan finished eating. His mother finished eating. His father savoured every mouthful of food or ale as though it was his last. It was at times such as this one when his father made everyone dance to his tune and Aidan knew the Beast of the Highlands relished it.

'Connor,' his mother said, 'we have waited long enough. There is news, I know it, so just tell us what you plan to tell us. I suspect there are preparations to be made?'

He winked when his mother looked at him. They both knew his father's methods, but she dared to question him freely. A habit years in the making and one that his father never put a stop to.

'News of the Sinclairs' arrival here early has spread and I've word from both of the other families that they will be here within days. So, Aidan, you will have the chance to renew your acquaintance with Alys Mac-Kenzie and to meet Elizabeth Maxwell.'

He must have reacted at the MacKenzie name, for his father's gaze narrowed at him then, realising why he might have raised an objection to one of that clan being considered for wife when she'd been named.

'So, I expect you to spend time with each of them as you did Lady Margaret.'

'I know my duty, Father,' he said. 'If you will excuse me now, I have things to see to.' He began to stand when his father grabbed his arm.

'Sit.'

Aidan took his seat once more, anger spilling into his blood.

'You have duties to attend to here. Stay out of the village until the Maxwells and MacKenzies leave. I would not have them insulted by your attentions elsewhere.'

'I have done whatever you've required of me these last weeks, Father. And I will do what is my duty when they arrive.'

'Do not make me take action to ensure that.'

He sucked in a breath, even as his mother hissed.

'Connor!' she whispered. 'That is not necessary.'

'Is it, Aidan?'

His father could and would do whatever was necessary to ensure his intentions were carried out. He would take whatever actions he needed to take to protect his clan, and if that meant ridding his son of a leman who was in the way of his plans, he would. So, at this point, Aidan did the expected thing and acquiesced as he would have to until he could come up with his own plan.

'Nay, Father. I understand what you expect of me.' Seething inside from his inability to challenge his father in this matter, he stood then and pushed back against the unwelcome restraints on him. 'Until the MacKenzies and Maxwells arrive, you know where to find me.'

He waited for his father to forbid him, but his mother's whispered words in his ear must have had some effect. With the slightest of nods, his father relented. Aidan strode from the table through the hall, all the time trying to rein in his temper and forcing himself to remain calm. His father had formidable resources and Aidan needed a plan if he was to go against him.

But right now, right now he needed to see Catriona. He missed her, missed her sense of humour and her way of seeing things clearly even when he wanted to ignore the reality of what they faced. Mostly, he just needed her assurance that she would not leave him.

'So, what do you think?' Catriona asked Muireall.

Days had passed since she'd spoken to Ciara. She avoided the woman now, afraid that what she'd suspected was true. Days during which Aidan remained at the keep or elsewhere doing his father's bidding and trying to decide which woman would be his bride. Her stomach quaked at that thought and threatened to erupt again.

As it did when she smelled any meat cooking. Or when she smelled certain herbs and flowers. Or when she woke in the morning.

At other times, she wondered if she was losing her mind, for she had no ill signs. Then an aroma would waft past her and it would begin. The vomiting, the dizziness, sometimes she even began to lose consciousness.

Two weeks of suffering had led her to do the one thing she did not wish to do—discuss this with Muireall. But, who else could she trust? Ciara's first loyalty was to the laird, so she knew it was but a matter of time before she shared this news.

'And your courses?' Muireall asked. 'Have they come at all these last years?'

'Aye, but not often and never in any kind of rhythm.'

The healer told her she could never carry and Cat had believed the woman. And she never worried over getting pregnant because she could not. Over the years with Gowan, it became nothing to think on because he'd left her bed very early in their marriage. So, when Aidan took her to bed, she never considered the possibility.

'Since Aidan began visiting you?'

'Not once.' The words echoed into the silence that gathered around them.

Now, she could think of nothing else.

'Here,' Muireall said, handing her a mug and waiting for her to sip the watered ale. It was about the only thing that did not make her sick. 'Sit.' It mattered not to her friend that they were not in Muireall's house, for she took command when she felt the need. Like now.

Catriona did as she was told, but then she burst into tears. Tears she could not stop or explain. Those came often these last weeks. Muireall's arm draped on her shoulders and her friend gathered her close.

'Hush now, Cat,' she whispered. 'All will be well.'

'What will Aidan say?' Cat said.

Never thinking she would ever bear a man's child, she wondered if Aidan would think she'd lied to trap him into this situation. Would he believe her? Would he want to acknowledge the child?

'Do you still plan to leave Lairig Dubh? Or will you tell him?'

Cat sighed and sat back. Ciara had asked the same question of her, but that was before she knew the truth. After the shock of it, came the thoughts about a future together that could not be. He would marry elsewhere and, even if his child was seen to, it guaranteed no place for her. And in her heart, she knew she could not stand by and watch him marry another.

'Leaving would be the simplest thing,' she admitted. 'But I think he deserves to know. I ask him for nothing more than that.'

'He will never let you leave if he knows,' Muireall said. 'You know that, do you not?'

'He asked me to stay as his leman and to move with him to Ord Dubh.' She'd not shared that with her friend—or with anyone—since he'd told her. 'He says married or not, he wants me by his side.'

'And what did you say to that?'

'I will be no man's whore and will not share the bed of a man married to another woman.'

'And has that changed? Have you changed your mind on such matters since learning that you carry his bairn?'

That was the heart of the matter, was it not? Could she continue to love him if he chose another woman? Oh, it was the custom and no one would think anything was awry when the heir of the most powerful man in the Highlands took a leman. Especially if she'd borne his child. But, after living with the shame and humiliation of failing her own husband, she really could not do that to another.

Muireall let out a sigh then and sat down, drinking her ale and pondering the matter. If her wise friend had not advice to give, she had no other place to turn.

'You love him, do you not?' Cat nodded. 'And he has declared his love for you…'

'Twas not so much a question as a statement, for Aidan had made it clear how he felt about her to one and all. He'd declared his love in his actions and his words before his people and in the privacy of the home he gave her.

'So, share with him this wonderful news and talk about the choices you have. If you wish to live somewhere else, he can still support the child and you. You must work this out between you.'

Catriona knew she must talk with him. Standing, Muireall stopped her from leaving with a hand to her arm.

'You should think about seeing the midwife soon. If you had problems before…'

She did not have to finish the words, for it was something that already filled Catriona's dreams with terrible images. She might not carry long enough. There could be problems with the bairn. It might not live past delivery.

'Gunna is a kind soul and very experienced in matters like this. Fear not to speak to her, ask her advice. She has saved many women and bairns over the years.'

'I will do that,' she promised.

First, though, she would share the news with Aidan.

She began to walk back to the house and realised she was already much closer to the midwife's house, so she turned around and decided to seek the woman's counsel. She would rather be able to give Aidan more knowledge about her condition and her chances of delivering the bairn safely when they spoke.

'Mistress MacKenzie!'

Before she could turn, a small, hard body ploughed into her, nearly knocking her over. She grabbed him and held him up and realised it was Alasdair.

'Alasdair,' she said, with a laugh. 'You must have a care when running through the village. You could knock someone down.'

'Lord Aidan…' he said, pointing towards the main

road. Was Aidan on his way here now? She did not think to see him until nightfall when his duties finished with his family at supper.

'Is he come?' she asked, peering in the direction in which the boy pointed.

'Nay, nay,' he said with a wild shaking of his head. Oh, the boundless energy of childhood, she thought. 'He is there. Fighting with Munro. Like this.' Alasdair began throwing punches into the air around him.

Aidan fighting Munro? Why? She gathered up her skirts and ordered the boy, 'Take me there, Alasdair. Quickly, if you please.'

They scurried along the path to where it crossed the main road and Cat discovered that wee Alasdair was right—Aidan and Munro were involved in a vicious fight there for all to see. Knowing she must stop them, she ran up to where they now rolled in the dirt and called out their names.

Now close enough to see them, she saw the blood streaming from Aidan's nose and from a cut over Munro's eye. She began to call out to them again when the ground beneath her tilted and she had to fight to remain standing.

It took only a moment more of witnessing the bloodiness before her for her world to go dark. She heard Aidan screaming out her name and then her world went silent, too.

Chapter Nineteen

Aidan saw Catriona crumpled to the ground and tried to reach her, but Munro grabbed him by the hair and pulled him back to the fight. He used the motion of Munro's action to swing around and punch his former friend in the jaw. A satisfying crunch told him that he'd broken something.

That satisfaction was short-lived, for Munro was the best fighter with fists and feet among his group of friends and a well-delivered blow to his stomach reminded Aidan why he needed to stay at least a pace away in a brawl. Landing on the ground again, he pushed to his feet and tried to reason with Munro.

'Munro, I must see to her,' he argued.

'You bastard! Why her? Why could you not leave her be?' Munro yelled at him as Aidan tried to get past him to Catriona. Why had she fainted so?

'I love her, Munro.'

'My father loved her! She was his wife!' Munro tripped him as he took a step towards her and kicked him back to the ground. 'She was just a game to you. You should have listened when she said nay, you…you did not!'

'Munro!' he called out again. 'I order you to cease this now.' Aidan backed up his demand with his own fists, gaining his feet and pummelling the man until he fell back a step.

'You are good at giving orders, are you not, *Lord* Aidan. You ordered him away so you could seduce her. You ordered him to his death. And she does not ken the truth of it, does she?'

Aidan paused in shock at hearing his sins exposed and that brief moment allowed Munro to knock him down. He waited for the next blows and instead saw Munro grabbed and pulled away by Young Dougal. Climbing slowly to his feet, he looked around and realised that others had probably heard his claim. Dougal kept hold of Munro while Aidan ran to Catriona's side.

'This is not something to settle in public, Aidan,' Dougal warned. When Munro began to argue, Dougal shook him and warned him off. 'Bring her and finish this between you in private.'

Dougal dragged Munro down the path that led to Catriona's house. Muireall reached his side and tried to help him, but he brushed her off.

'I will see to her, Muireall.'

The woman looked as though she wanted to say something more, but she nodded and let him pass. Catriona did not rouse as he followed Dougal down the paths and lanes to the edge of the village. Dougal kept Munro outside when Aidan carried her in and laid her on the bed. Sitting at her side, he stroked her cheek and whispered her name.

'Catriona, open your eyes and look at me.'

He went out to the common room and found a cloth and brought the jug of water with him into the bedchamber. Pouring some cool water on the cloth, he touched it to her face and neck and watched her rouse. She tried to sit up, but fell back, clutching the air.

'Here, now,' he whispered. 'You are on our bed,' he soothed. 'Lie in ease and get your bearings first.'

'Aidan?' she asked as her eyes seemed to clear and she met his gaze. 'You and Munro…fighting…'

'You fainted, love,' he said.

His stomach churned now, not from any damage done in the fight, but from knowing that he could not avoid her learning the truth. Munro would not let it lie and, unless he took drastic measures and got Dougal to drag him away now and remove him from Lairig Dubh, Catriona would find out the terrible way in which their love had begun.

'Where is Munro? Why were you fighting?' she asked, pushing herself up to sit next to him.

Did he stop it now by telling her the truth? Would it be worse if he did it or if he was exposed? Was there a better way to tell Catriona that he'd manipulated her life and caused Gowan's death? As he realised the inevitable results now of his stupid shallowness and lust then, he knew he was facing the end of…them.

And, though knowing he did not actually cause the man's death and though knowing he'd tried to make things right after it, Aidan knew that the true consequences of his acts faced him now. He'd gained what he wanted only to watch it, and her, be torn apart.

Would she survive this betrayal? He looked at her face, her eyes widened in confusion and fear, and he prayed that she would not pay the price for his selfishness. But how many times could a person's world be shattered for them to fall apart themselves?

Munro called out his name then, the sound of it loud enough for them to hear. She startled and looked at him.

'I beg you to give me a chance to explain,' he said, taking hold of her hand.

Munro's call drew her attention once more and she walked out of the bedchamber towards the door. Before he could reach her, the door slammed open and Munro burst in. Dougal was right behind him, but Aidan waved him off.

'I must speak with you, Catriona,' Munro said.

'Munro,' she said, standing at Aidan's side now, 'I know how upset you are about me moving here and Aidan and my...' He could tell she did not know what to call what existed between them. 'But I love him, Munro. Your father is gone and I—'

'Do you know how he died, Catriona?' Munro asked in a harsh tone. Both of them carried wounds from their fight and both still bled. Munro must have continued struggling with Dougal for he was out of breath.

'Do not do this, Munro. If not for the friends we were, then for her,' Aidan pleaded with the man. The last time her world had collapsed, he was there to pick up the pieces and help her regain a life of her own. This time...who would do that?

Catriona looked at the two men, facing off now just as much as they had in the road a short time ago. She knew that the blood of young men ran hot and fights were commonplace among the laird's strong warriors, but what had happened between these two was more personal. Sighing, she should have realised it was inevitable that they come to blows at some point over what Munro thought had happened.

'Aye, Munro, I know how he died. His horse went lame and threw him on his journey back here from his assignment.'

'Ask him how my father was sent on that assignment. Go ahead, ask him!' Munro demanded. She jumped at the ferociousness of his tone. Looking to Aidan, she was shocked by the sad resignation in his gaze.

'Aidan? What is he talking about?' she asked, turning to the man she loved and whose bairn now grew within her. There was barely a pause and no chance for Aidan to answer when Munro said the words that would shock her to her soul.

'He did it, Catriona. He asked his father to send your husband away so he could seduce you without a care. He sent my father away and to his death just to be able to rut between your thighs.'

If not his coarse words, his tone condemned her again of unfaithfulness to Gowan. She wanted to defend herself, but if what he said was true, then Aidan… Aidan….

'You planned it all along? Did you?' She looked at him, but he would not meet her eyes. 'Did you?' she screamed at him then.

He said nothing then and she threw herself at him, pounding her fists against his chest and crying out. His silence said more than any words he could say would. He took her by the shoulders and held her back a bit.

'Cat, let me explain,' he whispered.

'Just tell me…is it true? Did you send Gowan away to…seduce me?' She held her breath, hoping, praying, wishing he would deny it to her face, but he smiled that sad smile that always made her want to take his worry and pain away. Now, it damned him. 'Is it true, Aidan?' she cried out.

'Aye, Cat. I told my father to send him away.'

Though she heard the words, she could not take them and all they meant in. Her mind rejected it all and showed her images of the two of them since she became Aidan's leman…his whore. And all at the cost of a good man's life.

For a moment this morning, after sharing her news— her news!—with Muireall, she'd begun to accept the idea of remaining here and raising her child, his child, there in the place where he'd grown up, around his kith and kin. But all of that crumbled as did all her hopes and dreams as the ground on which they were built were washed away by the treachery of his act.

'Get out.'

Neither man moved, so she shouted it. 'Get out now!'

She pushed Aidan towards the door, moving him only because he allowed it. 'Get out. Get out,' she repeated over and over again, only knowing she must rid herself of him and Munro, who was right all along. Unable to face her part in the sin, she needed them gone.

Neither one resisted or refused her then. When she reached the door, she noticed Rurik's son standing there with an expression of shock that must have resembled her own. She slammed the door and was left alone in the house Aidan had given her and now she understood his actions better.

He'd sent her husband off to be able to seduce her without interference.

He'd sent Gowan to what would become his death.

He'd paid her blood money to ease his guilt.

He'd made her his whore and she'd loved every moment of it.

God forgive her, she'd accepted it all and never looked at the real cost of it.

For the longest time, she stood there, in the centre of the room, unable to move, unable to think really, unable to put all the pieces in this terrible puzzle together. Then, the silence was broken by a knock on the door. Still unable to do anything, she began to tremble as *his* voice spoke from the other side of it.

'Cat, I beg you to listen to me. I know you are not ready to hear me now, but I pray you not to do anything until you hear me out. Please, Cat.'

Once his pleading would have warmed her heart. Once his pleading led to indescribable pleasure. Now, it chilled her from her skin to her soul. She would not answer him, even if she could. Closing her eyes, she prayed he would leave before she lost the last bit of dignity and control she held on to.

The sound of his heavy footfalls echoed into the silent chamber as he left.

* * *

Aidan followed the path back to where Munro stood waiting with Dougal. Without pausing, he punched the man who used to be his friend, knocking him off his feet. Dougal gave him a look of frustration, but did not intervene now. Hidden from view of the rest of the village, Aidan planned to say the things he could not say to her.

'You had to do that, did you not, Munro? She was your father's wife. I was your friend.'

'That gave you no right to her,' Munro argued back. But it was the tone of his reply, the hints of jealousy and possessiveness that Aidan had never realised before.

'So you wanted her for yourself and I got in your way?'

The shock of his accusation flashed across Dougal's face, but Munro's reaction was more of the guilt he probably wore on his own face.

'What did you hope to gain from telling her? That she would run to you and beg for your help? That she would be shamed into returning to you?'

Munro scrambled to his feet. Brandishing his fist, he fought with his words this time. 'But I did not send my father to his death, you did that, Aidan MacLerie.'

'Did I, Munro? I sent him away, I admit it. I wanted her from the first time I saw her and I sent him on a mission that would keep him away from Lairig Dubh so I could get her in my bed.' Aidan shook his head. 'But my aim was never to kill him or harm or hurt her. You did that.'

Munro gasped and shook his own head in reply. 'I did

not. I could not stand by and see my own father turned cuckold by you. So, I summoned him home to see to his own wife and her unfaithfulness.'

'Munro,' he said, talking now, not shouting. 'Did you ever ask her if she'd broken her vows? You were my friend—did you ever ask me?' He paused. 'Nay, you did not. Instead you summoned your father back with some stories drawn from rumours and not the facts. Catriona was faithful to your father until and even after the day he died.'

Munro's face drained of colour as the truth struck him then.

'Between the two of us, we have destroyed two lives,' he admitted. 'I hope that God forgives us, for I doubt that Catriona will be able to now.'

There was nothing else to say now between them. Two men who had been friends and rivals for the same woman without knowing it and now were nothing. Only the thinnest of blood connections remained, leaving them related.

'Come. Your father will have heard about this by now,' Dougal counselled. 'You should speak to him.'

Aidan did not wish to speak to his father—he wanted to go back and beg her forgiveness. He wanted to hold her and tell of her of the youthful madness and indefensible attempts at seduction that had driven him to have her. That he truly had not wished Gowan ill mattered not—he had, directly or not, brought about the man's death.

Worse, he'd convinced Cat that he was better than the other men who had betrayed her in her own life. Just when she might have believed that he'd helped her, the truth came crashing into everything and she was left with a life in tattered pieces...again.

At least this time she had property and coins saved. At least this time she could walk away and live her own life with no ties to the MacLeries, if she chose to.

But he prayed that she would do nothing until they could talk. He wanted her to stay, to let him explain, but mostly he wanted her to wait until the shock of what she'd learned passed.

Aidan feared for her. He feared for their love even more.

When she was alone again, all control vanished and she crumpled to her knees and then fell to the floor.

He'd professed his love for her, to her, making plans and begging her to stay at his side. And yet, all the while, he was the one responsible for sending Gowan away. He'd given her the means to an independent life, more than she'd ever had before—property she could have called her own, money to use as she needed. He'd urged her to better herself and even his cousin offered her a place in her household.

She laughed roughly as she remembered the time she'd said something about his guilt driving all his actions and generosity to her, never dreaming she was right.

She'd been about to reveal the one thing to him that would chain her to him for life. At least God had some mercy and this happened first. An ill-begotten child from an ill-begotten love and life.

* * *

Minutes turned into hours and day became night, all without her moving or making a sound. Chaos reigned within her, her thoughts and feelings jumbled together like a tangled ball of yarn. When she noticed that the sun had risen again, she fought her way to her feet, changed her gown to one of the old gowns she'd brought with her and went to ask Ciara to set up a meeting with the laird.

By the time the sun hit the highest point in the sky, her life here in Lairig Dubh was done.

And two days later, Catriona MacKenzie was no more.

Chapter Twenty

Connor was in Gair's chamber when Aidan crashed in. He saw everything he expected to see in his son's eyes— fury, loss, frustration, mistrust, confusion. It was only a matter of time before he discovered his leman was gone. And then, only a matter of minutes before he came to see the man he knew would be responsible for such a thing.

He'd kept Aidan busy preparing for the visitors who would arrive at their gates this day and only when he disobeyed and went to see her did he find the empty house, the deed to it and the coins returned in the sack.

'What did you do to her?' Aidan said in a deadly calm voice. 'Where have you sent her?'

'She is gone from Lairig Dubh, that is all you need to know,' Connor admitted as he closed the door. He did not want Jocelyn in the middle of this. 'And since you have others things to put your mind on, I think it is good timing.'

Aidan resembled Jocelyn when she became irate and their son was certainly that. His hands balled into fists.

Would he take that step and strike out at him? It was a time coming quickly and Connor knew, if not now, very, very soon. And that thought did not displease him. Every man must reach the time when he challenged his father. Connor was just disappointed that it was over this woman.

'She should not be punished for my mistakes, Father,' Aidan said.

'What makes you think this is some kind of punishment? Your leman's very existence was causing problems right now. The brawl in the village was only the latest. Now she is gone and you can move on and choose an appropriate wife without her as a distraction.'

'So, you are punishing me by removing her?' Aidan walked up closer to him. 'I would not have thought you, even at your most ruthless, would do something like that.'

'Aidan, it is time for you to marry.'

'Why not...?' Connor put his hand up in front of Aidan's angry, red face to stop him.

'My son will not take a whore to wife. Not while I am living and in charge of the people and lands of the MacLerie clan.'

'She is not a whore!' Aidan yelled.

Connor knew the moment Aidan's control snapped and prepared as his fists came at him. He let his son take a few, good, close swings, before knocking him down. When Aidan regained his feet, wiping his face, Connor pushed him into the chair in the corner.

He'd discovered how Catriona MacKenzie had married Gowan and, though he did not condemn her for any of it, that knowledge became useful to him. He also understood how a man in love felt and saw the world. But, as Earl of Douran, laird and chieftain of his clan, he could not let his son's first true love influence the decisions made—all must be done for the good of the clan.

'I have spoken to most of the men who served with Gowan when he married Catriona those years ago. He was travelling through the edges of MacKenzie lands and came upon a man whoring out his daughter. Gowan bought her from him and brought her to our lands, kept her until he knew she did not carry another man's bairn and then married her.'

Connor could see that Aidan was surprised to learn this about the woman he loved. He turned away and gave his son some time to think about it before continuing.

'She had, at some point, given birth to some man's bastard and resisted going back into her trade. Her father did not countenance her refusal and forced her to take customers whether she said aye or nay. Gowan took her from that life.'

'I do not believe you.'

''Tis the way of things, Aidan. But you needed to know the truth of it. And the reason why she cannot ever be wife to you, my heir. Not when we can choose from the most virtuous, wealthiest women in the surrounding kingdoms. From women tied to every clan and family in power in Scotland, England and most of the Continent and the north. I will not accept a common whore as your wife.'

The strangest thing happened then, something Connor did not expect. Aidan matured before his eyes, his temper quelled, his face and expression grew calm and he nodded as though he understood. Connor knew he did not accept what had been done or said or decisions made, but he gathered his opposition under control. His son stood and nodded at him.

'I have only one other question for you, Father,' Aidan said as he walked to the chamber's door. 'Is she well?'

'Aye. She is well.' Connor could tell him that.

Aidan walked away then and Connor let out the breath he did not realise he was holding. Sinking into the chair where Aidan had just sat, he considered what his son would do next.

If it were him, he would begin sending out men to the MacLerie holdings and looking from village to village for a woman who'd just moved there. He suspected that was what Aidan would do now. It would do him no good, for Catriona was not on MacLerie lands—he'd sent her to Robert Matheson and asked for a place among his people for a widow who'd lost her husband in the service of his laird.

Although he allowed Aidan, and would allow anyone else who knew of his involvement, to believe he forced the matter, he did not tell his son that it had been Catriona's choice to leave.

She'd arranged to speak to him at Ciara's house and asked for his help in return for leaving and staying out of Aidan's life. He paid her the fair value of the house and made arrangements for a woman called Coira MacCallum to travel to Matheson lands and live there. She said she did not want Aidan to find her and now he would not.

The strange thing was that she did not reveal her

condition to him, when she could have used it to gain support for the bairn and for herself. Ciara had told him quietly before Catriona arrived at her house and bade him to let her tell him. She did not.

It would not be surprising that his son had fathered a child on her for many MacLerie men had natural children. His own father produced several, including his half-sister Margaret. So it was not unusual at all. But her not wanting Aidan to know spoke of a woman who was cutting ties completely.

He would abide by their agreement, even if he pondered on it. It made things easier for him and he tried never to look for trouble.

He pulled open the door and he watched as the one person who did always seem to seek out trouble walked towards him. She would never understand the wisdom in what he'd done, so he had no plans to speak of it to her.

'I went to see my son's leman, after hearing about the fight, and she is gone.' She crossed her arms over her chest, tossing her auburn hair over her shoulder and taking what he called her 'fight' position. 'What have you done with her, Connor?'

He tried to look aggrieved, and part of him was that, at always being blamed for the things that happened that she did not like. He was laird. He was chieftain. He was earl. And with those titles and positions came great responsibility and the need to make decisions even when they were unpleasant, ruthless, expedient or wise. He could not reveal the truth about Catriona, for this time he'd only assisted someone who'd already made their decision.

'Jocelyn,' he drawled out, 'I did nothing to the woman. She is well, as I told Aidan. She is gone. She is no longer our concern.' She studied him in silence, so he held out his arm to her. 'Come with me so we can watch for the guests who arrive shortly. What did Lilidh write to you about the MacKenzie girl?'

From her intelligent gaze, he knew he had not convinced her to desist in her concern for Catriona nor deflected whatever actions she would take. He only hoped that by the end of this visit, a betrothal would be in sight and her attentions must turn to that.

He could only hope.

Neither of the young women there to meet him reminded him of Cat and Aidan supposed that was a good thing. Their looks and manners never mimicked anything about her. But their presence did not ease the pain in his heart over her departure or over his betrayal of her trust.

Days filled with pleasantries and journeys and meals and polite conversations were followed by nights of dreams that brought back every moment of passion… and love that they had shared. And then, just before he would wake, he would see her lovely face washed of all colour and her eyes fill with condemnation as she looked at him in that moment when his part in her seduction and downfall became clear to her.

He would wake up sweating and pleading with her to hear him. To an empty bed in an empty chamber that had once been filled with love.

Aidan used these days while forced to attend to Lady

Alys MacKenzie and Lady Elizabeth Maxwell to send out men to search MacLerie villages and lands for her. He used what coins he could to pay for it and sent only men who could be discreet. And he tried to arrange it all without his father knowing of it.

The busy days passed. The endless, empty nights passed. Soon, the Maxwells and the MacKenzies left and Aidan's life returned to what it been before he saw Cat by the well that day months before.

He trained with his friends, except for Munro who had moved to another of the MacLerie's holdings. He drank with them. He still could not bring himself to go carousing with them and seek out women as he had before…before Catriona. No matter that he understood why she would refuse his love, it did not stop him from loving her.

He continued to try to find her. His father's assessing gaze sat on him many times and he fought the urge to confess it to him. A time of reckoning was coming for them and Aidan did not think it would end well for either of them.

Two horrible, miserable, lonely months passed and Aidan knew what he must do. His efforts to find her were unsuccessful. So, he finally accepted that there was only one thing to do—tell his father he was going to find her and marry her, in spite of his opposition.

He waited to speak to his parents after the evening meal, telling them he'd made his decision about which woman he would marry. Although his father nodded at him and his mother had the gleam of tears in her eyes, the tension built through the meal and followed them into his mother's solar. Once the door closed, the first of his two battles began.

'So,' his father began once his mother was seated and he stood next to her chair, 'who is it to be then?'

'None of them.'

'None of them? What do you mean?' his father growled.

'I will marry none of them.'

'Oh, you wish for us to seek other women for you to consider?' his mother asked. 'I thought that Elizabeth suited you well. In spite of her being from England, she seemed at ease here.'

'I have decided on my bride, Mother,' he said.

'Aidan…' His father shook his head, warning him off.

But Aidan had made too many mistakes with Catriona not to learn from them. He would find her. He would make her understand how much he regretted his terrible actions and the consequences of them. He would make her understand that the love they'd found was worth saving. He was worth saving and she was the one person who could.

'I do not know where you have hidden her, but I will find her,' he promised. 'I leave on the morrow to begin my search.'

'You have duties here, Aidan. I forbid you to leave on this foolhardy quest to find a woman unworthy of my heir.'

He faced his father now and shook his head.

'I will leave.' The decision had been made.

'Will you risk my displeasure to seek a woman who does not want you to find her?' his father asked.

'Connor, what do you mean?' his mother asked, coming to his father's side and touching his arm. 'You sent Catriona away.'

'Nay, wife,' his father said, shaking his head. 'She came to me and bargained for my assistance to get her away from our son. She swore she wanted to never see him again and I agreed to help her…and promised her I would not reveal her whereabouts to him.' He nodded at Aidan then.

'Connor!' his mother cried. 'Why did you not tell him, tell me, this before? Why did you say it had been your plan to send her away?'

'It matters not. Until I hear it from her mouth, until she hears my explanation, until she can say that she does not return my love, I will not stop searching for her.'

'If you leave without my permission on the morrow, if you break your oath of loyalty and obedience to me, you are no longer my heir.' When his mother would have cried out again, his father held her off with his arm as he took several steps towards him. When they were scant inches apart, he uttered the threats that Aidan knew would come.

'Nay, Jocelyn. The boy needs to understand the consequences of refusing my orders and what his actions will bring about. He will no longer stand in my favour. He will be an outcast. No MacLerie will stand by him and remain bound to me. Is that what you want, boy?' his father asked him.

A loud knock interrupted any answer he would have given. The door opened and Duncan stepped inside.

'Is there aught that I can do, Connor? We can hear you out in the hall.' Duncan looked from one to the other and back again.

'Nay, Duncan. We are finished here,' his father said, walking past him and out of the chamber. 'Come, Jocelyn.' He held out his hand to her and waited for her to follow.

'Aidan, please,' she whispered to him. 'Do not...'

'Hush now, Mother,' he said, taking her shoulders and kissing her cheek. 'I know what I am doing.'

She returned his kiss and took a step towards the door, looking back at the last moment. 'Men, I have discovered, rarely know what they are doing.'

Her anger cheered him somehow and the thought of his father having to deal with her now lightened his mood. Duncan yet remained there, so he bade him a good night's rest and left.

There really was no choice in this for him. Living as his father's heir would cost too much for him to stay. He was a good fighter, good with a sword, and he had battle experience. He could find someone who would hire him for that. Part of his training had been menial labour, and he'd not been spared that because of his position as heir. So, he was not afraid of working with his hands or his back, if he must.

By the time the sun rose and the other inhabitants of Broch Dubh keep awoke, he was packed and ready, taking only what could be considered his. As he rode through the yard, anyone there going about their chores and duties turned to watch him leave. Aidan dared one last look behind him and found his father high on the battlements watching him as well.

He touched his legs to the horse's flanks and spurred him to move. Aidan passed through the village, forcing himself not to look at the familiar places there. Only as he reached the last lane did he realise that something was tucked inside his leather jacket. He grasped it and pulled out a small bit of parchment rolled and tied. Sliding the small length of ribbon from it, he recognised his mother's writing.

Go and visit with your sister.

Aidan laughed aloud then, knowing that somehow his mother had discovered Catriona's hiding place and shared it with him. He did not miss the irony in this situation, for she had done the same thing—sending a written warning about his sister to the man she loved—to warn him, too.

To Keppoch Keep, and hopefully Catriona, it was that he headed now.

Chapter Twenty-One

Keppoch Village— the lands of the Clan Matheson

Catriona accepted the small bundle from the little lass with thanks. The girl's mother had welcomed Cat to the village outlying Keppoch Keep and continued to send her food. Everyone here had been welcoming to the widowed kin of the MacLerie's wife. Everyone accepted the story that Lord MacLerie created for her—she was the widow of a loyal retainer and distant kin to his wife and sent here under his protection.

Though it was close enough to the truth, it was the new name she could not get herself accustomed to using—Coira MacCallum. It mattered not for the villagers had accepted her when she arrived nearly three months ago and made her welcome. When her condition became obvious, the women were even nicer, providing her with meals and inviting her to their cottages and including her even in some of their chores. Though some looked at her with questions in their eyes, none stared at her the way they'd done in Lairig Dubh.

This had become the kind of life she always wanted and could never have in Lairig Dubh.

Without him.

She sighed as she went back inside and opened the cloth to find some bread and cheese and roasted meat. Now, she could inhale the smells of food without her stomach rebelling. Her appetite had returned and she could keep down everything she ate. Cat wrapped it once more and put it aside for her noon meal. But first, the sun was shining and she had work to do outside.

The cottage she had was smaller than the house given her, but it did have an open area for a garden. Working the soil, pulling up weeds, nurturing the herbs and flowers she'd planted had saved her during those first weeks here. She had hired a few, strong lads to do the heaviest of the work and moving out the rocks, then she'd done the rest. Now, a nice crop grew and it needed her attention.

The hours passed by easily as she worked. She was just glad that she could now tolerate the smells of the growing herbs and plants. Some women told her that those symptoms went on through the whole of their pregnancies. Others never experienced it, but shared what other ones did assail them through the carrying.

The sun rose higher in the sky and Cat knew she'd had enough. Wiping the sweat from her eyes with the back of her arm, she sat back on her heels and caught her breath before trying to stand. She'd learned to pause for a few minutes after toppling over, off balance and winded, the first day she had worked the soil. Closing her eyes, she lifted her face to catch the breezes.

That's when it happened—well, really the two things happened.

A group of guards returning to the keep rode along the road not far from her cottage, laughing and calling out to each other. She lost her breath when she heard *his voice*. Even though it could not be, she tried to push to her feet and look. Her body did not react as she wanted it to and the extra weight she carried already slowed her. By the time she reached the low stone wall encircling the garden, they'd long since passed and were too far in the distance to tell one from another.

It could not be Aidan and yet she would swear she recognised the voice. Aidan's deep tones always made her body tremble in anticipation. She would know it. She would…

Just as she began berating herself for such a foolish thought, the babe within her moved. Catriona clutched her belly and waited as the wee one inside her jabbed and rolled, taking her breath with it. When it finally stopped, she dropped onto the wall and tried to breathe once more.

She missed him.

She'd refused to think about him, but this mistaken sound forced all her regrets to mind…and heart. The pain of losing him sliced through her now. The babe kicked again and she began to cry. Had she made the right decision?

Aidan had saved her in so many ways. He had shown her that she could love, even after the tragedies she'd suffered. He'd shown her that she could be worthy of the love of another person. He'd pushed her to try new things and to learn new skills. He'd made her happy and made her feel like she mattered when she had never felt that before.

But…he'd been involved in Gowan's death.

Since she'd not given him a chance to explain and had accepted the laird's help in leaving in exchange for never contacting him again, there was little chance she would ever know the whole truth of it. Was it possible to forgive him when he'd admitted it and used that to manipulate her into loving him?

Or had he?

She knew that guilt had driven him to provide for her. She knew that much. And she did not doubt that he loved her, but did that justify the means he'd used to make it happen?

Sometimes, she wondered if he had not been surprised by the love that had happened. The first time he'd said the words to her, his eyes filled with wonderment, as though he could not believe it himself.

Even if she could forgive his part in Gowan's death and accept that his love was genuine, she could not share him with another woman, even his wife. Even if it was the natural ways of things with wealthy men of power. Even if his family and his wife would accept and allow it.

So, Lord MacLerie's offer made things easier— taking her away from Lairig Dubh and giving her a new life and a chance to survive and mayhap even thrive.

Without him.

She was guilty, too. Guilty of thinking she could simply enjoy the passion she'd shared with him and not involve her heart. She could blame it on her inexperience. She could blame it on her need to feel loved.

Well, none of that mattered, for he was out of her life for ever. Most likely, he had chosen his bride and married by now. The babe kicked again and she smiled sadly. The one thing she had not thought about was what would she tell the babe about their father when he or she was old enough to ask?

Catriona had managed not to let herself wallow in pity since arriving here and yet the sound of a voice had sent her deeply into it. Shaking off the maudlin, sad feelings, she took a deep breath and let it out.

Since the weather might not hold for long, she went back to her task. Later, she made some soup that would be her contribution to the village's ceilidh planned for the next night. They were celebrating the wedding of one of the miller's sons to a girl from one of the families there with a gathering of food and music. She'd not felt like celebrating very much, so this might be a good thing.

If nothing else, it made her feel part of the lives of those who lived and worked around Keppoch Keep and for the Matheson laird.

Aidan kept a close watch each time he rode through the village or while on duty at Keppoch Keep for signs of her. Assigned as a guard by his brother-by-marriage, his duties took him to places all over Matheson lands and he hoped he would find her here. He'd done as the note suggested and travelled to his sister's home, gaining the approval of her husband to remain there in spite of breaking with his father.

Rob laughed when he told them how he was reclaiming his life and would not bend to his father's will any longer. Aidan saw some of the knowing and then heated glances exchanged between his foster brother who was now his sister's husband and he understood then that they had gone through the same thing with his father. For whatever reason, Rob agreed that Aidan would be taken into his service and be allowed to live here. If Rob and Lilidh had thought his request to be called something other than his full name was silly, they never said. So, Alastair MacLerie, distant cousin to the lady, came to live with the Mathesons of Keppoch Keep.

Though he wanted to blend in so he could search for Catriona, Rob would not hear of him living in the village. He was assigned to one of the small chambers that housed several men who served in the household. Other than seeing his sister in passing, he worked just as all the others did.

Days and nights passed and the dreams of her came each time he rested his head. And still he could not find her.

One of the men he served with invited him to the ceilidh in the village this night. His cousin was marrying and there would be a celebration. Ronald talked of his very eligible, very comely sister and his intention was clear to Aidan.

It mattered not to him, for his only goal was to find Catriona and beg her forgiveness. So, after finishing his duties, he walked down to the village, hoping that Catriona would come out of her hidey-hole and show herself.

He followed the sounds of pipes and drum into the village centre. Though much smaller than Lairig Dubh, it had a place around which everything else grew and it, too, was a well. Ronald greeted him and drew him over to tables where food sat ready. Aidan filled a bowl with some soup and took some bread while Ronald found a cup of ale for him.

As he followed the man and was introduced to all manner of people, Aidan kept an eye on the smaller gatherings and groups that formed along the lane. Women near the tables where they prepared and served food, men nearer to the barrels of ale. Children ran along, darting and weaving around the legs of the adults who stood talking.

Though the sun set late this far into the summer and the darkness would soon take hold of the night, torches burned brightly, lighting the area and allowing them to celebrate. Aidan found a spot near the well, drinking his ale and talking as people passed him by, but watching, always watching, and listening for her name or her voice.

Ronald's comely sister made her way to him, with Ronald close behind, and introduced herself to him. Andreana Matheson was indeed a comely lass and they enjoyed a few minutes of conversation as she pointed out various kith and kin and named them to him. He waited, holding his breath as a group of women walked by and until they passed and Cat was not among them.

He followed Ronald and Andreana to where their family gathered, in a clearing between two of the cottages. Accepting a new cup of ale, he sat with them, listening to the gossip and the music. The evening was enjoyable, not unlike his own family's celebrations. Aidan discovered no false airs or pretences living among these people and did not find himself yearning for the position he'd left behind.

Though he did miss his family, even his overbearing, domineering father, at times such as these. But, if he found Catriona and could convince her to forgive him, he would have his own family. Ciara had shared with him that Catriona could not have children of her own, but at least he would have her.

Deciding to return to the keep, he stood and thanked Ronald and his family for inviting him. Walking back to the main road, he noticed a group of women sitting partly in the shadows. Some held sleeping children, some chatted quietly. Some were younger women with bairns and some were older. He smiled, thinking on his mother and the wives of his father's closest friends who would sit in just such groups, sharing gossip and making plans.

One woman moved about in the shadows and he watched her, unable to look away. He cocked his head and listened for her voice. It had to be her. It had to be…

Catriona MacKenzie stood in the midst of the women, smiling and helping with some task.

Catriona was here.

His feet moved before he thought of it and then he stood before her.

'Catriona?'

Chapter Twenty-Two

The evening was a pleasant one. Catriona sat with other women, most of whom had children and most of whom were married. Now that the impossible was going to happen and she would have a child of her own, she began listening more carefully to the advice given by experienced mothers. And she began watching how they handled the small situations and big ones with their children in the hopes that she would know what to do when her bairn was born.

She'd been holding Seonag's older daughter on her lap while Seonag nursed the youngest bairn. Now, Seonag passed the bairn off to her own mother and so Catriona stood to hand off the wee one to her. Stretching her back, she began saying her farewells for she tired more easily now and wanted to seek her bed when she heard the name spoken of one who did not exist any longer.

By the man whose voice she would know anywhere… any time.

'Catriona?'

Turning to face him, she stepped out of the shadows to make certain she was not dreaming this.

It was him. Aidan MacLerie there a few paces away from her. Before she could say anything, he was striding towards her. The women around her missed nothing—not the wrong name, not the handsome young man calling to her, not even her hesitation.

'Are ye well, Coira?' Seonag said, walking to her side. 'Who is he looking for?'

'Who might he be?' asked one of the younger women.

Aidan would never go unnoticed as long as women were around, that much she knew. But he looked neither left nor right, at anyone other than her as he approached.

Did she pretend not to know him?

They clearly did not know him. The beard he wore now had fooled her for less than a second. The larger, muscular shoulders were new. Her heart pounded in her chest and her mouth went dry. The bairn tumbled within her.

Even while she drank in the very sight of him, she only knew she was not ready to face him. She pulled her shawl around her, letting it hide her growing belly, and she walked away.

Thoughts fled and judgement went with them as she trotted down the road, away from the gathering, away from him. The others must think her mad now, but she cared not. She was winded when she reached her cottage. Without pause, she entered and closed the shutters and barred the door.

Did he follow her? She knew not and would not chance to open the shutters to look down the lane. Why had he not left her alone? Why had he followed her? How had he found her? Surely the laird had not given up her secret, for he played a part in it, too.

After some time had passed, when no one approached her cottage, she put out all the candles and sat in the chair in the dark. Too riled to sleep, she sat there, thinking of all the things she would say to him. Or maybe she should leave the Matheson's lands and seek refuge in some other place?

Hours passed and she turned over all the possible plans in her thoughts. The only one she dared not think on was the one where she listened to him and forgave him. As the dawn's light crept into the sky, Catriona wondered why she was so afraid to face him.

Did she fear him? Or did she fear exposing her past to him in order to tell him of the bairn she now carried? Would he think she had lied to trap him somehow? Other women did such things, gaining the favour of a lord and bearing his child to be supported. Would he believe her words if she did not believe his?

Sitting inside the cottage like this made her a prisoner, a prisoner of her past and his. She could not and would not go back to the person she'd been—one who waited on her husband's pleasure, one who turned herself into a nothing more than a serving woman to pay back some debt she thought she owed. She'd lost so much of her life before she'd met Aidan, but she'd sworn she would not go back to a time when a man made her decisions for her.

So, when the day was fully awake, she realised that

in order to make her decision, she must listen to his explanation and judge it. Opening the shutters, she let the light flood inside the cottage. Seeing no one outside, she lifted the bar and latch and opened the door.

She expected to find him there. She expected that he had followed her back and would press his case. Instead, she found herself standing alone as the village around her began to wake to the new day.

Aidan wanted to run after her, but did not. Afraid she might fall or hurt herself, he watched until she was just a shadow moving away from him down the road.

This was not how he expected it would go once he'd found her. Nothing about Catriona went as he expected it to. Never.

'Alastair?' Ronald said, stepping up next to him. 'You are mistaken. Her name is not Catriona. That is Coira MacCallum.'

'Ah. Just so,' he said, nodding at Ronald. She was hiding in plain sight by using another name. His mother's family name. 'She looked like someone I used to know. My error. I hope I have not frightened her?'

'Seonag!' Ronald called out to one of the women in the group there. 'Is she well? Coira?'

'Oh, aye,' this Seonag said. 'She's a bit tired from all the work preparing. And from the bairn.' Cat must have been helping with the children there amongst the women.

'Is she married, then?' he asked, trying to keep his voice even as he found out more about the story she used here.

Ronald slapped him on the shoulder and laughed. 'She's a widow, though a bit old for ye, dinna ye think?' he asked. 'And she's carrying.'

Everything stopped around him for just a moment as the words sank into his mind. Every sound, every movement, every person around him seemed to stop.

She's carrying.

Catriona was pregnant with his bairn. He stumbled then and Ronald reached out for him.

'I warned ye about the ale,' Ronald said, holding him until he steadied. ''Tis stronger than most.'

'I will see you on the morrow,' Aidan mumbled out.

He walked down the road, towards the keep, but his heart wanted to follow her. How was it possible she was pregnant? She was barren. She could not have children.

He laughed harshly at the truths before him.

She knew that she carried his babe when she left him. His father must have known—for there was little or nothing the Beast did not know about those under his protection. She lived here and made no secret of it.

Confused and unable to sort through it all, he made his way back to the keep and to his chamber.

He thought he would ride in, find her, make her listen to his explanation and then she would forgive him.

If, knowing she was pregnant, his father sent her away and she made no attempt to contact him, it spoke of a reason he did not wish to consider.

She would never forgive him for what he'd done.

His mighty plan of making her see reason in his role in Gowan's death would accomplish nothing. It might make him feel better, but she had already turned away from him.

And even while she carried a babe she thought she could never have. The pain struck him then as all of his hopes and dreams came crashing down around him. This could not end well for him.

Lairig Dubh, Scotland

Jocelyn waited for her husband in the solar. His mood and the mood of everyone here deteriorated more with each day that passed since Aidan rode out of the gates. Oh, she'd witnessed tests of will between her eldest son and his father since the first time Aidan could say the word 'nay' and more recently there had been some serious ones. But nothing came close to the stupidity of both of them in this matter.

She now had no choice left but to step in and meddle as Connor liked to call it. Jocelyn thought of it as taking steps to prevent catastrophe and disaster. And to save those whom she loved the most from self-destruction. Pacing around the chamber, she realised that she was part of the problem, too.

All good reasons for her to take some action of her own before it was too late—if it was not already.

The sound of his loud voice, calling out orders to this one or that one, echoed through the hall and into the chamber where she waited. Jocelyn cringed at the tone, at the sound of servants crying out and dropping things and then at the silence as they, no doubt, watched him walk by, hoping he would not focus his attentions on them.

It had not been this bad when she first moved here, nor since. But this falling-out between father and son, between chieftain and heir, was tearing the MacLeries apart. And pride and anger was not going to heal this breach.

The door opened and Connor strode in, his pain evident to her in every step he took towards her.

'You called for me?' he asked, going to the table and pouring a measure of whisky into a cup and swallowing it in one mouthful.

'This turmoil is not good, Connor,' Jocelyn said, walking towards him. Many would stand away, but she needed to touch him, to soothe him when her words would inflame him. 'And I have been searching for the real cause of it.'

'Your son's pigheadedness and immaturity!' he shouted. 'He is stubborn, like you, and questions my decisions and my authority.'

At one time, she would have run at such words, but she and her Beast had been through too much for this bluster to frighten her off. She needed to take the proverbial thorn from the lion's paw, but it was going to hurt in doing so. Taking a deep breath, she walked to his side and touched his arm. He almost pulled it from her. Almost. But he calmed the tiniest amount and let her hand remain there.

'I discovered two secrets you are keeping, from me and from our son, and I wonder if, in keeping those secrets, you are not feeling guilty?' The muscles in his arm tensed and she waited for him to withdraw from her touch. When he did not, she pressed on.

'One secret you keep would have helped Aidan and might have averted this whole situation. The other would have helped you get your way with him and yet you did not use it when you could have. So, would you like to hear what I have discovered?'

Connor glared at her and ground his teeth together, but did not move away.

Men liked to think that only women gossiped or spent time passing tales around, the juicier the better, but, truth be told, men were just as good at it as women were. And no man in Lairig Dubh could share gossip, and in the right circumstances share secrets with her, like Rurik Erengislsson.

She had developed a relationship with the half-Scot, half-Norse warrior in her first days here, even if they did not recognise it. He became the one man she could count on, no matter the situation, and he stood at her back at times when Connor could not. Though things became strained recently when her brother pursued his daughter, Rurik had seen the love between them and given up his resistance to the match.

So, when she needed to know what was truly going on with her husband and the clan, she spoke to Rurik. He probably did not even realise the importance of what he'd shared with her, but she had. A good challenging game of chess and the man spilled out information he would never have shared if he wasn't concentrating on and distracted by his next move.

'Aidan was not the one who decided on Gowan's assignment that day. The one that took him from Lairig Dubh and began…' They both knew what it all started. 'The names of those being sent had already been chosen. Aidan only thinks it was his decision.'

'So, what of it? It was a test of his abilities and he failed,' he growled out.

'But instead of stopping him, you let Gowan go. You knew of Aidan's attraction to the man's wife and you let him go.'

He let out a breath filled with pain and guilt and his eyes confirmed her suspicions. *He* had made the decision. *He* allowed the situation, even knowing what would most likely happen.

'Gowan was the best man to go. We needed his experience and his training skills with those new soldiers,' he explained in a voice that showed his conviction wavering. 'I made the decision for the good of the clan.'

'That is why you were willing to give Catriona the house and the settlement when Aidan asked for them. Not because of his guilt, but your own?' she asked, not expecting an answer. Jocelyn walked over to one of the large chairs and sat down. When Connor did the same, she continued.

'You just did not realise that his heart was already engaged. That this woman was different from all the rest who came before.'

'I believed that when Gowan died and Aidan thought he'd caused it, he would lose interest in her. She's too old for him. She's too poor. She's uneducated. She's—'

'She's not a whore.' His eyes flared then in surprise, something not common to her husband.

'How do you know that?' he asked. 'The men I spoke to said she was.'

'I spoke to the ones you did not. The ones who saw the whole of the incident that led to Gowan's marriage to her. Her father was trying to force her into selling herself and she fought him and the men he tried to sell her to. Gowan heard the commotion, took her from there and handfasted with her the next day. Their marriage in church happened later when they arrived back here some weeks later.'

'I should have asked you to gather the information I needed,' he said with a harsh, sarcastic chuckle.

'Aye, you should have, for I also found out she thought herself barren because she'd just lost a babe and had nearly died from it.'

He stared at her for a moment, his gaze filled with admiration. But, that moment passed and the anger flowed back. It would take more than just a secret to break down his resistance to the whole truth of the matter.

'That led me to the second secret you keep.'

'What secret is that, Wife?' he asked, shifting on the chair to face her.

'You did not tell Aidan the truth when he confronted you about your role in Catriona's departure. You allowed everyone to believe that you forced Catriona from here. That you decided to exile her to some secret place to get her away from Aidan.'

He glared at her, but remained silent.

'You only told Aidan part of it when you admitted that she asked for your help.'

'I told him the truth,' he argued.

'Liar.' She leaned closer to him. 'Aye, Catriona came to you when she discovered what she thought was the truth from Gowan's son—that Aidan sent him away to seduce her.'

'He did.'

'You sent the man. You could have stopped it. You could have told Aidan from the start and it would never have got to this point, Connor.'

'Your point, lady?'

'That she asked for your help in escaping. She asked for your help because she also discovered she is carrying Aidan's child, our kin, and she could not face him, knowing…' Jocelyn paused. 'Or believing what you let her believe.'

Connor pushed out of the chair and began walking around the perimeter of the chamber, beginning and stopping whatever words he wanted to say several times before any came out of his mouth.

'I thought he would tire of chasing a woman who did not want him. I thought that if he tried and failed, he would move on to another woman, as he always had before.' Connor raked his hands through his hair and stared at her. The thorn was still there, waiting to be pulled free.

'I thought he would see the wisdom in choosing another woman, a woman better than her in so many ways. Yet, he clung to her.'

'He loved her, Connor,' she whispered.

'Then, when Munro told her his version of what had happened, the one Aidan also believed, she asked me to help her leave. She would make no claim on our son if I found a new place for her to live. The daft woman would take nothing more than a small settlement and did not even admit to me that she was carrying.' He paused and looked at her then. 'It was exactly what I wanted to happen. So, I did as she asked.'

'So, why did you not reveal her secret to him? That she knew she carried his child when she left him?'

His voice shook with sadness and resignation as he said the rest. 'Because it would have broken him to let him know he would lose her and his child. I could not stand to have him suffer that way.'

'So, you kept that very important matter to yourself?'

''Twas better not to reveal it.'

When he met her gaze, she saw the pain of a father trying to protect his son. Yet, he'd put them together when he thought they would fall apart. Then, in separating them, he forced his son away.

Now she needed to come up with a way to bring them all—Aidan and Catriona, father and son, kith and kin, back together. Jocelyn walked to the door and called several servants to her.

'What are you doing?' Connor asked.

'Preparing to visit my daughter.'

'Lilidh? Now? Why?' he asked, watching as she gave orders that would see trunks packed and horses and supplies prepared.

'Because I also discovered where you sent her and sent Aidan there. Now, you have to devise a plan to heal this breach before we arrive there.'

'He is the pigheaded, wrong...'

'Stubborn one. I know. He is the very image of you, my love,' she said, walking to him now. 'He is the best of you and the worst. And if you do not mend this tear, you will never survive it. We will never survive it.' She smiled as he considered her words. 'You may even have to apologise.'

'Jocelyn!' he drawled out. 'I should not have to—'
She reached up and put her hand over his mouth to stop him.

'Ah, but you are the stronger, the wiser, the more experienced man in this situation. It is your place to lead by example.'

He mulled over her words, but the doubtful expression in his amber eyes showed he did not think much of it. So, she used the threat she kept away for those times when reason and rational thought did not work.

'If my son does not return to his home, I will not return either.'

She needed Connor as she needed the air to breathe and she knew he needed her in the same manner. Their love was tempered by fire and challenged and strengthened over the decades since their marriage. But part of that love included their bond with their children. Breaking that bond damaged everything between them. This was no idle threat and she held her breath, praying he understood it the same way that she did.

He walked past her, pulled the door open even wider and called out in his battle voice to those outside. It took little time for their journey to begin.

She did not ask and he did not say what his plan was, but she knew her husband and little that he set his mind to do was ever left undone.

The thorn was loosening a bit.

Chapter Twenty-Three

T hey circled each other over the next sennight, acknowledging the other with the slightest of nods or glances. But Aidan had decided not to press her at this point. He did, however, find ways to observe her when she did not know he was there.

The people in Rob's clan had accepted this stranger into their midst and seemed to have a care for her. A small girl brought messages and bundles of food to her from the girl's mother and other women in the village. A strong older boy helped her with the harder tasks, such as cutting and carrying peat and wood for her fires. She spent time during the day working in the new garden she'd carved into the small plot next to her cottage. He wondered if she grew betony yet.

Aidan accepted the duties he was given and let everything else ruminate while he looked for a solution. The one thing that had not changed was his love for Catriona.

And when a note passed to him from someone in the keep informed him that his parents were now travelling towards Keppoch Keep, his path became clear to him and the cost of his youthful stupidity must be paid by him and no other.

Catriona finished her tasks, put away her mending and put out some of the candles. She poured the last of her tea into her cup and sat sipping it before going to bed. Tired from staying busy and from the demands that pregnancy put on her body now, she had been finishing up and seeking her bed earlier each night.

Her cold, empty, lonely bed.

The one in which she tossed and turned every night, examining her conscience and the same question—could good come from a bad beginning? Or did the bad taint everything that came from it?

Though she would love the babe as much as she loved his father, could she accept him and be happy when a man's death had been caused by them?

She was no closer to an answer, in spite of knowing he was there in Keppoch village and keep.

Though she'd seen Lady Matheson and now knew of the connection between her and Aidan, she could not figure out why Lord MacLerie had sent her here. If Aidan had not found her, she could have been happy here among these people.

Since that night when he'd recognised her, she waited for him to appear at her door, demanding that she listen to his side of things. Instead, he gave her a wide circle, not approaching directly or even too closely. It was almost as though he was giving her the time and distance she wanted.

The problem was that she wanted him. Now that this babe seemed firmly in place and growing well, she wanted to share the small joys with the man she loved. The last time, she had lived in fear through the whole time, never knowing what to expect and then getting worse than she could have imagined. What would it be like to go through this with Aidan at her side? With both of them wanting this babe? With both of them...

The soft scratching on the door startled her. She put her cup down and went to open it. Sometimes, one of the village women, Seonag or Isobel or one of the others, would send over their leftover food from their suppers for her. When she put her hand on the latch, he whispered through the door.

'Catriona? I would speak with you, if you would grant me a few moments?'

Damn her traitorous heart, for it raced in reaction to his voice, his whispered words, and even just knowing he was so close to her now. She tugged the door open and forgot how to breathe once again.

He looked wonderful and terrible at the same time. She wanted to push him away and take him in her arms. She loved him and wanted to hate him in the same moment, but love won out. She knew then that she could not hate him, not even knowing that he thought he was responsible for Gowan's death. For in the long and lonely nights filled only with time for thinking, she'd realised that Munro played just as much a part in his father's death, maybe more so than even Aidan.

If Munro had not believed the worst, for whatever reason he chose to do so, he would have let things lie and never summoned his father home. In his attempt to punish her and humiliate Aidan, he'd sent the message that forced Gowan on to that road that night and to his death.

Up to that time, nay, up until Gowan was long dead and buried, she was a faithful wife to him. Aidan's sins were of lust and pride and for coveting a woman who was not his to covet.

With that knowledge in her heart, she waited on his words, hoping he would ask for her forgiveness so she could do so. Instead his words shocked her.

'I have come to say farewell to you, Cat.' He did not try to come in, but only stood there outside her door. 'It is unfair for me to disrupt the life you have found here on your own. I thought…I thought that if I could say the right words, you might…' He paused then and gazed at her. 'I have realised that I expected what every other man has expected of you—that you would do what I wanted because I wanted it so. I thought that if I came and said the words I wanted to tell you, you would accept them and forgive me.'

He looked away then and she felt the tears beginning to gather in her eyes. 'But I was wrong. The things I did were wrong. The way I forced you into my protection and manipulated you into caring for me was wrong.' Aidan laughed sadly. 'I thought you were like all the others and, in that, I was truly and completely wrong.' He cleared his throat and glanced back at her then.

'Aidan, I…'

He shook his head. 'I pray you let me finish first?' She nodded.

'On the morrow, I journey to a cousin's lands in the

north. I will tell my sister where I am so that if you have need of anything…' His gaze fell to her belly and she instinctively placed her hand there. 'She will know where I can be found. My father is supporting you and the bairn?' he asked.

'Aye,' she forced out, the tears now tightening her throat and spilling over and down her cheeks. 'He paid me for the house.'

'I am sorry for devastating your life and causing Gowan's death. It does not change anything, but I am sorry. Farewell, Catriona MacKenzie.'

With those simple words, he began to tear down her defences. But the next ones destroyed them.

'I hope you are happy about the bairn?' he asked. She could only nod then. 'Good. Have a care for yourself, Cat.'

And he walked away. He did not look back. He did not stop. And Cat knew if she did nothing, she would regret it for the rest of her life. For the one thing she had always ever wanted was to be loved and Aidan did love her.

Bad beginning or good one, she was loved.

'Aidan,' she called out, running after him. 'Do not leave me.'

He stopped and turned, the nearly full moon above lighting the ground where he stood.

'I was wrong, too,' she said. 'You had the right to know about the babe and I kept it from you.'

'I think you had good reason, Cat. How could you trust me not to take it from you when that is my nature?'

'I know that you sent Gowan away, but you did not cause his death. You never intended him harm.'

He sucked in a breath at her words. 'What are you saying?'

'I know not how this will work out, but I would stay with you, so you can see and know your bairn.'

That was not the only reason. Cat would take his love however she could. If that meant being his leman, she would do that. She did not want to give him up.

'How this will work? If you will have me, I would marry you.'

Now it was her turn to stand wordlessly before him. 'Marry? Your father would never permit such a thing!' She almost laughed, the thought of a penniless, unlearned, twice-married daughter of a whoremonger as the wife of the MacLerie's son.

'I should make it clear, that if you say aye, you get only the man before you. I have given up all claim to my father's titles, lands and wealth. He has disowned me likewise.' He sounded light-hearted and happy, if such a thing was possible.

'Why would he do such a thing? Why would you?' she asked. It was simply a thing not done.

'I wanted to marry you. He refused permission. Now, I do not need it.' He shrugged it off as though an everyday occurrence. 'Now, I have accepted a position with my sister's husband and work for my living. It is not a bad thing, to have to prove myself instead of expecting it as my due.'

'Aye,' she said.

He realised what she'd said and still did not move.

'Truly?'

'Aye.'

He crossed the gap between them and pulled her to him, lifting her off the ground and swinging her around. His laugh echoed through the lanes and around the cottages and she tugged on his arms so he would put her on her feet.

'Will you regret this? How can you give up your family? You love them and I know you will miss them.' She did not want to come between them or have him hate her for causing this break.

'Now, we will begin our own family,' he said, drawing her close. He held out his hand as though to touch her belly and stopped just inches from her. 'May I?'

Cat covered his hand with hers and placed it where he could feel the bairn within her. As if the most obedient child, the babe pushed against the weight of their hands. He laughed then, pressing gently where the babe had pushed and waiting to feel it move again.

Then, as she tilted her head back to watch the joy that covered his face, he leaned down to kiss her. Catriona closed her eyes and waited to feel the touch of his mouth on hers.

'I love you, Catriona MacKenzie. I think I have from the first time I saw you,' he whispered. Then his mouth took hers as she'd wanted him to do. She wrapped her arms around him, holding him close.

'I love you, Aidan.'

How long they stood there, in the moonlit night, she did not know, but when she felt the night air's chill, she tugged him towards the house.

'No, lass,' he said, not budging from the spot. 'You know what will happen if we go inside together.'

Sinfully, she did and she hoped he would banish the memory of all those lonely nights without him.

'If we are to be married, we should wait,' he said.

'Wait, my arse!' she said, then she covered her mouth after saying such a coarse thing. 'I have a mind to seduce you, Aidan MacLerie. To have my way with you.' For this time it was her choice and he was the one she'd chosen.

'I may let you,' he promised. He bent over and lifted her in his arms.

No words were spoken nor needed through the rest of that night. Though Catriona worried over the changes in her body wrought by the pregnancy, Aidan did not seem to mind at all. His attentions drove her mad with desire and then he satisfied her. And she satisfied him from the sound of it.

Now, lying together, with him wrapped around her, she slept soundly and dreamlessly for the first time since she'd left him. For why dream of him when she had him with her now?

She woke for some reason just past dawn and found him staring at her. Cat did not move, enjoying the feel of his body next to hers, his heart beating under her hand. She could have remained like that for hours or days, but the arrival of a large, noisy group of people outside her door told her that would not happen. When she would have climbed from the bed and found a gown, the door burst open and the Earl of Douran strode in.

Chapter Twenty-Four

Aidan pushed Catriona behind him and turned to face his father. Then his mother entered, took in the situation and whispered furiously to him.

'Connor, let us wait outside. Now.'

He watched as the petite woman commanded the most fearsome warrior chief in the Highlands like a serving woman. He almost laughed as his father did exactly what he was told to do. Once the door had closed, he stood and found his trews and shirt. Helping Catriona from the bed, he avoided touching her as he wanted to. Her lush body blossomed now, her soft curves filling out and her breasts swelling as her belly did. He'd explored every inch of her last night, kissing and caressing all the changes in her body.

'Aidan, what does he want?' Catriona asked, as she reached for her garments and dressed quickly.

'I do not know. His agreement with you was that you not see me again,' he said. She blushed at his words.

'Aye. I know you went to him for help. It saddens me that you had to humble yourself because of me.'

'And you came for me in spite of his orders.'

'Aye, love, I did.' He kissed her on the forehead. 'And I will be with you no matter what he says or does. Fear not. You are mine now and I will protect you, even from him.'

'Aidan!' his father called from outside.

Aidan walked to the door and pulled it open. Not only were his father and mother there waiting, but he saw his sister and her husband, along with Duncan and a large group of MacLerie warriors. Not to be outdone, Rob had sent along his Matheson soldiers, so it looked like a war camp outside Catriona's house.

'Aye.' His mother slipped past him before he could stop her, with some words about speaking to Catriona.

'I would speak to you,' his father said, or ordered.

'To what end?' he asked. 'We said all we needed to say weeks ago. You should know that I am marrying Catriona.'

'Walk with me.'

Aidan looked at his father, for the softer tone and request was most unexpected. He nodded and followed his father down the lane to where they could not be heard by the others. They stood in silence for a few minutes before his father spoke.

'I asked for your opinion that day as a test of your knowledge and your abilities. One day as chieftain, you will have to make decisions like that.' Aidan did not pretend to not know which day he spoke of or which decision. 'But you—'

'I failed. I know it, Father,' he admitted. 'I sent a man away for an unconscionable reason and he died as a result.'

'Nay, you misunderstand. I had already chosen the men to go. Asking you for your opinion did not change my decision, it only confirmed it. I chose to send Gowan in spite of knowing why you spoke his name.'

Aidan stood in shocked silence then. So, his father had sent Gowan away? Still…

'I still failed, for my decision was based on my own personal desires and not on what was best for the clan. Not a very good choice for a man who would have led the clan one day.'

'Will lead the clan.'

'Nay,' he said. 'You disinherited me if I chose to marry Catriona and I will not give her up for you, Father. Not for the MacLeries.'

His father looked over his head and up at the sky. Then down at the ground where he shuffled his feet with the expression of a recalcitrant lad on his face. When he spoke, his words carried both guilt and hesitation.

'I think she has been good for you. When you thought you'd caused Gowan's death, you took responsibility and tried to right things with her, for her. I would have preferred a different way, but you did not shirk your duties.' From the painful grimace on his father's face, Aidan did not mistake these words for what they actually were—an apology, or as close to one as he would ever get from him.

'And now? Do you think that I will say you were right

and allow her to be taken or leave me again? We will be married, have no doubt of it.'

'From the way that she faced me down, even in her darkest hour, I suspect she will fit in. Even now your mother is no doubt explaining how it will be to be the wife of a MacLerie laird.'

Aidan turned as the door opened and the two women he loved walked out, arm in arm. Instead of fear or nervousness, the two shared some jest and laughed aloud.

'You will learn to rue the day when you let your mother get her clutches into your wife. It cannot be good for either of us.' His father held out his arm and Aidan clasped it.

A short time later, they arrived at Lilidh and Rob's keep and summoned a priest to perform the marriage. When the man of God raised the question about the banns being announced, the growl from his father, the severe glare from his mother and the obvious condition of the bride prevailed quickly.

By the noon meal, he had married the woman he set out to seduce. And by the evening meal, she had seduced him again.

By the time the sun rose again, Aidan MacLerie decided that he could happily live without his former womanising ways now that he'd found the woman who'd said no to him until she said yes.

It took some time to return to Lairig Dubh. They made the journey at a slow pace in consideration of

Cat's condition, so it took over a sennight to reach his, their, home.

And once they reached his bedchamber, with its large, comfortable bed, it took them more days to leave that.

Connor watched as Rurik and Duncan and their wives approached the high table. A celebration marking the wedding of Aidan and Catriona was almost at an end. The bride and groom had not been seen in some hours, and would not likely appear again for even longer. Jocelyn had not spoken a word about what he'd done to bring Aidan home, but she was happy and that mattered to him.

'I thought he favoured the English lass,' Rurik said.

'Nay, 'twas the Maxwell girl who had the better chance,' Duncan argued.

He waited for Jocelyn or one of the wives to explain how Catriona was the only correct choice for wife for his son, but none said it. Puzzling. Jocelyn slipped her hand in his and rested it on his leg under the table.

'She meddled again,' he said, exposing her weakness to their friends.

'Jocelyn!' Margriet and Marian said, laughing. Neither one looked or sounded surprised.

'So, if we had wagered on this match as we did on the others, I would say you forfeited by meddling,' he said. Duncan and Rurik quickly agreed, claiming a victory for the men.

'I think I am glad that we have some time before the younger ones will be ready to wed,' Margriet said. 'I cannot believe that our Isobel is married.'

'And our Ciara,' Marian said. 'I think they will be announcing another bairn soon.' Duncan looked very pleased by that news.

'Now that Lilidh and Aidan are both happily married,' Jocelyn said, 'I think I could even admit defeat in this match.'

Connor looked at his closest friends and their wives and then at the woman he loved more than life itself. Raising his cup, he smiled. 'To the happy couple!' They all called out the words in reply and drank from their cups.

As he watched his friends leave the table to seek their beds and the forfeits due them from this last marriage wager, he turned to Jocelyn and kissed her. When they were the only ones remaining in the hall, as was their custom, he lifted her in his arms and carried her to their bedchamber.

After he showed his mate the depth and breadth of his love for her and she slept in his arms, he offered up a prayer that his son would find in Catriona what he had found in Jocelyn.

If he did, Connor knew that all would be well and good in the Clan MacLerie.

* * * * *

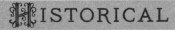
BRIDE BY MAIL
Wild West Weddings • by Katy Madison
(Western)

Expecting a plain, dependable woman to reply to his advert, Jack Trudeau is taken aback by Olivia Hansson. She's pretty, yes, but can she handle life in a simple log cabin alone with him?

SCARS OF BETRAYAL
by Sophia James
(Victorian)

Cassandra Northrup had believed Nathaniel dead...until now. Once, she had loved him, given herself to him, in the hidden depths of the snow-covered Pyrenees. But then she had betrayed him....

SCANDAL'S VIRGIN
by Louise Allen
(Regency)

Heartbroken Lady Laura Campion transformed herself into the infamous Scandal's Virgin of high society. But now she must change her ways to win her daughter back from the powerful Earl of Wykeham....

SURRENDER TO THE VIKING
Victorious Vikings
by Joanna Fulford
(Viking)

Hot-tempered Lara Ottarsdotter has seen off many an unwanted suitor! Then Finn Egilsson comes seeking vengeance on a mutual enemy and Lara's father offers him help. The price? Finn must take Lara as his wife!

REQUEST YOUR FREE BOOKS!

HARLEQUIN® HISTORICAL:
Where love is timeless

2 FREE NOVELS PLUS 2 **FREE GIFTS!**

YES! Please send me 2 FREE Harlequin® Historical novels and my 2 FREE gifts (gifts are worth about $10). After receiving them, if I don't wish to receive any more books, I can return the shipping statement marked "cancel." If I don't cancel, I will receive 6 brand-new novels every month and be billed just $5.44 per book in the U.S. or $5.74 per book in Canada. That's a savings of at least 16% off the cover price! It's quite a bargain! Shipping and handling is just 50¢ per book in the U.S. and 75¢ per book in Canada.* I understand that accepting the 2 free books and gifts places me under no obligation to buy anything. I can always return a shipment and cancel at any time. Even if I never buy another book, the two free books and gifts are mine to keep forever.

246/349 HDN F4ZY

Name _____ (PLEASE PRINT) _____

Address _____ Apt. # _____

City _____ State/Prov. _____ Zip/Postal Code _____

Signature (if under 18, a parent or guardian must sign)

Mail to the **Harlequin® Reader Service:**
IN U.S.A.: P.O. Box 1867, Buffalo, NY 14240-1867
IN CANADA: P.O. Box 609, Fort Erie, Ontario L2A 5X3

Want to try two free books from another line?
Call 1-800-873-8635 or visit www.ReaderService.com.

* Terms and prices subject to change without notice. Prices do not include applicable taxes. Sales tax applicable in N.Y. Canadian residents will be charged applicable taxes. Offer not valid in Quebec. This offer is limited to one order per household. Not valid for current subscribers to Harlequin Historical books. All orders subject to credit approval. Credit or debit balances in a customer's account(s) may be offset by any other outstanding balance owed by or to the customer. Please allow 4 to 6 weeks for delivery. Offer available while quantities last.

Your Privacy—The Harlequin® Reader Service is committed to protecting your privacy. Our Privacy Policy is available online at www.ReaderService.com or upon request from the Harlequin Reader Service.

We make a portion of our mailing list available to reputable third parties that offer products we believe may interest you. If you prefer that we not exchange your name with third parties, or if you wish to clarify or modify your communication preferences, please visit us at www.ReaderService.com/consumerschoice or write to us at Harlequin Reader Service Preference Service, P.O. Box 9062, Buffalo, NY 14269. Include your complete name and address.

HH13R

SPECIAL EXCERPT FROM

H **HARLEQUIN**®

ℋISTORICAL

*Next month, follow Louise Allen's SCANDAL'S VIRGIN
as she leaves a trail of broken hearts across London's
ballrooms, and discover the only man who can heal her
own shattered dreams…*

Now he carried Laura to the bed and set her carefully on her feet beside it before returning to the door. His hand hovered over the key. "I will lock the world out, not you in."

"Leave it, I trust you." She smiled faintly at his raised eyebrow. "In this, at least."

"Why, Laura? Why have you come to me?" Propose to her now, or afterward? Afterward, instinct told him. Do not complicate this moment. In passion, in the aftermath of passion, surely he would see the truth in her.

She half turned from him and ran her fingers pensively over the old chintz bedcover, tracing the twining flowers and stems that some long-dead lady of the house had embroidered. The curve of her neck, the elegant line from bare shoulder to ear, was exposed to him, pearl-pale in the lamplight. Between her breasts was a shadowy, mysterious valley where a gold chain glinted.

"It has been a long time," she said finally, without looking up. "You think me loose, but there has not been anyone since…since before Alice was born. And there is this thing between us. This desire. I feel cold inside almost all the time. Flirting and laughing is no longer enough. And with you there is heat, even if there is nothing else but dislike and suspicion."

Avery had not expected this frankness, this simple confession of need. His body stirred, eager, but he did not move. She spoke of nothing but desire, dislike, mistrust. Could he ever replace that with even the basic tolerance marriage would require? He probed a little, testing how open she would be. "You know you are fertile. Why take such a risk again?"

Laura did look up then. The brown eyes that could look so cold seemed pansy-soft in the lamplight. "We were young and foolish. We were to marry, so what did it matter? And Piers was inexperienced. You, I think, are both experienced and not inclined to be careless."

Avery could argue that all the care in the world was sometimes not enough, but somehow his prized self-control was slipping away, sand through his fingers. Tomorrow he would take that huge risk with his life and his heart and with Alice's love. Tomorrow he would disregard all the lessons of his own parents' disastrous marriage.

Tonight he would lie with this woman who was ruining his sleep, haunting those dreams he could snatch from a few hours of slumber.

Don't miss
SCANDAL'S VIRGIN
Available from Harlequin® Historical
June 2014

HISTORICAL

Where love is timeless

COMING IN JUNE 2014

Scars of Betrayal

by

Sophia James

Cassandra Northrup had believed Nathaniel dead…until now.
Once, she had loved him, given herself to him in
the hidden depths of the snow-covered Pyrenees.
But then she had betrayed him….

Relief at the sight of Nathaniel turns to darkest shame as Cassie
sees the hate in his eyes. Years have passed and their physical scars
have faded, but the pain runs deeper than ever. Yet passion can be
born out of betrayal—and as desire crackles between them once
more, will Cassie reveal the secret she's long kept hidden?

Available wherever books and ebooks are sold.

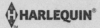

HISTORICAL

Where love is timeless

COMING IN JUNE 2014

Surrender to the Viking

by

Joanna Fulford

A hot-tempered redhead with a talent for sword craft,
Lara Ottarsdotter has seen off many an unwanted suitor! Then
the Viking warlord Finn Egilsson comes seeking vengeance on a
mutual enemy and Lara's despairing father offers him a bounty of
ships and swords. The price? Finn must take Lara as his wife.

Finn has no wish to endure marriage again, yet his reluctant bride
fires his blood with one passionate kiss. Her courage means she
will never yield in battle, but soon all he wants is her ultimate,
willing surrender—in the marriage bed!

Available wherever books and ebooks are sold.